THE

LAST BOAT

THE
LAST BOAT

A Novel

Michael Hite

iUniverse, Inc.
New York Lincoln Shanghai

THE LAST BOAT

iUniverse books may be ordered through booksellers or by contacting:

iUniverse
2021 Pine Lake Road, Suite 100
Lincoln, NE 68512
www.iuniverse.com
1-800-Authors (1-800-288-4677)

Because of the dynamic nature of the Internet, any Web addresses or links contained in this book may have changed since publication and may no longer be valid.

This is a work of fiction. All of the characters, names, incidents, organizations, and dialogue in this novel are either the products of the author's imagination or are used fictitiously.

Cover photograph "Woman with dory on beach, Cod Fish Park, Sconset" courtesy of the Nantucket Historical Association, GPN505

ISBN: 978-0-595-42033-9 (pbk)
ISBN: 978-0-595-67962-1 (cloth)
ISBN: 978-0-595-86378-5 (ebk)

Printed in the United States of America

For Diane

Acknowledgments

I remain indebted to all those who provided invaluable assistance along the way:

Organizations that provided assistance in my research: the Nantucket Atheneum, Nantucket Historical Association, National Archives and Records Administration, New Bedford Public Library, New York Historical Society, New York Public Library, Columbia University Library, and the International Red Cross.

The following authors and their books on the First World War: Martin Gilbert, *The First World War: A Complete History*; John Keegan, *The First World War*; Yvonne M. Klein, editor, *Beyond the Home Front: Women's Autobiographical Writing of the Two World Wars*; Michael Stevens, editor, *Voices of the Wisconsin Past: Letters from the Front 1898–1945*. For Nantucket sayings: William F. Macy, *The Nantucket Scrap Basket*.

The following family and friends, who read various drafts of the novel, providing insightful comments and support: Mary Catherine Bolster, Sherri Bustad, Anne Castine, Lisa Caviola, Leonard Cox, Susan Duff, Marcia and Homer Dunn, Randy and Steve Goldberger, Mary Hite, Richard and JoAnne Hite, Robert Hite, Gretchen Irmiger-Poitier, Carolyn Keating, Nancy Larsen, Lynda and Biff Levy, Peggy and Larry Levy, Andrew McCrea, Morgan and Allen Morton, Alex and Lynnette Mautner, David Near, Patty Pennington, MJ Roach, Judy Seinfeld, Terri Spilman, Valorie Thompson, and Blaine Zuckerman.

Paul Bresnick, whose early editorial notes and professional recommendations were instrumental in shaping the story.

Sarah Flynn, for her spot-on critique, direction, and support.

Shea Spindler and Jennifer Gilbert, my editors, for their talents in fine-tuning the manuscript.

Linda Loring, whose friendship and stories of old Nantucket inspired the idea for this book.

Finally, my wife, Diane, who read every draft, believed in the work, and provided unending support throughout the process.

Author's Note

Although the places, settings, and some of the characters portrayed in this work are real, it is a work of fiction nonetheless.

CHAPTER I

Wearied and bedraggled, Samantha dropped her worn suitcase at her side and stood on the lower deck. She slouched forward, planting her elbows on the safety railing to prop herself up. Her eyes fixed on the horizon.

She didn't know that I had followed her onto the ferry (at least, I didn't think so). We had left Nantucket for the mainland—or America, as we say—and we were two hours into sail. There was no land in sight, save for the faintest flash of light coming off Great Point Lighthouse.

The raw, damp, and chilly October evening didn't seem to affect Samantha. Nor did the cold spray from the murky waters crashing against the steamship *Uncatena* divert her attention.

She pulled something out of her coat pocket (a rope, perhaps?), then bent over her suitcase, fussing with it. Was she afraid that the contents would fall out if the suitcase weren't tied shut?

She struggled to lift the suitcase, but couldn't. It must have been packed full of all of her belongings, along with some dresses and blouses of mine—borrowed, but never returned.

Drained of all energy, she dragged the suitcase and staggered toward the bow of the boat, trying to keep her balance. Then, in a blink of the eye, she did it. She mustered up her last ounce of strength, picked up the suitcase, forced her arms through the roping, clutched it close to her bosom, and threw herself overboard.

I ran pell-mell to the place she had last stood and searched frantically for her in the water. There was no one—not a soul. No suitcase. No air bubbles. Nothing. I tried to scream, but I was choked with fright. *Speak, damn you! Speak!*

"Man overboard! Man overboard!" a voice behind me cried out.

Did it matter that it was a woman instead of a man? I wasn't in any condition to argue. I swung around to see a crew member running for a life preserver. Thank God he had found the words that had me by the throat.

Still, nothing surfaced on the water. I don't know what possessed me, but I jumped in. The shock of the frigid sea made my nerves wild as a Tuckernuck steer. I felt freeze-dried as the icy cold electrified my vitals. An instant, sting shot from my temples down to my toes. Adrenaline surged.

Looking up, I saw faint lights from the steamer filtering down from the surface and gained my bearings. I tried to locate her but could find nothing. I dove deep into the gray-green black. I kept swimming toward the bottom, hoping to catch up to her. *Why did she do it? Why?*

I kept picturing the blood in my legs slowly becoming slush; I felt as if someone was driving nails through every part of my body. I had to keep my blood moving. I touched my legs to make sure they were still there.

The frenzied dance of the ferry's searchlight caught my eye and illuminated for an instant her figure, a few feet in front of me, drifting to the bottom. I swam toward her and grabbed her. Her eyes seared me, telling me to go back.

I scrambled to free her arms from the rope securing the suitcase. She held on tighter. I couldn't let her do this. But time was running out. She was pulling me down. I swallowed the last gasp of my held breath. I was losing the battle. I couldn't force her up; she was hell-bent on making me cry uncle.

I was powerless to her resolve. She was in a dark place that I couldn't access. As much as I tried, I couldn't reach her. She spiraled further and further away from rationality. I loved her more than anyone. I was her only hope, but she wasn't going to let me save her. As always, she dug her heels in, and no power on heaven or earth was going to change the circumstances.

I had little air left, and I finally said it to myself: *uncle.*

I stopped struggling.

And then she smiled the way she had when we were children. "It's OK. Despite it all, I love you, too," she seemed to say. Her smile faded, and I peered into her eyes. I had seen those eyes many times before: in soldiers just before they passed away on my watch, during late-night vigils when loved ones passed. That mix of defeat and peaceful resignation always collected in their eyes, which were watery with bittersweet tears. Letting them go somehow seems like the only thing to do. It is the hardest part—knowing when to let go. The time had come for her.

I let go. It was the worst moment of my life.

She clutched the suitcase tighter and continued her journey to the bottom, fading before me.

As quickly as she vanished, instincts tugged at my heels. My empty lungs, tightening chest, and the light above called me back. I wasn't going to die like this. Suddenly, a strict head nurse's voice coached me along.

"Keep going. You'll reach the surface. Ignore the pain, the cold. You're almost there. A little bit more. The light is close. Move, missy. Move your pithy ass."

I couldn't reach the light. Where was it? It was as if the light surrounded me, but I couldn't touch it. It was blinding. I couldn't go farther. I swallowed water. Salt instantly went down the wrong pipe and scorched my throat. I gagged. Choking, I broke the surface, gasping for air.

I awaken.

This morning is like so many early mornings since that October afternoon many years ago. I've never understood why no one believes me. That she did jump. That she perished that day.

The official record tells one story, but it is not true. Unlike those who testified, I was there. I saw it with my own eyes. My good name suffered for some time, because I refused to believe anything but the truth.

I wipe the night sweat from my brow and caress my cheeks. My fingertips feel time's ravages.

This dried salted-cod face. These bloodshot eyes. What happened to my baby blues? And my skin—it hangs on me like an oversized coat. I'm not sure when old age happened, but look at me: it most certainly did happen.

And then there's my heart, which progressively weakens. It's no wonder; I survived a heart attack in my seventies, had a pacemaker put in during my eighties, and suffered a stroke in the past year that has left me feeling numb from my right elbow to my fingertips. The doctors have told me my heart stops beating for periods of time while I'm asleep, but I'm not aware of it.

Yet, I plow on. It's just awful to see what time does to you. It's terrible. When I drag myself into the bathroom and look into the mirror, the sight is hard to comprehend. My reflection could kill a baby. But what's harder to comprehend is that I was ever desirable. That someone could be attracted to me. Caress me. Love me. Make love to me.

I can't look anymore. It's too hard to bear.

The moon glows silver outside my window. Branches from the elm trees my grandfather planted long ago scratch the sea-worn cedar shingles of the house. I've got to replace them, but haven't gotten around to it ... and probably won't.

I'm out of sorts. Wadgetty. Rattled.

"Is someone there? Who's calling me?"

No one answers; no one ever does. I usually turn over and pay no attention. But to tell you the truth, I'm a bit spooked, especially tonight, because that feeling is there again. I know she is here with me. The hairs on the back of my neck are standing straight up. She's visiting me this last day—my birthday.

My name is Amelia Moorland. This morning, I'm one hundred years old.

"Congratulations," you might say.

"Thank you, my dear."

You might ask, "What does it feel like?"

I would say, "It feels like winning the lottery. Like I have a new lease on life. Like spring has sprung again. I feel like a million bucks."

Truthfully? It feels like a rusty fuck.

I feel let down. Disappointed. There is so little left to see. Nothing can shock me, move me. I've seen it all. I never dreamed I would be the type of person who would say such a thing. I was always curious. Mischievous. A jadehopper. A (very) few I've recently met on the street who think I'm such a cute little old lady might say I was as clean and dainty as something in the bureau drawer. Still, others might say I was untidy—a slurrup, a slattern. Whatever I was, I lived. I was an adventurer, determined and persistent to go masthead high.

Nevertheless, I'm exasperated to wake this early morning a celebrity. A "been there, done that" veteran of life. A walking encyclopedia. A veritable know-it-all.

"Ask Amelia, she knows everything," I hear people say.

It may come as a surprise to you that I don't feel good about that. I've never turned my back on flattery. Placement on a pedestal as the grand dame was very attractive to me while it was happening. But to know everything leaves one with no desires, senses, or passions. Everything becomes a stretched-out yawn, a big "so what?"

And people start to prod. They want a piece of you. You become the toast of dinner conversation: "May we all live to be her age and with her mind."

"Hear, hear!"

You are invited to all fêtes, fund-raisers, inaugurations, memorials and—thank God—cocktail parties. I'd never make it through these social exercises without the aid of good ole Uncle Jim. Uncle Jim Beam and I have been introduced to the rich and famous.

"Amelia Moorland, may I present to you the president of the United States."

"Ms. Moorland, I am charmed."

"Likewise." (Even though I didn't vote for you.)

The pleasure of your company is always requested. Well-wishers you don't recognize knock on the door and ask you to tea or to have dinner and cocktails always trying to get to know me better.

"Perhaps another time." With a faint smile on my face and a wave of the hand, I close the door behind me, wondering, *Who the hell was that?*

Worst of all, you are the subject of history lovers' laments. They act as if at any moment, you're going to take your last breath. The urgency of capturing a part of you before you die obsesses them. And it's as if they think you're so far gone that you can't hear their wailing.

"She is the last of her kind."

"There can be no one like her."

"Get her on tape before she's gone."

Unfortunately, they're not interested in what I'd like to have recorded. The events surrounding the night Samantha jumped are of no concern to them— nothing more than the ramblings of an eccentric old lady. The one time I let them come in and interview me, they were far more concerned with the stories surrounding my Chinese export collection. They kept asking questions about where I got this piece or that painting, and I'd answer with a question: "Don't you want to know about what happened that evening on the ferry?" They'd look at each other as if they were in the presence of a madwoman, and after an hour, they turned their recorder off and gave up. I never let them in again.

The town is all abuzz about my birthday. The chamber of commerce wanted to block off Main Street and have a picnic in my honor. At an earlier age, I would have blushed and been honored. I might have even thought I deserved it. But looking and feeling the way I do, I want nothing of the spotlight. I declined. They kept asking. I continued to decline. Other organizations followed suit. It was very kind of them, but I don't think they understood. I wanted to spend the day by myself. They sent letters and cards begging my attendance. The telephone seemed to ring off the hook. I turned away dozens of people knocking on my door, hoping to change my mind. Cornered by their badgering, I finally had to act like an old, ugly, matted cat that stays under the bed day and night, out of sight, and only comes out to eat and go to the bathroom. I exuded a "don't touch me, please" aura. They finally got it and left well alone. Honestly, I'm quite content to be alone and around all of my things.

I have many mementos lying about. Every so often, I sift through them, sorting them out, discarding those whose value has diminished and safely storing away those that remain priceless: my father's timepiece. The program from the Hippodrome, where I saw Harry Houdini. My ERA button for the Equal Rights

Amendment, that I wore every day during the seven-year ratification process, which fell short (a terrible moment in our history). And all the letters from my family and Samantha during the war.

But my house is still a mess. It's going by the board, crumbling under layer upon layer of stuff. I can no longer walk into the living room, dining room, library, sunroom, or three guest bedrooms. The basement, garage, and toolshed are stacked with row upon haphazard row of past correspondence, matchboxes, photographs, paintings, newspaper clippings, ball gowns, summer dresses, records, lamps, bicycles, playbills, magazines, and so on, piled high from floor to ceiling (with mouse droppings in between). I have left a path to my bedroom and bathroom, to the kitchen sink and refrigerator (I take my meals out most days). In the end, I believe I will be known more for my pack-rat prowess than for my wisdom. At my memorial service, the town will talk about the state of my house.

"What a disaster."

"That house should have been condemned years ago."

"She should have been condemned."

"How could she live like that?"

"What else, besides her, died in there?"

Wouldn't they all like to know.

Archivists will have a field day cataloging my spoils of war. They'll comprehend the connection of some things to my life, like the extensive collection of Da's Nantucket baskets and photographs of my service in the Great Wars. Others, like the key to room 323 of the Hotel Jerome in Aspen, will confound them, as I've never stayed at the Jerome, nor did I enter that room. I thought about it, but I never walked through that door. Suffice it to say that he was still gorgeous. And who knows? A stay in that room could have changed the course of my life. Only the fates know. But I'll get to that and other juicy bits later.

It took me one hundred years to collect these things; I believe it could take them as long to go through them and document their relevance to my life. Unfortunately, they will discard many gems in their haste to empty this house and ready it for the next owners.

But the only possessions left that are of any real value to me are my memories—and they, like life itself, are failing me. Before they do, I'd like to clear my name once and for all. To let you know what really happened—what they failed to believe. I've got to get this out before I go. You must take it in. Register what I have to say. Gather up the evidence. Perhaps in doing so, you'll find it in your heart to believe me.

You may pass judgment as you see fit. I'll leave nothing out. And I'll tell the truth, at least as I see it. I've never been one to tell a lie. "Liar" would never be imprinted on my tombstone, at least not by my closest friends. "Odd as Huckleberry Chowdah" is a more likely epitaph.

No one living today remembers. But I remember. It has haunted me all these years and eaten away at me. And tonight is my last night. Now is my last early morning.

She is here because of it: This is my last day. I'm sure of it. I have a feeling in my bones. I can feel it in my heart ... whatever's left of it.

I'm tired. It takes everything in me to move. My body doesn't have much oomph left in it, and my heart can't beat much longer. It won't. I'm heading out on the last boat. *arrivederci, mon amour. Mon amour. Mes amours ...*

I've jumped ahead. You need to hear everything from the beginning. Don't let me jump ahead. I have a habit of doing so. Perhaps that's how I came to be one hundred years old—always jumping ahead.

I live on Nantucket Island and have nearly all my life. I wasn't, however, born here. I'm not blessed with that privilege, which is how the natives of the island see it. Unfortunately, I'm a coof. Don't bother checking the dictionary; you won't find an entry for that word. "Coof" is the Nantucket word for those who are not born on the island, simple as that. But no one knows for sure where they got "coof" or when it was first used. The word was, however, derogatory. Or at least that's how Mama perceived it.

Thus, I've been plagued with the "coof" distinction since the day I was born on the morning steamer from New Bedford to Nantucket on what I was told was a crisp, steel blue sixteenth of June in 1901. Mama had held me in during the five-hour sail as best as she could, racing to give birth on Nantucket, for she knew I wouldn't be considered a Nantucketer (part of the family) unless I was born on the Gray Lady's soil. As we entered the head of Nantucket Harbor and rounded Brant Point with less than ten minutes to docking, I popped out of Mama, an impatient coof.

Mama tried to push me back in. I refused. There was a struggle. In the end, I won. I was persistent and had no intention of returning to the womb. It scarred my relationship with her for life. This kind of struggle would play out over and over again throughout the next forty-five years of my life, until her passing.

Defeated, but stubborn as a mule, Mama took me in her arms, threw me over her shoulder, and carried me off the steamer, despite multiple protestations by fellow passengers and crewmen who were horrified that a woman who just gave birth would walk, let alone without assistance. She stomped up Main Street, her head bowed to the ground, embarrassed and humiliated. She turned down Pleasant Street and headed for our house.

Upon entering, she was greeted by my father—my da. "Is it a boy or girl?"

She handed me over to him like a wet dog. "It's another coof. Get me a bourbon." Mama collapsed on the staircase leading to the bedrooms in a fit of anger, disappointment, and tears.

Da looked at me and kissed my forehead. "You may be a coof, but you're the prettiest little coof I've ever seen."

It seems reasonable to wonder why, if it was so important for her to give birth on the rock, that she would decide so close to my due date to travel to New Bedford on a shopping spree (so I was told) for summer clothing. Mama placed the blame on me. According to her, I was premature by one month. Her physician told me that he estimated the birth date to the day. He stated that my mother was insistent upon her estimation and would not listen to him. Such a stubborn error came as no surprise to me, for Mama lacked the basic skills of mathematics, and most likely miscounted the months, thus making the incorrect estimation. Her incompetence with numbers had brought forth another Moorland coof. While this devastated Mama, it had no effect on Da.

And so my life began.

We must backtrack a bit for you to completely understand from whence I came. I base everything I know about my family's history on conversations I had or overheard—and probably had no business listening to—from my parents and grandmother. Whether they're absolutely true, I suppose I'll never know. It's the hand I've been dealt.

My da, Obed Moorland, was a strikingly handsome man. He was tall and thin, but fit as a fiddle, with the most charismatic smile. It made people melt (or at least me). His eyes were blue, and his hair was a mousy blond that turned silvery white in his old age. He was born and raised on Nantucket and, as such, was always considered part of the family. His father, Ebenezer, a fisherman, was lost at sea on a fishing trip during a gale somewhere between Nantucket and Boston in the autumn of 1879. His body was never found.

Da's mother, Eliza, was one of the last orthodox Quakers on Nantucket. She never gave up hope that Ebenezer would once again walk through the front door of their house, as her father had many years before, after falling overboard and being presumed lost on a whaling expedition in the Pacific. She simply couldn't believe that Ebenezer was lost forever.

Being an orthodox Quaker, Eliza lived by the old rules and ways of life. She dressed in black; she kept a simple house with austere furnishings and little decoration (nothing ostentatious); she wanted none of the modern-day conveniences.

Just after Da's father was lost at sea, my da, at the age of eleven, became the sole supporter of his mother (he had no siblings). Thus began his seafaring career as a third-generation fisherman. But Da had no stomach—or nose—for fish. He especially hated cod. As surely as the town clock rang on the hour, Da threw up at the sight of cod. He could manage striped bass and bluefish (which only gave him dry, heaving gags), but cod would lead to his demise. He began having difficulty finding anyone to go fishing with him, and garnered the nickname "Head Overboard," for his head was constantly hanging over the side of the boat, releasing his distaste. Finally, after eight miserable years, and at the suggestion of the master wharfinger, Captain John Killen, Da decided to look for another trade.

He would not, however, bid farewell to the sea. His unwavering sense of duty to the Moorland name and its seafaring legacy were the backbone of his search for an occupation that served the good of mankind—indeed, a contribution proved many times over. At nineteen, he secured a position on the Lightship Number 1 Nantucket, New South Shoals, working eight months on board and having four months' land leave: two months in the spring and two in the summer. I've heard more sailors and captains say that the Nantucket Shoals are the most dangerous waters to navigate with their unpredictable currents, shifting sands, and inclement weather. This was so even with the lightship warning the way.

Da proved a worthy shipmate, doing his duties and staying even-keeled in the most brutal of winter gales and densest fogs, not to mention when ships would head directly into the path of the lightship, just missing it on several occasions. The lightship, however, never moved from its position, chained in place. The crew was ordered never to cut line unless relieved by another ship.

You can imagine the stories my da told my brother, Bernard, and me of his exploits on the lightship. Like a soldier recounting tales of war, Da rattled on until the day he died. As children, we were captivated; as adults, we did everything we could to ignore the recitation of stories already branded in our minds, much like a catchy tune that outlives its welcome.

Though he feared for his life on days when a nor'easter with hurricane-force winds, salt ice, and twenty—to thirty-foot swells pounded the deck as the crew was being battered from one side of the ship to the other (to paraphrase his description), he always felt exhilaratingly alive. He and his shipmates thumbed their noses at the elements, hunkered down, and lived to tell of their harrowing experiences.

Da's stories won him membership into the Pacific Club, whose membership requires the telling of a great tale. The original members were whalers, but their breed was dying out, and the club was opened to all sailors with experience on the seas. He honed his tale-telling skills through many a horrible day and night on board the lightship.

It was a story of culinary craving, not a horrific storm, that Bernard and I heard most often. Da frequently shared an experience that served as the catalyst for his occupational epiphany.

"It was April of 1891 ..." Da used to begin. The captain of the lightship had underestimated the amount of butter the crew needed during one of their long tours of duty. With less than a pound of butter and six weeks before the next supply-ship visit, the good captain had panicked. He couldn't possibly live without butter and would never be so cruel as to expect such a sacrifice from his crew. The captain looked out across the shoals on a clear winter day and decided he would send a crew rowing to Nantucket to bring back butter. The weather seemed in his favor. Da was taken aside by the captain and apprised of the situation. Da tried to protest. "But it's twenty-five miles! Are you mad?"

The captain was enraged. "I will not be without butter, and you will obey my orders."

"Yes, sir."

Da dutifully made the arrangements for the long row home. No sooner had they pushed off than a thick fog surrounded them. Keeping his crew calm, Da pressed on, determined to bring his captain butter. They had rowed for two days when they finally came upon Nantucket Harbor. Da raced to the general store and bought the entire butter stock. The crew reaped their reward of an overnight stay in town before rowing back to the ship.

Da told us he believed there must be a better way of communicating with the island during these times. He said it would be a great convenience to be able to contact town and tell the harbormaster, or any ship's captain, that they were out of butter.

His face would light up, and his eyes would sparkle, and he'd say, "Imagine— during fair weather, the butter could be brought to the ship, instead of the crew going to the butter."

Then he'd put his hands on his chin and furrow his brow. "But how would this be accomplished?"

He said he didn't have the answer to that question at the time, but he knew deep in his heart that the answer would come to him eventually.

Back on lightship duty, it was the boredom, not the life-or-death situations, that got the best of Da. While the weather made the job interesting and provided a plethora of material to weave into dramatic tales, eight months on board a ship that didn't move could put any man in the doldrums. Partly to fight the boredom, but also because they made extra money doing so, the crew, like the lightship crews before them, took up basket weaving. Da was no exception. The baskets they wove became known as the Nantucket Lightship Baskets. What distinguishes these baskets from others is that they are mold woven and have a hardwood bottom. Some weavers signed their name to identify each basket as their own. Da glued an Indian-head penny in the bottom of his baskets.

Today, baskets woven on the lightships back in the 1800s are highly sought after and collected. In fact, baskets attributed to Da can bring several thousand dollars, especially at Nantucket's renowned Raphael Osona Auctions. Weaving, however, didn't stave off the restlessness in Da.

In 1893, he had a conversation with Captain Killen. The captain was thinking about installing the first brand-new hygienic ice machine at the Straight Wharf. This was inspiring to Da; he marveled at the industrial advances happening around him and embraced their elevation of mankind's quality of life. He took leave of the lightship and set out to meet the engineers of the Frick Company in Waynesboro, Pennsylvania, to discuss the possibility of installing such a machine. He was to report back to Captain Killen.

On his way to Waynesboro, he stopped in Brooklyn, New York. He had never seen Manhattan or Brooklyn and thought he should take in the sights while traveling through America. But he took in more than the sights while in Brooklyn. He found himself a wife.

My mama, Catherine Cannon, was thin as a waif, with porcelain white skin and silky, long, black hair that she wore in a bun. She came from Irish stock—the kind that had left the old country during the Great Famine in search of a better life. Her father, Patrick, was an officer with the New York City Police Department who had saved every penny in order to purchase a house. Unfortunately, he died in action with a self-inflicted wound: he swallowed his whistle. In a state of panic, and as he attempted to breathe, he sounded like a chirping canary. A crowd gathered near his post, amused, not knowing the severity of the problem. Patrick Cannon choked to death. Mama was ten. Her mother, Mary—my grandmother, whom I called my nanna—was left with a ten-year-old, a house, and the determination not to lose either. She pulled herself up by the bootstraps and converted their home into a boardinghouse. My da walked into that boardinghouse on Mama's eighteenth birthday. They both said it was love at first sight.

Da never made it to Waynesboro, and he married my mama in the spring of 1893. Upon Da's return to Nantucket, Captain Killen expected a report on the ice-making machine but instead met Mama. When Captain Killen met her, it was understood that Da would never work on the wharfs, let alone in the ice-making industry. Captain Killen eventually got his ice machine, and my parents made it a point to buy ice from him whether they needed it or not—out of recompense, I'm sure.

When Da introduced his new bride to his mother, Eliza coldly embraced her daughter-in-law and immediately excused herself from their company. Mama told me that Eliza had run upstairs to her room to change into another black dress. She felt violated by having touched a non-Quaker—and a Catholic, no less.

Mama had the ears of a watchdog and heard Eliza sobbing in her room and speaking to herself: "Now I have no choice but to read Obed out of the meeting. It was bad enough when he didn't attend meetings. But marrying a non-Quaker … and a Catholic! It's inexcusable. He's no longer fit to be part of the Religious Society of Friends."

Eliza hadn't learned much from the past. The Quakers had thinned their membership down throughout the 1800s on Nantucket by kicking out those members who supported the American cause in the Revolution and War of 1812. You see, pacifism is a central belief of the Religious Society of Friends, but many members fought in or helped finance American efforts. This pitted family members against each other. It caused many to miss meetings and to seek out other religions. This discord also was responsible for many marriages into other faiths. When Eliza read her son out, there were a handful of Quakers on the island (including her).

As history is apt to repeat itself, once he was kicked out, Da, like many of the read-out Quakers before him, joined the Unitarian Church. While he loved his new wife, he had no desire to convert to Catholicism. He did, however, agree that when they had children, Mama could raise them Catholic. Religious instruction was much more important to her than to him.

Shortly after, in the winter of 1894, Eliza succumbed to pneumonia. Mama was relieved; she felt spared of years of icy receptions from her mother-in-law. But it wasn't just Da's mother who seemed standoffish.

After my parents' marriage, Da went back to work on the lightship, despite the objections of Mama, who was quite lonely during the eight months he was away. You have to remember that Mama was not a Nantucketer and did not come from a seafaring family. Unlike the Nantucket women, Mama was not used to being separated from a family member, let alone a husband, for what to her was a long period of time.

The Nantucketers' bone-chilling coolness (as Mama described it) didn't help matters. She was rarely invited to social gatherings. Storekeepers conversed with Nantucketers but would fall silent when she entered their stores. As much as she'd try to carry on a conversation with them about the goings-on in town, she never got beyond small talk. She would have loved to have gossiped with someone, but in those early days, no one would let her into their confidence. They were never rude to her, but she longed for the warmth she observed among them. It was hard to accept their inbred exclusion of foreigners. She would never give up trying to break in. With a wild-eyed, stubborn, "I'll show you sons of bitches" Irish attitude, Mama resolved not to allow her children to be treated the same way, and most likely saw giving birth on Nantucket as a way for her to be redeemed, if not renamed, within the community. Unfortunately, that was not to be.

Their first child, Bernard, my older brother, was born in Brooklyn while my parents were visiting Nanna in 1897. Mama went into hysterics, and a wet nurse had to be brought in. It took a year for her to accept the defeat—not to mention Bernard. My parents had a second child, Nora, in the winter of 1899. Nora was born on Nantucket (thank the Lord), but she died three weeks later (God rest her soul). My parents would wait until 1900 to conceive me.

When Da was on the lightship, Mama counted the days until his return. By 1900, however, the stress of caring for my brother, with me on the way, and the prospect of Da gone for another eight months was overwhelming. She couldn't find the mental strength to survive another year living most of the time with her husband absent. She had endured it for the first seven years of her marriage, but she would have no more of it.

As luck would have it, Da heard about an Italian gentleman from Bologna who was setting the world of science and technology on fire. His name was Guglielmo Marconi, the inventor of the wireless telegraph. Although Da had difficulty pronouncing his first name (as did all Nantucketers—I still can't to this day), he dreamed of meeting Marconi. This was the man who set up the first wireless telegraph across the English Channel. This was a man, about the same age as my da, who was finding solutions to the same questions Da had grappled with. Da imagined wireless communication between the Nantucket lightship and Nantucket Island. It would solve the butter problem he had thought about years ago.

Da was not the only man thinking of the implications of such instantaneous communications. The muckety-mucks at the *New York Herald* imagined the implications of communication with transatlantic ships and set up the Marconi Wireless station in Siasconset (or simply Sconset, as we just call it), a quaint little village on the eastern shores of Nantucket that overlooks the Atlantic Ocean.

If ever there were a company Da dreamed of working for, it was this one. He immediately set his sights on working at the station. Da never met Marconi. He did, however, shake the hand of Marconi's representative, Mr. Bradfield. In August of 1901, Da landed a job with the station.

He spent the rest of his life working in wireless, shuffling back and forth to the lightship to adjust the instruments.

On his deathbed, Da pondered why, in all those years of service at the wireless station, he never got a request from the lightship for butter.

You now know of my parents. It's time to get back to me.

United States Coast Guard
Special Report upon the
Incident on the Steamship *Uncatena*
October 16, 1921
Excerpt, Testimonials, Deckhand Ripley "Rip" Barker

"I was on the lower deck, and Tiny was on the upper, closest to Captain Swain. I yelled up to Tiny, 'Over there!' And he yelled back, 'Where?' And I said, 'Starboard.' And he asked me if I was sure, and I said yes. And he told me to keep my eyes on her, which I did. Then, I heard Captain Swain yell, 'Hold on.'"

CHAPTER II

Since I can remember, I have always started my day with "strangled" eggs and bacon. The smell of bacon is better than sex—at least the sex I'm getting at my age. Which is to say, I'm not getting any, and therefore, it's the smell of bacon that sends me to orgasmic heights. Isn't it tragic that the old are forced to derive their joy from items as basic as bacon and baked apple pie? It's the simple things in life that help us get by. I haven't had sex in thirty years, but I've consumed pounds and pounds of bacon in hopes of keeping my yearnings in check. It doesn't suppress the hunger. All in all, I feel like a nun—and a frustrated one at that.

That may shock you, but by the time I reached eighty, I decided that I'd tell it like it is, and I don't give a rusty what anyone thinks. At the time, I thought I'd only last a few more years. You can imagine how many people I've offended in twenty years, but that's the chance one takes. At eighty, I was regarded as such a nice old lady. At a hundred, I'm regarded as a crude old bitch. No, it's true. Though I'm highly regarded because of my age and experience, the *Inquirer and Mirror* would be hard-pressed to quote me verbatim on most subjects. I believe, however, that if most people would just tell it like it is, words that now make them shudder would become soothing. There is no better remedy when I'm feeling angry than to just let the obscenities flow. Such linguistic release is my cure-all.

I believe I inherited my flair for the obscene from my older brother, Bernard, who claims Nanna handed it down to him. My first introduction to this vocabulary happened when I was six years old. I was such a cute little girl. I hadn't lost my baby fat, so with my curly, blonde hair, blue eyes, and button nose, I looked like a cherub out of a Michelangelo painting. But as you'll see, I didn't act like one.

It was on a Sunday, just seconds before the church bells tolled noon, and just seconds after the ice dropped, clink-clank, into the glass of Mama's midday nip. I walked out onto the front porch to witness Bernard, who was always thin as rail and sported short, kinky, carrot-top hair, falling off his bicycle in the street. Suddenly, he roared a stream of profanities that, quite honestly, made me tremble—not out of shame or fear, but out of sheer excitement.

"Shit, damn, hell, bastard, witch, bitch, bastard, shit, shit, shit!"

The bells continued to toll. Bdong, bdong, bdong …

I called back, "Shit, damn, hell, bastard, witch, bitch, bastard, shit, shit …"

Bdonggggg. The bells ended. I closed my eyes and let out a long scream: "SSShhhiiiittt!"

I opened my eyes to find Bernard looking at me in utter shock. I smiled at him and then noticed the entire neighborhood looking my way. In what appeared to be slow motion, our neighbors came out onto their porches. Everyone on the street turned, dropped jaw, and gasped at my newly found words.

Having conveniently left her drink indoors, Mama ran out of the house, screaming, "How dare you?"

She slapped me across the face.

"Where did you learn something like that, young lady?"

"From Bernard."

"I never taught her that."

"You said it before I did."

"Who told you those words?" Mama asked my brother.

"Nanna," Bernard replied.

"You have the audacity to accuse your nanna?"

"It's true." Whack! Bernard jumped. "She said it when she burned her hand on the stove." Another whack. His face crinkled into a frown. "Ouch! It's true. Honest."

"You children will be the death of me. Come into the house, now." She tried to shuffle us in as quickly as she could, bowing her head to the neighbors in complete humiliation. Mind you, she wasn't humiliated by our public beating (in those days, hardly anyone thought twice about whipping a naughty child), but that such a commotion would involve her and her front yard.

"But I don't want to go inside," I complained.

"Missy, you get in that house, or I'll have your hide."

"I won't!" God, I had titanium balls.

Smack. My face received the back of her hand.

"Go on. You're embarrassing me."

It wasn't the first or the last time Mama would utter those words. She slammed the door shut and grabbed us by the arms.

My da came down the stairs to see what the noise was about. "Catherine, do you have to—"

Mama interrupted. "Not now, Obed."

She hustled us past Da, then ushered us into the bathroom, where she washed our mouths out with soap. "This will cure you of your evil tongue."

The taste made us gag, but it was easier to stomach than the brutal strength of my mother's hands as she scraped the bar of soap over and over our gums until they were bloody and bruised. I wanted to fight back, but I couldn't. She was too strong and unrelenting. I was scared to death of her when she got this way, because she never knew when to stop. We had to endure it, get through it. At times, I think she enjoyed it; hitting us staved off the frustrations of her everyday life. And she was unpredictable—she could snap at any time, like Dr. Jekyll and Mr. Hyde.

Finally, when Mama had had enough, she sent us to our rooms.

"Stay in your rooms, and think about what you've done."

"Yes, ma'am." Bernard was always so proper.

"I expect an apology from both of you, and if I don't get one, don't bother coming out of your rooms for the rest of the day, so help me God."

"Does that mean dinner, too?" The only way I could fight back was to ruffle her up again.

"I'll have no insolence, little lady." I took that as an affirmative: no dinner.

Slam. Slam. The sound of doors banging ricocheted through the house. I could hear her footsteps galloping down the stairs. I heard mumblings of Da and Mama arguing in the parlor. I couldn't make out what they were saying, but I knew they were at odds over how she disciplined us.

Suddenly, the house turned silent. Then I heard Bernard whimpering behind the closed door of his bedroom. He broke within the hour. I could hear his teary-eyed apology through the door: "I'm sorry, Mama."

"You'd better be."

"I didn't mean to." Snuffle, sniff.

"There, there."

"I'll never do it again."

"You swear to it?"

"I'll never use a curse word for the rest of my life."

"That's a fine boy, Bernard."

A fine boy, indeed. To my knowledge, he kept that promise. He was so impressionable. I, on the other hand, immediately retreated to my bed and chanted under my breath, "witch, bitch, witch, bitch, witch, bitch …" until I fell asleep. She would never break me.

Upon waking the next morning, I tiptoed down the stairs and sat at the breakfast table. My da was reading the newspaper. He peeked his head around the paper and winked.

"Good morning, sweet pea. Strangled eggs and bacon for my princess?"

The mispronunciation of my toddlerhood had become an affectionate family joke. I gave him a hug and smiled. At least he forgave me. "Yes, Da."

I grabbed the egg basket, and Da and I set out for Gardner's Market to pick up our usual dozen eggs, and then to Burgess Market for a slab of bacon. As we walked out the door, Mama fired up the Magee Imperial Range.

We brought the goods back to Mama, who refused to speak to me but asked Da the same question she asked him each morning. "How much a dozen?"

"Still twenty-five cents."

She grabbed the egg basket out of my hands and proceeded to prepare breakfast. Da tried to keep her mind off me by talking about the prices of this and that.

"There's talk that they're going to raise the price on milk and cream."

"I doubt the Gardners will allow that to happen anytime soon."

"Don't be too sure. We all have to live, you know. Prices on everything keep going up. I don't even want to think of what the price of coal is going to be this year."

As calmly as she could, Mama handed me my plate. She never looked me in the eye. She would ignore me for the rest of the week, until she finally got over it. However, the unwritten cease-fire would not last, as I would surely provoke warfare once again.

To be fair to Mama, I was, to say the least, a handful. Disciplinary actions only fueled my resolve to turn the screws even tighter. I have to admit that if I had a child like me (and fortunately, I didn't), I most likely would have put it up for adoption. I reveled in making Mama mad, and I did so frequently by pitting Da against her. He, of course, had no idea that he was being used. Mama always saw through my design, but she could never convince him that I could be so devious.

I learned at a very young age that baby blue eyes always proved a powerful weapon to getting what I wanted. I just flashed those eyes, fluttered the lids, and saw everyone but Mama melt before me. Yet, in all cases, such manipulation ended in Mama's disapproval and wrath, and that was, at times, difficult to

endure. A ride in a Maxwell proved to be one of the worst (if not the worst) epi-
sodes with Mama, for the consequences of taking such a ride almost ended my
life. Were it not for my da, I believe my life would be ninety-four years shy of the
hundred years I'm celebrating today.

The arrival of the steam-driven horseless carriage on the island prompted bot-
tled-up enthusiasm from my da and loathing from my mother. I don't believe
that she really hated automobiles, but found that in pretending to do so, she
gained membership (albeit with the caveat that she wasn't island born) into the
community she longed to be a part of.

You see, Nantucketers saw the introduction of the automobile as an attack on
the local economy, since the horse, buggy, and wagon ruled the transportation
sector. It didn't take long for the horses to start throwing their drivers at the noise
of an automobile rolling down the cobblestone streets. Livery drivers would
curse, fists clenched, at the operators of the passing trainless locomotives. Something had to be done to quickly halt this intrusion of modern life on the island's
peace and tranquility.

Mama raised her flag in protest alongside the liverymen and their wives, and
the selectmen acted swiftly to order restrictive speed limits, defying the Massachusetts Highway Commission and the complaints of the Massachusetts Automobile Association. Two years later, they would further their cause by banning
the automobile from Nantucket streets and ways.

Mama became a master orator at town meetings. "We Nantucket citizens are
taunted by this modern fad that does nothing but fill the atmosphere with dust
and the stench of gasoline. It is a nuisance to our everyday existence, not to mention a deadly hazard to the future of our community and our children. My own
children were almost hit by one of these contraptions, while the driver never batted an eye. It's a disgrace, I tell you—a disgrace!"

The crowd cheered. Mama bathed in their acceptance. Bernard and I looked
at each other, perplexed, trying to recall such an event. We didn't know what she
was talking about. After the meeting, a newspaper reporter cornered Bernard and
me and asked us to recount our terrifying brush with death.

"Come along, children." Mother hustled us away before we could get a word
in edgewise. Deep down inside, Bernard and I relished the fact that Mama had
lied; she was human after all. We finally had something on her, but we dared not
use it against her.

The majority of islanders were against the steel contraptions. Da, on the other
hand, fancied himself a future automobilist. He kept his delight to himself,
thumbing through the *Saturday Evening Post* and other publications, secretively

perusing the automobile advertisements while drooling like a pubescent boy discovering pornographic material. In such instances when Da gawked behind the paper, Mama made it a point to break his gape by pulling the paper from his hand, gritting her teeth, and turning red in an attempt to elicit guilt and shame from her husband.

Da looked at her innocently. "Now I can't read the paper in my own home?"

"You're not reading. You're looking at those satanic machines."

"I was reading Jack London's installment."

"I tell you, we'll never have one. I won't have it."

My da got up from his chair and went over to the Columbia gramophone he purchased at C. W. Austin's on Main Street and put on his favorite cold-mold record, "In My Merry Oldsmobile." Da always filled the house with music, and most times, it had a way of softening my mother's firmness.

"Come dance with me, Mother," Da invited.

"Don't be ridiculous."

He put his arms in the air as if he were holding a partner and danced over to her.

"Come on. You know you love to dance."

Mama blushed. "No, Obed. Not in front of the children."

He began singing and forced her up into his arms. Mama loosened up and giggled. Bernard and I got up and mimicked their steps. Da's voice bellowed throughout the room as we all glided across the parlor floor.

When the song ended, we all caught our breath, and Da kissed Mama on the cheek.

"Don't think that a peck on the cheek, let alone a song and a dance, will get you a merry Oldsmobile."

Da sighed heavily. "Sometimes, Mother, you're impossible."

"It's all in the course of the voyage."

He took the paper from Mama's chair and went back to his dreamworld. Mama, slightly defeated, went back to her needlepoint. As she stitched, her brow furrowed in apparent concern with the prospect of losing her newly found acceptance in the community because of Da's fascination with the automobile. She seemed determined to quell his desires at every twist and turn in the road.

I didn't understand how Mama could love my da and still refuse to do everything to make him happy. If he dreamed of automobiles, why didn't she dream with him? She approached everything with fear and negativity and didn't seem to enjoy life. It was Da who taught me to be adventurous, to embrace what life has to offer.

Unlike Mama, I shared Da's excitement about automobiles. I'd sneak into the parlor and flip through Da's magazines, fantasizing over advertisements of people smiling and laughing as they drove down the road with their scarves blowing in the wind behind them. I imagined Da driving, me sitting next to him, and Bernard in the backseat. Mama, however, wasn't with us. We toured the island and had the time of our lives. We even took the ferry to the mainland and drove around the Cape. The three of us were in heaven. Wouldn't that be the berries? I prayed that our dream would come true.

Then came the summer of 1907. By that time, I was a professional at batting my baby blues. A summer resident decided to drive his Maxwell Tourabout from town to the village of Siasconset in protest of the automobile ban. On his way down Broad Street, he was flagged down by a darling six-year-old girl with golden hair who wanted more than anything to take a ride in his satanic machine.

"Please, mister," I begged. "Please take me for a ride."

"Oh, I don't know if I can do that."

"Why not?"

"Well, I think you'd have to get permission from your parents."

"Oh, they'll let me. I'm sure of it."

"You don't think they will mind?"

"No. My da likes automobiles."

"And your mother?"

I couldn't tell him she hated them and would probably tar and feather this motorist if she got hold of him. "I don't know. She probably wouldn't mind. Please? Won't you take me for ride?" I batted my blues. He caved in.

"Well, if you're sure your parents won't be upset …"

"Oh, I'm sure."

"Then hop on board."

I let out a scream and jumped into the Maxwell as quickly as I could, before he could change his mind. He tooted the horn, and we headed out of town.

For those who don't know automobiles of the past, the Tourabout was a two seater with no doors, windows, or windshield (if you can believe that). That might have terrorized some, but not me.

The ride down Milestone Road was euphoric—six and a half miles of complete bliss. The feel of my hair blowing in the wind, the kiss of the sea air on my brow, and the exhilaration of moving at such a fast speed gave me a sense of power for the first time in my life. I vowed never to forget that feeling and always to replicate it—or at least seek it out.

"Go faster. Faster. Faster, mister!" I held my arms up to the sky, feeling the air pass through my fingertips. The resistance of my arms and hands against the wind was electrifying. The man smiled and chuckled. He shifted gears, and the Maxwell roared on.

We drove through the village of Siasconset, past the small, cozy, rose-covered cottages. I remember the roses were just coming into bloom. The tips of the buds were pink and ruby red, and seemed seconds away from bursting open. I can tell you that there is nothing as wonderful as seeing them in bloom, especially when they cover the sea-worn cedar shingles and low roofs of the old cottages. Those enchanting flowers look as if they're out of some fairy tale. They can't be real. I've always thought they were the eighth wonder of the world.

As we drove down Broadway, one of the main drags in the village, the man honked his horn continuously, and the summer bohemians (as Mama used to call them) came out of their houses, roaring with cheers and laughter and waving us on. Being in the Maxwell, with everyone watching me, made me feel part of something special.

After the ride to Siasconset, he drove me home. I felt as if I had been to the moon and back. When we entered the center of town, everyone was watching, terrified at the sight of the forbidden automobile making its way through the streets. Jeers erupted from the liverymen who worked for Lawrence Ayers. "Damn wash-ashore! You should be arrested!"

Women and men scowled at the horrific sight. The pastor at St. Mary's fainted. I felt like a despotic queen. The neighborhood children ran behind the carriage, to the disdain of their parents. *What a sorry lot, these lowly subjects of mine!*

They hated my position and power; I had no use for them. If the mood had swayed me, I would have proclaimed, "Off with their heads!" I had no worries and no need for friends. I was omnipotent.

He dropped me off in front of our house, where Mama, Da, and Bernard stood dumbfounded on the porch. He tooted his horn twice before rumbling away.

Mrs. Macy, our ancient, blind, and decrepit next-door neighbor, was completely taken off guard. She came out onto her porch and looked up into the sky. "Was that a flock of geese?"

I strolled past my family with a grin the size of Nantucket Sound. No sooner had I entered the house than the fireworks began.

Mama was so livid, she had gone pale. "I have had it with you, young lady."

"What did I do?"

She grabbed me by my hair. I felt it grow an inch. "Ow!"

"Don't get smart with me."

"I'm not."

"Quiet!" She tugged my hair again.

"You're hurting me."

"I haven't begun to hurt you."

Da took a step forward. "Catherine, don't."

"You stay out of this, Obed."

This was my cue to play Da against Mama. "Da?" Of course I was batting those eyelashes in between wincing.

Mama would have none of it. "I said quiet!"

This wasn't going to be easy. With one hand maintaining a tight grip on my long, silky, blonde hair, she slapped me across the face. The shock, not to mention the quick burn, snapped me to attention. I began to scream. This wasn't like any other licking.

"Amelia?" Bernard cried out. He clawed Da's pant leg. "Da, do something!"

"Everything will be fine, Bernard." Da turned back and put his hands out, as if to defuse the situation. "Catherine, that's enough."

Mama ignored him and put her hand over my mouth to try to silence me. I wanted to bite her hand, but knew better not to.

Bernard's lower lip trembled. "Da, I'm scared. Mama?"

Da bent down and knelt in front of Bernard. "It's all right, Bernard. Go out back and play. Go on."

Bernard reluctantly walked slowly out the front door. Da started toward us. As he did, Mama tugged at my hair yet again.

"Get away from us, Obed. I'm not finished with her." Mama quickly led me up the stairs to her sewing room and slammed the door shut on Da's face. My vocal cords burned as I screamed bloody murder. She locked the door.

Da slammed his fist against the door. "Catherine, open this door now!"

She slapped me across the face again and again. "Keep quiet," she hissed, "before I wring your neck."

My lips bled. I sucked my lower lip in my mouth in an effort to stifle my screams and sobs. I could taste the salty blood and heaved to keep my cries in. Da pounded on the door.

"I've had it with you, Obed!" Mama screeched. "You always protect this little witch. She does nothing but cause trouble and makes my life hell. I won't have it, Obed. She's going to pay for this."

"She's six years old!"

"She's an insolent instrument of the devil. She's evil, I tell you. Evil. And I'm going to lick it out of her."

Mama had beaten me before, but not like this. I thought she was going to kill me. Instincts told me to run from her, but I couldn't get away. I tried to block her blows with my arms, but they were reddening with every slap. Could I really deserve such a beating? Had I really done something so terribly wrong? I wished she were "back of the rip," as my da used to say—in a place beyond the shoals and sandbars off Nantucket that allowed for no return. I wanted her gone forever.

She took a yardstick and slapped it across my legs. I became a Mexican jumping bean. I couldn't hold the screams in any longer. "Ahhhh!"

I heard Bernard yelling downstairs. "Amelia?"

Da screamed, "Open this door, Catherine!"

She continued the licking. I continued to wail and jump.

Da's tone was more forceful. "Catherine!"

She hit my shoulders with the yardstick. Snap! The yardstick snapped in two and flew across the room. I thought that was it. I thought she would let me go to my room. I prayed it to be over.

Mama was furious. "You broke my yardstick."

I broke her yardstick? I couldn't believe her insinuation.

She grabbed my hair again. It hurt so badly that I thought my hair was coming out of my head. "You think you're so cute? I'll show you how cute you are."

She pulled me over to her sewing basket, took a pair of scissors, and began cutting my hair.

"Noooo. Nooooo!"

I was furious. How could she do this to me? How could she humiliate me? In her fury, she clipped and jabbed my head. With each scrape, I screamed. I thought she was going to kill me.

"Nooooo! Stop it, Mama. Stop it."

I clenched my fists and gritted my teeth. I closed my eyes and began to shake. How was I going to get through this beating? Where was Da? Why couldn't he rescue me? I saw mounds of my hair falling to my feet. Streamers of my beautiful blonde locks tumbled, lifeless, around me. I felt naked and violated.

I heard the frantic beating at the door. Boom. Boom. Boom.

"What are you doing, Catherine?"

Boom. Boom. Boom.

More jabs. More hair. More screams. I hated her.

Ka-BOOOOOM! He finally broke through.

Mama took me by my throat and held the scissors up, ready to strike. Da stopped dead cold in his footsteps. I didn't know what was happening. I shook in agonizing fear. All I wanted was to escape from her.

Da spoke matter-of-factly. "Put the scissors down."

I swallowed air and held my breath to stop the tears.

Mama screamed back at him. "I will not! She's got to pay for this."

"She's had enough. Get ahold of your senses."

"And you, yours!"

"Look what you've done to her!"

Mama looked down at me, and then at the scissors.

Da pleaded with her. "Catherine? Catherine!"

Her eyes welled up with tears.

"For the love of God, Catherine. Please."

She shook her head and dropped the scissors. "Oh, God."

She began to cry and embraced me. Thank God it was over. But I had to get away from her. "Oh God, forgive me. I love you, Amelia."

I wiggled free and ran to my da, who took me into my bedroom and shut the door.

Mama yelped like a bitch in heat in the hall. "Amelia? I love you. It was for your own good. Mama loves you. Amelia?"

"There, there, angel. Mama didn't mean it. She didn't mean it, sweetheart."

He kissed my forehead, held me tight in his arms, and rocked me back and forth.

How could she not mean it? What could I have possibly done to deserve this? It was all so confusing. I hated her.

I heard the screen door open and the reluctant footsteps of Bernard coming up the stairs.

"Mama?"

"Mama loves you, Bernard," I heard her say. "Mama loves Amelia, too."

Da tried to reassure me. "Mama won't hurt you again. Mama loves you. She loves you."

I heard Bernard cry outside my door. I couldn't understand why he was crying. I had just gotten the shit kicked out of me—welts swelling by the minute, hair hanging in a jagged mess, scalp bleeding with scrapes and scratches from the fierce chops of Mama's sharp scissors—and here he was, bawling. It wasn't until later (in fact, much later) that he said he cried in response to the sounds of terror he had heard. He couldn't imagine that amount of brutality coming from Mama or anyone else.

I cried myself to sleep. Da came up with a tray of food and woke me at some point during the evening. I refused to eat; I had no appetite. My stomach was in my throat.

In the morning, I awoke with a headache. My legs stung as I got out of bed and walked to the mirror. I was afraid to look. All I could remember was all of my hair at my feet. I tasted the scab on my lip and looked up.

I had a playmate, Patience Hardwicke, who liked to give her dolls haircuts. She'd snip their long hair off, with no regard to appearance. Chop, chop—she'd cut so close to the scalp that all that was left was a prickly patch of hair. You could see the holes that the strands were glued into. After Patience got through with them, she'd twist their heads off. I felt like one of those dolls.

Mama and Da didn't speak to one another in front of Bernard and me for days. I stayed as close to the walls and as far out of sight as possible. Da wouldn't let Mama be in a room with me alone. At night, through the bedroom walls, I heard her crying and Da scolding her. A couple of weeks later, Mama went away to Nanna's in Brooklyn for a month or so. I was ashamed to go out in public.

After my sores went away, Da took me down to Miss M. J. Brooks on North Water Street for a shampooing and styling. He insisted that he bring me after hours. "M. J.? Take care of my little angel."

I was so afraid that Miss Brooks would scream in fright when she saw me, or tell me I was the instrument of the devil and had gotten what I deserved. Instead, she picked me up, placed me in the chair, and put an apron around me. "You are the prettiest little thing. We're going to make you even prettier."

I smiled with relief. With every snip of the scissors, she moved my head from side to side, trying to find symmetry. Eventually, she made me look presentable, even though I looked like a little boy.

At the end of the summer, Bernard and I went back to our school, up on Academy Hill. It was called the Academy Hill School, but it wasn't one of those hoity-toity New England private schools. It was public.

After school, I'd watch Bernard and his friends playing a new game. They called it basketball. Of course, I wanted to play, and I pushed my way on to the court.

"It's not for girls," one boy said.

"It is too," I protested.

"I bet my sister could whip any of you in a game," Bernard challenged.

"Could not."

"Anyone want to challenge her?"

"It's not for girls."

Defeated, I stomped away. Little did I know how many times in my life I would hear that.

I did my best to stay out of trouble. It didn't last too long. My teacher, Miss Sanford, spent the first few weeks of class trying to warm up to us and pepper small talk into the various subjects she was teaching. It was our geography lesson that planted a wedge between us.

"Have any of you children been off island recently?"

"Why, yes," I said.

"And where and when have you been off island?"

"Well, Bernard and I were wading in the water off Brant Point just yesterday, so we were off island."

The classroom erupted in laughter.

"Amelia, don't be flippant."

I had no idea what flippant was, but I knew it must not be good. "I'm sorry."

That was it. She never liked me after that and never called upon me when I knew the answer. She had this way of knowing when I didn't know the answer, and certainly didn't hesitate to call on me then.

For some reason, I couldn't stay out of trouble that year. I was either deliberately causing trouble or falling into it blindly. Either way, I just couldn't win.

Mama came back sometime in September. Da met us after school to go meet her ferry down at the wharf. That day, he was so excited—but not necessarily about seeing Mama.

As we walked down to the wharf, Da smiled like a Cheshire cat. "You'll never believe what came across the wire today."

Our eyes widened with curiosity. "Tell us!"

"The *Lusitania*."

I thought he was speaking a foreign language. "The Lusi-what?"

Bernard placed his hand on my shoulder, acting as if he were my teacher. "The *Lusitania*, Amelia."

"That's right, Bernard."

Bernard grinned at me. I hated when he showed off, so I shoved his arm off my shoulder.

"And do you remember what I told you about it?"

"It's the biggest ship out there," Bernard answered.

"And how many can it hold?"

"Almost three thousand people."

"Wow," I said, trying to visualize the enormity of that number.

"Amelia, do you know how many people that is?"

"That's a lot."

Bernard continued to try and impress. "That's almost as many people as on Nantucket."

"Right again, Bernard."

"So we all could sail away on her?"

"Technically."

"We could get everybody on that ship?"

"You bet. Just think, your old da talked to the *Lusitania* crew on its maiden voyage across the Atlantic."

We got to the ferry and picked up Mama. She was waving from the top deck. We blew her kisses in the wind. She got off and embraced us all.

"You two have grown so much since I left. I'm not going to leave you again— I promise." She pulled us even closer and ran her fingers through my hair. "There, see? It's growing back prettier than before."

I shook her off me. She frowned in disappointment. The memories of that horrible day had not faded, and wouldn't for a lifetime. Though she never went after me with that much fervor again, I was always on my guard. Children rarely forget.

As for the summer resident who took me for the ride of my life, he was arrested for driving an automobile on Nantucket, but later found not guilty (Nantucket's automobile laws were always stricken down in state courthouses). For punishment, I would have rather been arrested like the driver than feel the pain of Mama's hard hand, but I was happy to be alive and to have taken that ride.

The court decision didn't stop Nantucketers from banning automobiles. Nantucketers (and Mama) continued their vigilance against automobiles, always promoting peace and tranquility.

It wasn't until May 16, 1918, eleven years after my scalping, that the automobile came to Nantucket via a town ballot. The ballot read, "Shall the operation of automobiles be allowed on the island?"

By a margin of forty votes, the town repealed its automobile-exclusion laws, and the horseless carriage became accepted. The automobile war was over; eighteen years of anti-auto protests had come to an end. Nantucket kicked and screamed its way into the twentieth century just as the Great War was coming to end. I don't have to tell you how I would have voted, had I had the opportunity. But women didn't have the right to vote—and anyway, I was away. But I'm jumping ahead … I'll get to that later.

On May 17, 1918, Da woke up and set out to order a Maxwell before he'd even had his morning coffee. Mama looked for another cause to maintain her acceptance within the community. The Maxwell was delivered in a matter of weeks. Ironically, Mama drove it all the time, leaving Da to his bicycle. Da considered buying another Maxwell for his own personal use.

United States Coast Guard
Special Report upon the
Incident on the Steamship *Uncatena*
October 16, 1921

Excerpt, Testimonials, Deckhand Samuel "Tiny" Crosby

"So I asked Rip if he was sure that it was her. And he said yeah, it was her. And then he pointed her out in the water, so I told him to throw her the line. He missed on the first try, so I told him to try again. He went to throw the line, but lost sight of her. I looked out and saw her bobbing in the water and yelled, 'Over there.' He saw her, and I told him not to lose her. He threw her the line, and then I said it looked like Amelia. He said you're right, and then yelled out to her."

CHAPTER III

I don't know why I'm bothering with cleaning the kitchen today; it's not as if I'll be around tomorrow. I hate doing the dishes and taking out the garbage. Perhaps I'll treat myself this last day and pile the dishes in the sink and let the damn garbage sit until God-knows-who discovers my body.

Maybe I won't bathe. They won't be able to discern whether the stench is my decomposing body or the garbage. If they found me reasonably quickly, they could piece together the meals of my last day without opening me up for autopsy. I can see the coroner sifting through the sink, perhaps sneaking a morsel of leftover bacon. "Hmm. Yummy."

Isn't it odd that the last meals and requests of criminals on death row are always of interest to the populace, but rarely is any thought given to the last meals of citizens who innocently go about their own business? I have yet to see the last meal of any law-abiding person mentioned in an obituary.

Obituary … my obituary. I'm not quite ready for that.

It's settled: the egg-crusted pan will sit unattended.

Mama wouldn't approve. She'd be mortified if she were alive. She kept the house clean as a whistle and expected us to keep our rooms shipshape. We'd have to have our beds made and chores finished no later than the first whistle of the steamship.

There it is. Do you hear that? Beckoning, sweet music. It's the morning ferry's whistle.

In the summers of our childhood, Bernard and I used to drop everything and run to the dock to meet the ferries, looking for other children (troublemakers). We'd see Bostonians, New Yorkers, Philadelphians, Baltimoreans, Washingtonians and others walk the plank clad in resort-wear, smelling the blessed salt air. Some searched for loved ones. Others searched for someone to love. Dogs and children would bound out of the ferries as well, tugging at their owners. Some kids screamed; others laughed, playing "catch me if you can." The occasional bullet-smart "Get over here right now!" whizzed past the ill-behaved, turning the heads of locals and holidaygoers who ducked for cover.

And then there were the sages. They departed the boat and knew. Just knew. They knew about life, love, loss … being. Their stories were written on their foreheads, orated in their strides, beamed from their eyes, and stamped on their hands. Wisdom flowed from their garments, whisk-whisk-whoosh.

Back then, I had a mission: I was going to be a sage. I willed myself to have visions of shipwrecks, violent storms, crashing waves—all the ingredients tempests are made of. I thought about torrential downpours of toads … splat-a-tat-tat. I imagined droughts affecting the cranberry harvests with infestations of locusts eating the earth raw. I spent several afternoons in the graveyards, holding gams with the dead ladies and swapping stories with the dead whalers. They enjoyed my sense of humor and imagination.

I went about town, willing doors to open, winds to pick up, people to trip on the cobblestones, couples to sneak a kiss, hats to fly off, horses to whinny. Every time such events occurred as anticipated, I reveled in my newly found powers.

I started looking at people between their eyes. I'd concentrate on the hairs just above the top of their noses and below their brows. I'd bow my head down while maintaining this gaze, which made my eyeballs roll slightly into the top of my head. Then, for the final touch, I'd make my eyes cross. I looked as if I had been born in the middle of the week and was looking both ways for Sunday. I practiced in front of mirrors until I had it perfected. I looked frightening.

Then I started making appearances at meetings of the Daughters of the American Revolution and scaring the bejesus out of the summer residents in attendance. I'd sit in a corner and stare at a few of the women—the ones who smelled of a secret. They fidgeted, always fixing their hair and wringing their hands. They couldn't sit still. They were experts at whick whacking. I would unnerve them to their breaking point.

"That child looks like the devil."

"Poor little creature."

They would usher me out the door like a backyard pet that had broken loose from its chain and made a beeline for the antique sofa.

"Shoo, girl. Shoo."

"She must be possessed."

"You have to be careful of some of these locals."

"Stay away from that one. She's trouble."

"You know her family wasn't on the *Mayflower*."

The door would close, and with two little clicks, the latch would be set.

I began to will things to happen. One particular instance comes to mind. Mama was adamant about having her children's pictures taken each year. She'd dress us in our Sunday best and haul us down to John Johnson, the photographer. She'd have a dozen photo postcards made of us for one dollar. As my brother and I headed toward one such photo session, we walked down Main Street in front of Mama.

I spotted prey. "Bernard. See that baby over there?"

"Where?"

"In front of the bank. I can make it cry."

"You cannot."

"Can so. Watch me."

The baby boy rested on his mother's shoulder with his eyes lazily shut. I whispered my incantation.

"Boy. Sweet baby. Sweet baby boy. Awaken and look my way. Awaken."

Mama heard me say something, but she clearly couldn't make out the words. "Stop mumbling." She tugged at my shoulder, moving us along Main Street. That didn't deter my concentration.

"Open your eyes. Open your eyes."

The baby slowly opened his eyes and looked in my direction. I saw right through him. He whined. I grinned from ear to ear.

"See, Bernard. I have powers."

"That doesn't prove anything. Babies cry."

I countered with a blow to his arm.

"Ouch. Why'd you do that?"

Mama reeled me in by my ear. "Don't hit your brother in public. We're on Main Street, for heaven's sake. Act like a young lady."

If she only knew that I wasn't a young lady. I may have been young in years, but I was convinced I was an old soul. Perhaps I was a witch. Mama had called me that in the past; perhaps there was truth in her accusation.

Or maybe I was a saint. They'd have to burn me at the stake to rid me of my powers. Like St. Joan of Arc, I would be a martyr: St. Amelia of Nantucket, the patron saint of sages. The town would rename St. Mary's in my honor. Schools, government offices, stores, and businesses would close on my feast day. A somber parade would wind its way down Main Street. My statue would sit at the top of the steps of the Pacific National Bank, and people would kiss my hand in hopes of receiving a special gift from me—maybe even a blessing. Pilgrims would camp out in front of our house on Pleasant Street. The pope would come every year to sleep in my bedroom. At midnight, I would make an annual appearance from the dead to those who truly believed in my powers. A new order of nuns would be created (the Amelia-ites), and they would follow my teachings and would distribute prayer cards with my picture. Stained-glass windows would be made in my effigy. Great artists from around the globe would devote their lives to painting scenes from my life. To top off my popularity within the church, the college of cardinals would begin procedures to rename St. Peter's Square in Rome to St. Amelia's Square.

Life as a future saint came with all sorts of powers. On August 20, 1910—a Saturday I will never forget—I had a revelation as I ran down to the wharf to meet the morning ferry. I stopped in my tracks. Bernard continued to run.

"Come on, Amelia. We'll miss it." He looked back at me. "What's wrong?"

"I will meet the love of my life today."

Bernard burst out laughing. Granted, these were silly words from a ten-year-old girl. "What man would fall in love with you?"

Exasperated, Bernard ran ahead of me, leaving me to digest my premonition and mull his counterprediction (which, unfortunately, would have some merit—he must have had powers too).

The steamer *Sankaty* arrived from New Bedford with the usual fanfare. Bernard found a couple of boys to play tag around the dock. Mr. Kittridge, the baggage master, busied himself organizing the various trunks and luggage and barking orders to all of his underlings. I was content to look at the passengers, destined to find my true love. And then, I saw her, peeking around the waistcoat of her portly and very serious father.

She had auburn hair, blue eyes, freckles (oh, dear, did she have freckles), and a small, impish frame. She was dressed as common as a country post, and above her plain collar was the saddest smile I'd ever seen. Her forehead was furrowed, and she gave the appearance of someone old and wise, not a child. We locked eyes. It was just the two of us. Samantha Witherspoon—Sam. In that first exchange, she would rat me out as a charlatan. It wouldn't be the last time. She knew me (the only one in my life to do so, time and time again).

I followed her family up Fair Street to the house they had just bought on Ray's Court. They were moving to Nantucket—not for the summer, but for good. Like Mama, Bernard, and me, the Witherspoons were now part of that inferior group of "wash-ashores." They struggled up the steep steps with their luggage.

Her mother spotted me. "Why, Sam. I think you've found a new friend."

Sam looked me in the eyes (again) and slowly put her hand up to gently wave. I smiled and took off running, making a bee line for home. I was in love.

Before you get excited and think that I've just revealed some major titillating secret of Titanic proportions, the kind of love I'm talking about with Sam was more akin to finding the soul sister I never had. It was intuitive intimacy. It didn't require the physical or sexual. I was not a lesbian, but I was mad about Sam. No other relationship (and there were many physical ones with men) was the same.

We communicated on a different level. We could be together and not talk, but share a conversation all the same. Call it mind reading if you will. We carried on discussions in our sleep many miles from each other. At times, such a connection was disconcerting, as it often felt as if she had the ability to enter my mind and experience my life without being physically present. But she always seemed to come to me when I needed her the most. I drew comfort in that. She knew my thoughts, and I hers. That jeopardized our friendship once or twice, as you might imagine, but I'll save those stories for later.

She was something special—"some nice," as they say here on Nantucket.

But I'm digressing.

That first day I met Sam, I spent every aching hour thinking about her. I had a feeling she was going to be my best friend, and I was anxious to get to know her. Leave it to Mama, however, to put a damper on that.

When I tore through the kitchen door, I knew I was late for lunch. Sure enough, Mama, Da, and Bernard sat at the table, waiting for me. In those days, this was a common occurrence—the likes of which had prompted many a grounded afternoon in my room.

Before I could sit down, Mama was already interrogating me. "Where have you been, young lady?"

I was so excited about Sam that I didn't cower at her questioning. "I met a new friend."

Mama could not have cared less. "You're late."

I tried to appease her. "I'm sorry, Mama, but she's my new best friend."

She would have none of it. "So you're willing to keep your da, Bernard, and me waiting, all because of a friend?"

I turned to Da. "You understand, don't you, Da?"

Da gave me a stern look. "You know the rules, Amelia."

"But, Da—"

Mama interrupted. "Wash your hands, and make it snappy. You'll have all afternoon and evening to reflect upon your selfish behavior in your room."

After lunch, I went up to my room and looked outside. There was Sam, hiding behind the weeping willow in our backyard and gazing up at my window. We waved to each other. I had my mouth open to yell down to her when she placed her index finger to her lips, telling me to be quiet.

I whispered, "I can't come down and play."

She nodded. "I know. Sorry you got into trouble."

I was taken aback. "How did you know?"

Embarrassed, she started backing away. "When I saw you in the window, your expression gave it away."

My face lit up. "We'll see each other tomorrow?"

Mama yelled up the stairwell. "Who are you talking to, Amelia?"

"No one, Mama."

Sam smiled. "Tomorrow." And then she ran off.

I got through the rest of the afternoon and evening by thinking about the next day. But I didn't realize it would be a Sunday, and that meant the weekly argument with Mama, who insisted that Bernard and I go with her to mass. Bernard didn't seem to mind. He liked putting on his only suit and sitting through the sermon. I, on the other hand, hated it. The only part I enjoyed was the music; the rest was for the birds. I didn't understand most of it (in those days, mass was in Latin), and the priest had his back to us. I don't think Mama really enjoyed it either; it was just something you had to do.

Every Sunday's argument started with what I was wearing. I'd come down dressed in overalls, which I thought were appropriate, and Mama wouldn't approve. "Today's Sunday, Amelia."

"I know, Mama."

"That's not your Sunday best."

I stomped my foot down. "I'm tired of wearing that same ol' dress every week. Why do I have to wear a dress anyway?"

"It's mass. We always dress our best for mass."

"And why doesn't Da have to go?"

Her face turned red. "I've told you that is not for you to ask."

I stomped my other foot. "I don't want to go. I don't want to wear a dress."

Mama tried to restrain herself; instead of slapping me, she pinched my shoulder. "We've been through this a million times, Amelia. Don't ruin this Sunday for me by having me discipline you again. Now get dressed, or I'll run you up those stairs and dress you myself."

Mama let go of my shoulder, and I dragged myself up the stairs to change clothes.

In retrospect, my Sunday best was not that awful. It was a gray velvet dress with black buttons down the center, and a big, white silk bow at the waistline that I wore off to the side. At the time, I hadn't wanted to be bothered with dresses and girlie things. But when I look back at old photographs, it was quite becoming on me.

Mama, Bernard, and I sat in the same pew every Sunday. As I walked into the pew, I saw Sam and her parents in the same row. Sam and I smiled at each other as I took my place next to her. I immediately liked mass a whole lot better than before.

During the mass, Sam and I looked at each other and giggled quietly for no reason. Mama heard me and slapped my wrist; Sam looked at her disapprovingly. I looked at the back of the priest and pretended to understand what he was droning on about in Latin.

Then I heard Sam whisper, "My father is like your mother."

I turned to Sam, but she wasn't looking at me. I thought I was hearing things and looked down the pew at Sam's father, who was trying to keep his eyelids open as he dozed off. I didn't know what she meant.

I felt very strange. If she hadn't said anything to me, why on earth would I dream it up myself? Was I hearing voices? Was I going mad?

After Sunday dinner, I went over to Sam's house, and we played hopscotch in her driveway. I had to know if she had spoken to me about her father, or if I had imagined it.

"Did you say something to me in church today?"

Sam concentrated on hopping from square to square. "I don't know. Maybe I did."

"Did you whisper something?"

"Like what?"

"Like that your father was like my mother?"

She stumbled, but regained her balance. "I didn't whisper it … I thought it."

"What do you mean, you thought it?"

She picked up the stone and began hopping back to the first square.

"I knew you could hear what I was thinking."

"But how did I hear it?"

"It was only for you to hear, and you heard it."

She finished her turn and handed me the stone. I was ready to take my turn at the game when we heard Mr. Witherspoon scream. "Don't speak to me that way, woman!"

We turned toward the house and saw his shadow through the front window. We saw his arm swing as he slapped Mrs. Witherspoon across the face. She cried out, "I'm sorry!"

He continued, "Don't let it happen again." The house went quiet.

Sam looked at me with the saddest eyes. "You see it's true. He is like your mother."

I hugged Sam, trying to comfort her. She continued, "We share a gift, Amelia. I can tell what you're thinking and doing, and if you try hard enough, you can do the same. It's why we knew we'd be close friends the second we saw each other."

I was in shock. It had been fun to pretend I had mental powers, but such a notion didn't really seem possible. "But can you hear me?"

Sam shrugged. "You've never tried to speak to me that way."

None of this made any sense to me. I thought she was pulling a fast one on me, so I tried to tell her so in my thoughts. I looked at her intensely, thinking, "You're putting me on, aren't you?"

She didn't respond.

I blurted out. "Did you hear that?"

Sam's face was blank. "Hear what?"

I smiled like a fox. "Hey, I was right—you are putting me on."

Sam chuckled. "If you say so, Amelia."

I wasn't convinced.

In the weeks that followed, Sam and I were inseparable. We became fixtures in each other's families. She had dinner at my house, and I at hers. We went to the beach together with Da and Bernard, and I tagged along to the A&P with Sam and her mother.

Sam and I were also in the same class together. We walked to school and back home together and ate our lunch together. When teams were chosen, Sam and I always managed to be on the same team. We did our homework together and quizzed each other on our math tables.

During this time, I heard no whispers like the one in church. I had resigned myself to believing that I had heard voices, and that Sam was leading me on.

And then, in January of 1911, during a geography exam in Ms. Eagleton's class, I was struggling to answer one of the questions: "What is the name of the longest river in the world?"

Sweat poured from my brow. My mind went blank. The only river that came to my mind was the Mississippi, and I wrote it down. But as soon as I did, I knew it was the wrong answer, and I erased it.

Ms. Eagleton paced up and down the aisles. I began biting my nails. Ms. Eagleton looked at her watch and said, "One minute, then pencils down."

I bit my upper lip. I had no other choice but to leave it blank … and then I heard Sam speak from her seat behind me: "It's the Nile."

I turned around and saw that she was busy writing. I looked at Ms. Eagleton, whose eyes were glued to her watch. "Thirty seconds."

I turned around and wrote the correct answer down.

"Pencils down," said Ms. Eagleton.

On our way home from school, I asked Sam how she had given me the answer. She said she didn't know what I was talking about. Was it possible that her voice was becoming the voice of my brain?

School let out for summer vacation in late spring, and Sam and I spent even more time together. We road our bikes to Brant Point and went clamming in Polpis Harbor. And, of course, we met the daily ferry.

On one such occasion, Bernard joined us. I was in one of my sage moods and boasted to Bernard and Sam, "I can predict things. I know when something is going to happen before it happens."

Bernard made a sour face. "You're crazy."

Sam was intrigued. "What's your prediction?"

I swung around, held both of my arms up in the air, and looked them both in eyes. "There will be a fire this year. People will die."

Bernard knew I was a lot of puff with no pastry. "And there will be rainy days and sunny days. Amelia, you can't predict the future."

I pointed my finger at him like a crazed prophet. "Pay heed to my words."

He pushed me away. "You're annoying."

With that, he ran off to the wharf by himself. I yelled back to him, "I am not." I turned to Sam, needing reassurance. "Am I?"

"You're not annoying, Amelia. But I'm not sure you understand what you said."

"What do you mean?"

"Nothing. Now hurry up, or we'll miss seeing everyone get off the ferry."

We ran down to the wharf. I wasn't sure what Sam was getting at. I had thought I was having a little fun, pretending I was the great sage.

Then came the fire—the god-awful fire.

That doomed Saturday—June 24, 1911, to be precise—was a beautiful summer day, one of those top-ten days of the year. Mama made me lunch, and I went off to bed to take a lazy summer nap. I lay on my bed, thinking about Sam, and she spoke to me.

"You really do have visions, don't you, Amelia?"

"Yes. And you do too."

It was as if she were in the room with me.

Sam continued. "Your visions are mostly terrible."

"What you mean?"

"Destruction. Death. Pain."

I answered defensively. "Don't you have the same?"

"Sometimes death, but I always hope that even if it is death, that something good happens."

"Sam, is that possible?"

"People say it is. But I have to admit that I've never known it to be true, at least with my visions."

"We're talking to each other. Are we witches?"

"I don't know. You're the first person I've been able to do this with."

I kept fumbling for a logical explanation. "Am I dreaming?"

"Maybe. But I'm not asleep, and I hear you, Amelia."

"I know. I see you swimming at the jetties."

I saw her clear as day. She was wading in the water up to her waist in that bathing costume I admired, with the wide black-and-white stripes and ballerina tutu at the waistline.

"Amelia, pick a place to meet later today—as a test."

"OK. Meet me at the wharf at five thirty."

Sam became anxious. "But you've seen something terrible that will happen today."

"No, I haven't. Besides, even if I did, what does that have to do with meeting at the wharf?"

"You'll see."

"Wake up, Amelia. You can't sleep all afternoon." Mama shook my shoulder.

I awoke, disoriented. "Did you see Sam?"

"Sam?"

"Was she in my room?"

"You must have imagined it, Amelia."

"No. She was talking to me."

"Your imagination is going to get you into a lot of trouble, missy."

"I'm serious, Mama. Was she in my room?"

"You must have been dreaming. Now get ahold of yourself, and come with me to Worth's. I need to get some brick ice cream for dessert tonight."

I arrived early at the wharf. I was anxious to see if Sam would show, but I also loved going down to the wharf at the end of the day to soak in the action. There were always fishermen easing their boats into dock, or cleaning the daily catch. People would line up on the docks to see what could be had for dinner. Others, mostly tourists who had never seen a fisherman clean a fish, frowned in disgust as the fish were gutted. Some turned their faces away as if to throw up, bracing themselves upright by placing their hands against the outside walls of the boat-houses and wharf shacks lining the docks.

Day sailors would add to the bustle, tying up their catboats or taking them out for a quick sail before sunset. Interspersed among the fishing and sailing vessels were empty dories tied to one another. You'd hear the push and pull of the ropes tightening as the waves gently rocked the boats back and forth.

As I sat on the edge of the wharf watching all this, I prayed for Sam to arrive and prove that, contrary to Mama's explanation, I wasn't dreaming. I heard music coming from a phonograph. It was "Alexander's Ragtime Band," and it was coming from one of the boathouses where people were securing their boats.

I heard the distant chuckles and laughs of young men and women. I peeked through the door of the Barnes's boathouse. A man was teaching the others a dance step. Two women, one taller than the other, attempted the dance steps as the other men and women stood on the side, appraising the situation.

"Amelia." I turned around, and Sam was there.

"So it wasn't a dream."

"No, but we should go."

Sam grabbed me and pulled me up.

"Why?"

She seemed nervous and had her weather eye peeled on the Barnes's boat-house. I followed her gaze.

A man placed a cigarette in his mouth, then dragged a match along the sole of his shoe. This made a quick, brittle sound, like a twig snapping in the forest, and then the match ignited, fizzing like carbonated water.

He then lit his cigarette and threw the match on the floor.

Whhusshhh.

A corner of the boathouse suddenly was on fire. We heard a shout: "Fire! Fire!"

The men and women in the boathouse scrambled and screamed. Four of them ran from the building, which belched smoke. We heard screams, horrible screams. And then we saw one of the men in the boathouse take a bucket of water and pour it all over the floor. Instead of extinguishing the flames, it ignited them farther.

The music melted, stopped. The entire boathouse went up in flames. The scene before us looked like one of those moving pictures at The Dreamland, only this was real. We later learned it had been turpentine, not water, that was in the bucket.

Everything was all adrift. Sam and I couldn't move from that spot; it was as if our bodies were bolted to the wharf. I closed my eyes, hoping that when I opened them, this would not be happening. But it was. And we were shaking. I tried to stop by tensing my muscles, but that only increased the tremors. I began to feel cold.

Sam finally shook lose and grabbed me, and we ran for cover, finding shelter under an abandoned cart. People on the docks were in a panic. Cinders were raining down like Fourth of July fireworks gone awry. The sky flamed red, black, and blue. Smoke poured out of the boathouse and grabbed us by the throat, choking tightly. People around us put handkerchiefs up to their mouths. Mothers and fathers shielded their children from the sight as they sobbed. Tears flowed down our cheeks. All we could hear was the ferocious roar of the flames and bone-chilling screams. I prayed for them to stop; it was too much to bear.

We saw a man run into the building to help. In seconds, we heard his cries. "Help me! Ahh …"

We saw him go up in flames. He never came out.

Sam and I ran off the wharf and up Main Street, which was crowded with anxious people. A woman fainted. Another sat on a bench, mumbling incoherently. A couple of reporters dashed out of the offices of the *Inquirer and Mirror* and ran toward the wharf. They passed a young man who stood embracing his two babies and wife, refusing to let them go. People were yelling for their loved ones.

As we turned the corner onto Fair Street, we looked back. Smoke was rising above the Pacific Club. Our faces were streaked black from the soot. We were coughing up smoke. We wiped our tears away, smearing charcoal gray stains onto the backs of our hands and our dresses. Our clothes were ruined. Our emotions were shattered. We held each other, shaking and crying. Our legs gave way, and we collapsed curbside.

"It's my fault. I knew this was going to happen. I told Bernard there would be a fire, and there was." I began slapping my own face. I was a devil child.

"No, Amelia, it's not your fault."

"I should be the one who dies, not those people."

"You didn't really know this was going to happen, did you?"

I kept slapping my face. I was so raw, I couldn't feel the sting of my hand. She took hold of my wrists and stopped me.

"Did you?"

I wiped my nose and looked at her as tears welled up, and my tongue went back into my lungs. "No."

She took me in her arms and pressed me close. I felt warm and safe as I sobbed in her embrace.

Sam and I gathered ourselves as best we could and made a straight wake for our homes. Our parents hadn't known we were at the wharf, but they would have seen the smoke and heard all the commotion about the fire, and they were probably in a panic because we weren't accounted for.

When I walked through the door, and the screen door closed behind me, I heard a shuffle in the kitchen.

"Amelia?" Mama ran out of the kitchen and down the hall toward me. I thought she was going to attack.

"Don't hurt me!"

"What happened to you?"

I must have looked quite a sight. "Please don't hurt me."

"Your father and I have been worried sick. You were down at the wharf, weren't you?"

She reached out. I thought she was going to hit me.

"No. Please, no."

"Amelia, for heaven's sake. What's gotten into you?" She pulled me toward her and embraced me. I stood still as a mouse. "Did you see the fire?"

"I saw it. I saw the fire, and the people … they …"

I couldn't finish the sentence. I couldn't talk about the burning figures I had seen, or the mixed smells of burning wood, chemicals, and flesh. The anguished looks on everyone's faces. I felt as if I'd been to hell and back. I began to cry. Mama rocked me back and forth. At that moment, Da and Bernard came running through the door.

"May Congdon said she thought she saw …"

Mama turned around, and Da got a glimpse of me. "Oh, thank God."

He embraced us and prompted Bernard to do the same. "We were so worried, Amelia. Are you all right?"

Before I could answer, Mama answered for me. "She'll be just fine."

Mama pushed me away from her and placed her hands on my shoulders. "You shouldn't go down there alone. You're forbidden to go down there without Bernard or Da or me."

Bernard looked at me with raised eyebrows, questioning my silence. He knew I would never agree to live by such a rule. But for the present time, I went along with it, because it calmed me and felt soothing. It was one of those moments when Mama could be as loving and kind as Da always was. I could never figure out why she couldn't find it in her heart to be this way always.

"Let's get you cleaned up, sweetheart."

She escorted me up to my room, helped me out of my soiled dress, ran a hot bath for me, and washed me gently.

"Mama? Am I a bad person?"

"No, Amelia. You're not. What makes you ask such a thing?" She poured water over my shoulders.

"I don't know. You're always telling me I'm the devil or talk like the devil or something like that."

She took my face in her hands. "You're an angel."

"I don't feel like one."

"Well, you're my little angel tonight. Now, come on. Let's get you dried."

That night, we sat quietly at the dinner table. Nobody felt like eating. I ended up pushing my food from one end of the plate to the other. This behavior would normally launch a stern lecture from Mama, but in these special circumstances, she let it go.

Exhausted, I finally spoke up. "Can I please go to bed?"

"You don't want any brick ice cream? It's strawberry—your favorite."

"I'm not hungry. All I want to do is go to bed. Can't I? Please?"

Mama and Da looked at each other and had some kind of unspoken conversation. Da put his fork and knife down, and with a nod from Mama, turned to me and patted me on the head.

"Certainly, sweet pea. You have pleasant dreams."

"Thanks, Da."

He kissed my forehead.

"Come on. Let me tuck you in." Mama got up from the table, placed her arm around my shoulder, and led me upstairs to my room. She drew the curtains, turned down the bed, and tucked me in.

"Good night, Amelia."

"Good night, Mama."

She held me tight. I could hardly breathe. She was choking up.

"You forget everything you saw today. You're going to be fine. Just fine."

I hoped so.

She released me, kissed my cheek, and tucked me in. Just as she closed the door, she turned to me.

"I love you so, Amelia."

It was one of the first times I can remember thinking that maybe she really did.

I tried closing my eyes but couldn't fall asleep. I kept reliving the day. And then I heard Sam.

"Amelia?"

"Yeah?"

"Are you all right?"

"I guess. You can still see them, can't you?"

"Yes."

"Me too."

"Sam, I've never seen someone burn before."

"Me neither."

"Those two women, the ones who were learning the dance steps before the boathouse caught fire ... they were so pretty. I keep thinking about their skin and hair on fire. And the smell. And nobody being able to do anything to help them. And that man disappearing in the flames, crying for help. How could this happen? How?"

"I don't know, Amelia. My mother says we can't question these things. They just are."

"Every time I close my eyes, I see it over and over again."

"It will pass, Amelia."

"Are you sure?"

"Yeah."

To tell the truth, I didn't believe her.

Sam's voice cracked. "I saw them get into their catboat this morning, Amelia."

"You did?"

"The taller one was talking about a young man she was hoping to get engaged to, and how much she was looking forward to sailing that day."

"Did you know then that it was going to happen?"

Sam didn't answer.

"Sam, did you?"

I knew she was there, but she couldn't answer. "I think we'll be friends forever, Sam."

I'm not sure if she heard that. By that time, I couldn't feel her near. I turned over and closed my eyes. I finally got to sleep, but my dreams were filled with the fire.

The next morning, two coffins were placed on the *Sankaty* steamer. Two young women, Ms. Helen Wilson and Ms. Mildred DeHaven, seventeen years old and twenty years old, were dead.

I remember so vividly the image of two caskets, each adorned with a large bouquet of flowers, being carried aboard. And silence—an eerie silence pervading the air. The waters were still and smooth as glass. No wind blew from any direction. Even the seagulls were silent and out of sight, nowhere to be seen in the skies above or on the wharf. Life would go on. But on that day, there was nothing in the universe to be said.

The man we had seen run into the burning building was the Barnes's butler. He died shortly after. Another man, the one dancing (or so I thought), died the following Monday. The Barnes's son survived, but was severely burned. When I saw him later in life, I did everything I could to avoid him—not because he was a bad man, but because seeing him reminded me of that horrible day.

I didn't sleep soundly for months. Bernard never made the connection between my premonition and the fire; he must not have ever believed I had powers. I stopped pretending I was a sage. I didn't have the stomach for it. I did have the gift of telepathy with Sam. We shared some kind of power. But other than our ability to communicate on a different plane, I wanted no part of the supernatural. Unfortunately, many times during my life, I had feelings about the future that I would have given anything not to have experienced.

Do you hear it again? That sudden sound like the horn section of a symphony, blasting double forte. Then it stops and reverberates off the town buildings, softening, until it fades like a last breath. Silence, and it's over.

That's the last time I'll hear the morning-ferry whistle.

United States Coast Guard
Special Report Upon the
Incident on the Steamship *Uncatena*
October 16, 1921
Excerpt, Testimonials, Deckhand Ripley "Rip" Barker

"So I yelled out to her to take hold of the line. She wasn't going for it. It was like she was stunned or something. Then I yelled up to Tiny and asked him if I should jump in after her. But before he could answer, she took the line and waved at us. She was conscious. Tiny shouted to her to put the line around her. Then Captain Swain asked if the blankets were ready. I told him they were right next to me. She then dropped the line. She wasn't holding on. We told her to grab onto it. She wasn't responding, so I said I was going in after her."

C H A P T E R   IV

I've been invited to Boston next weekend for the Red Sox-Yankees game. You must think I'm half seas over, as they call drunks on Nantucket, for even considering going, especially at one hundred and with my heart condition.

But as you well know, I won't make it. I'm torn between telling Bobby to give the ticket to someone else, or letting him put one and one together. If I call him, it might upset him and put a damper over the outing. I can imagine the conversation.

"Hello, Bobby? Yes, it's me, Amelia. I'm fine and you? I'm calling to let you know that I won't be going to Boston after all. You see, I'm dying this evening. That's right. This evening, I'm dying. But have a hot dog with all the fixings in my honor, will you, dear?"

How I will miss baseball. I've loved it ever since I was a kid. In those days, you'd go out to the grounds of the Sea Cliff Inn on Cliff Road and watch the cottage clubs play. The Sea Cliff was one of the grand dames, if not the grandest dame, of Nantucket's hotels. It sat majestically on the cliff overlooking Nantucket Sound. People mostly from New York and Boston, but other areas too, would take up residence there for the summer.

There was always something going on at the Sea Cliff, including baseball. Calls would go out to the locals and summer residents to form a team, and they'd take on everyone from Falmouth Heights to the Hyannis Club and that other island over there in the distance ... what's its name? Oh, yes, Martha's Vineyard. It's a terrible island, full of old-town turkeys ... but then, they think we're a bunch of scrap islanders. It's a nice rivalry. However, when all is said and done, our island is much better, even if they claim the opposite.

Bernard and I also followed the professional teams. We made such a cadoo about the Boston teams, both the Red Sox and the Braves. We knew all the players and kept track of all their wins. We'd go down to Mack's on Main Street to get the latest scores from the wire. Everyone paid into the fund, so that Mr. Mack (or Dick, as my da called him) could keep the town abreast of the scores and news. Guest houses would ring him up for the latest reports. People would line up outside his store to read a headline or catch the scores.

On Saturdays, Bernard, Sam, and I would go with Da to enjoy Mack's Saturday Special, which was chocolate walnut fudge for thirty-nine cents a pound. Da got his smokes, we kids got our fudge, and Mr. Mack would tell us how our teams fared.

When the World Series was on—especially when the Red Sox or the Braves played (which in those days, seemed like almost every year)—people would line up in front of Mack's during each game and wouldn't leave until the final result was posted. Those who couldn't be there in person kept his telephone wires warm. It was a nice diversion from the everyday ups and downs and the impending cold of winter.

But the year the First World War broke out in Europe, Da would need a diversion more than anyone else who congregated in front of Mack's. You see, almost everyone felt the war was far away, and it wouldn't affect us. I was thirteen and had absolutely no idea what the war meant—or how, or if, it would enter our front door. Oh, I heard my parents and Bernard talk about it. Da would read us the news from the paper.

"It looks like war is going to break out at any moment. The stock exchanges in New York and Boston have closed."

"Has that ever happened before?"

"And it says London exchange has closed as well."

I didn't see the connection between Nantucket and Boston or New York—or especially London. How could this upset our summer?

One night, Bernard looked over Da's shoulder as he was reading the paper and saw a map of Nantucket. "Amelia, do you see this?"

"It's Nantucket. So what?"

"So what? You see that line there?"

"Yes."

"Ships have to get into that area to be safe from being destroyed or captured."

"Who's going to destroy or capture a ship out here?"

"The Germans would."

"You think so?"

"They say German warships have already begun chasing ships."

"I wonder if we could see that from the shore?"

"Maybe on a clear day."

"Do you think they'll try to take over the island?"

Da tried to calm the waters. "We've got nothing to do with that war, and we'll all be just fine."

Bernard didn't appear to believe him. And to be perfectly honest, at that point, I didn't really care.

The war ripples crossing the ocean didn't reach us until that late September day in 1914, when Da came in and gave Mama the news.

"What are you doing home so early?"

"They shut us down." He was pacing back and forth.

"Who shut what down?"

"The secretary of the navy. It's censorship, I tell you." He poured himself a bourbon and drank it in one gulp. That was something we rarely (if ever) saw him do.

Mama was flabbergasted, and rightly so: this behavior was expected of her, not him. "What happened?"

"We forwarded a message from a British cruiser to the British admiralty in New York about supplies for the warship."

"What's wrong with that?"

"Supposedly, the navy forbids it."

"Does this mean you've lost your job?"

"One of us has to stay on until the government decides what it's going to do. They chose me."

"Oh, thank God."

"But the others had to go, and I don't know if they're going to tell me to walk as well. Nixon, that rat from the navy, is going to be watching over me like a hawk."

"Will you still get paid?"

"Of course. Marconi has been good to me throughout the years, and I'm sure they'll continue to be so. They're trying to fight this in the courts."

Da poured another drink; this time, he sipped it. "It just gets me so angry. We're only doing our job. We would've done the same for any ship flying the flag of any country, including the Germans."

Mama wiped her hands on her apron, went over to Da, and hugged him. "Just be careful, Obed. We can't afford for you to lose your job."

"As if I didn't know that." He gulped his drink and went into the living room.

I had never seen my da brood so much as he did that evening and the following days. He was always good-natured, but this put him down in the dumps. The war had reached our house.

Thank God for the World Series. That year, the Boston Braves were playing the Philadelphia Americans. Da, Bernard, Sam, and I (to the consternation of Mama) made our pilgrimages down to Mack's to follow the games. Our excursions seemed like the only thing Da looked forward to.

The atmosphere at Mack's made you feel over the bay. The energy of people rushing in and out of the shop, asking Mr. Mack if he'd heard anything else, and the constant ring of the phone was testament that Mr. Mack was truly the busiest man in town during the series. One day, he estimated that he answered almost fourteen hundred questions, of which over thirteen hundred were without profit.

People would make wagers, and some would win quite a bit of money. Jim the bootblack, who knew more about baseball than the rest of us combined, made a wager on odds and won twenty-one dollars.

"I'd have to shine two hundred and ten pairs of shoes for that kind of money." He was so proud of his foresight.

After each score was announced, Mr. Genesky would get the crowd singing "Tessie." My da would join in and forget all about the wireless station and the war.

Those who cheered for Philadelphia protested, "No, no, not again!"

But the majority of the crowd would sing even louder.

Da jeered back at the Philly fans. "If this song helps the Red Sox win, it'll work for the Braves too."

Suddenly, Mr. Mack poked his face out the door. "Gowdy hits another double."

Sam and I cheered, and we sang that song at least fifty times each day, not counting the number of times we sang it in our sleep. It was one song you couldn't get out of your head. I think the reason the song helped the Red Sox win was because the challenging team got a terrible headache listening to it over and over again. Actually, there was talk about banning the song from Fenway Park, because it was so annoying to the visiting teams.

But that year, that repetitious Tessie came to the aid of the Braves. They won the series in a shutout—and in doing so, took away Da's anxiety (for at least a few days) and gave Sam, Bernard, and me a reason to hold our heads high for rooting for the winning team.

The war, however, knocked on our door again. Mama came home one day from one of her anti-automobile meetings in tears. She was almost inconsolable. I, of course, thought I had done something wrong, but I couldn't figure out what it might be. I feared the punishment that would follow. I must have turned white, for I felt as if I were struck with the dry wilt. Da wiped away Mama's tears.

"What's wrong, Mother?"

"Children, please go up to your rooms."

Bernard and I protested.

"Why, Mama?" Bernard asked.

"What did I do?" I asked.

"Do as you're told."

We hemmed and hawed on our way upstairs, then both kept our ears against our doors to steal a listen.

"Do you remember the Gardner's from Siasconset?"

"Yes."

"Well, she's originally from Belgium ..."

Mama was choking up. "... and she got word that some of her family ..."

I pressed my ear to the door, but heard nothing but sobbing. I finally cracked the door and looked out. Bernard had his door wide open. I whispered across the hall to him.

"What'd she say?"

"Shh."

Bernard signaled me to come over. I slipped out of my room and tiptoed as quietly as I could over to his room. He closed the door behind me.

"What was it?"

"I don't know if I should tell you."

"Come on, tell me."

"It might be too frightening."

"It won't scare me. Hardly anything scares me anymore ... except Mama sometimes."

"They might get angry at me for telling you."

"I won't tell them. Really, I won't."

"You swear on your life?"

"One hundred times. Now tell me, Bernard. Please?"

Bernard took me by the shoulders and half whispered into my ear just to make sure our parents wouldn't hear. "Mama said the Germans killed the Gardners' son-in-law in Belgium, and their daughter and one of their grandsons have gone missing."

"How'd they do it?"

"I don't know, but their other grandson is alive and trying to avenge the death of his father and find his mother and brother."

"What would you do if they killed Da?"

"I'd hunt them down and kill them too."

"Do you think the Germans will pass the three-mile line and attack Nantucket?"

"I don't know, Amelia. But I sure know that I'd kill them if they tried."

"Me too."

"Not a word about this, you hear?"

"Yeah."

"Get back to your room before they find us."

I slowly opened Bernard's door. My parents were still talking.

"But Belgium was neutral. We're neutral. What makes you think they'll respect us?"

I stopped to listen as Da eased Mama's concerns.

"We have to believe this war will be over soon," he said calmly.

"But they dragged England into it. What makes you think they won't drag us into it as well?"

"It's not our war, Mother."

"They're bullies. They're nothing but Huns."

The shadow of Mama appeared in the entranceway. I got back into my room without any notice and lay down on my bed, trying to envision Mrs. Gardner's grandson searching for his mother and brother among all the Germans who had taken over Belgium. I was thirteen years old, and I had never met a German—or at least I couldn't remember meeting one—but I immediately hated them.

During that late fall of 1914, Sam knew I had nightmares of the Germans invading Nantucket. She woke me almost every time I had one. She always woke me before they shot Da.

"Amelia?"

About one hundred faceless soldiers pounded on our front door.

"Amelia, can you hear me?"

Mama was screaming as Da tried to shove us into the cellar.

"You've got to think of other things, Amelia."

The door came crashing down, and guns were pointed at Da. I stuck my head outside the cellar door, and I saw the finger of one soldier on the trigger, ready to fire. Da was as good as gone.

"Wake up, Amelia. Wake up!"

I screamed, running toward the Germans. "Nooooooo!"

Suddenly I sat up in bed, surrounded by darkness. All I could hear was my heart pounding as I gasped to catch my breath.

"Are you all right?"

I slowly got my bearings. "Sam?"

"Yes."

"I had it again."

"I know."

"I can't stop thinking about it."

"You've got to try, Amelia. Think of something else. Think of us wading in the surf."

"I try, but it always comes back to this."

"They'll never reach us here, Amelia."

"How can you be so sure?"

"Because it's too far-fetched."

"I wish I felt the same way."

Sam was gone. I lay in bed, waiting for daylight, shaken by the thought that my nightmare could come true.

Christmas came and went without much joy that year. We went through the motions of celebration, all the while praying in church for the end of hostilities and to better days of peace. But a gray cloud seemed to hover over us, and quite frankly, it dampened our spirits.

The Marconi Company lost their suit against the government and made the necessary adjustments to comply with the government's rules. By this time, Da was less concerned with issues of censorship than with keeping his job. Prices for food and coal were creeping up, and Mama's constant worrying and complaining never helped the situation.

The wireless station reopened in January of 1915, and Da's nemesis, Ensign Nixon, was relieved of his duties. The first brushes with the war were behind us, but they would not be the last.

I always enjoyed the month of May. Mama, Da, Bernard, and I would take walks down Main Street after dinner to gaze in the shop windows, see who had arranged their storefronts for the season, discover new stores, and to rekindle friendships with those we hadn't seen over the hibernating winter. We called these walks our random scoots. And we always ended up at Mack's.

But on a beautiful May day in 1915, our random scoot was shattered by the headline written outside Mack's door: "LUSITANIA TORPEDOED SUNK!" We ran into Mack's, and Da pressed him for the details.

"Those poor people." My da looked as if he had been blown over by a squall.

Mr. Mack shook his head in disbelief. "It went down in less than thirty minutes. How could they do such a thing?"

Da had to find the nearest bench to absorb the blow. His beloved *Lusitania* was gone.

Bernard went off like a firecracker. "I told you they'd stop at nothing. We should do what Roosevelt says. We should enter the war."

Mama grabbed him by his shoulder. "Bernard, don't say such a thing."

"Why not, Mama? They've just attacked a civilian vessel, not a warship, with innocent people aboard, killing over a hundred Americans—not to mention the thousands of other civilians. When are we going to stand up and say enough is enough?"

I took hold of Bernard's hand. "Would you go and fight, Bernard?"

Mama didn't give Bernard time to answer. "Amelia, don't ask those kinds of questions."

Instincts told me not to provoke her with talk about war.

Bernard stood up straight as an arrow. "I'm thinking of joining the French Foreign Legion."

Mama exploded. "You'll do no such thing, and we'll have no more discussion about this."

Bernard protested. "I can't stand by and watch them kill innocent people. Today it's the *Lusitania*. Tomorrow, they'll decide Nantucket would make a great base for their submarines. Then what are we going to do?"

I began to wonder if Sam had been wrong about the likelihood of my nightmare becoming reality.

Mama pleaded with Da. "Obed, say something, for heaven's sake."

Da must have had visions of that great voyager sinking to the bottom. "Let's not frighten your sister, Bernard."

Mama furrowed her brow. It was not the response she wanted to hear.

Bernard wasn't ready to give up. "She's not frightened. Besides, it's our duty to speak the truth, however much the truth may hurt."

Mama wanted this discussion over. She grabbed Bernard by his collar. "Your duty right now is to respect your mother and do as I say. And right now, I say nip this talk of Germans, the war, and the Foreign Legion."

I could see Bernard's jaw jutting out the side of his head. He was turning red. "Yes, ma'am."

Mama let go of his collar and gently straightened it by pressing it with her hands. "Come on, Obed. We're going home."

That night, I went over to Sam's house and told her Bernard's intentions.

"He's very brave, Amelia."

"I know. But I don't think a day would go by without me worrying about him. And I can't imagine how it would be for my da and Mama. What if he were injured or killed by the Huns?"

"That's not going to happen, Amelia."

"Can you be sure?"

Sam took both of my hands in hers. "Bernard will make the right decision, and he'll keep safe. Don't worry about it."

That was easier said than done.

By the summer of 1915, Bernard had graduated from high school and had begun working for the New England Telephone and Telegraph Company (like father, like son). He was a salesman, and a pretty good one at that. He signed up more guest houses and private homes than anyone else working on the island at the time—or at least that's what he told me. When we got our first telephone (you'd be correct in assuming Mama was against it), Bernard taught me how to make a toll call.

"OK. You call the local operator."

"Right."

"She's going to ask you for the number. You tell her you want the toll operator."

"Toll operator."

"Correct."

"Then you give her your number."

"123–13."

"Your name."

"Amelia Moorland."

"The town or city the party you want to speak to is located."

"Washington DC."

"The telephone number, if you know it."

"I don't."

"Or the name of the person you want to speak to."

"President Woodrow Wilson."

"Come on now, Amelia. This is serious."

"I am serious. I want to speak to the president about the war."

"Well, so do I, but you don't see me trying to make a toll call to the White House. That's just plain crazy."

"Well then, maybe I'm crazy."

"I'd say you've gone to Hyorky."

"Well, it's nice here in Hyorky. You should visit sometime. So tell me what happens after I tell them who I want to speak to."

"The toll operator will then tell you that they'll call you when they reach the party you want to call. In the case of the president, don't expect a call back any-time soon."

"This is a lot to remember just to make a toll call."

"You'll get the hang of it. Just don't be calling President Wilson, or Mama will be over you like whalers to whale oil. The last thing she needs is for you to embarrass her by becoming the talk of the town."

Bernard told me that on his lunch hours, he often went to the Atheneum Library to scour the newspapers for news of U-boats, specifically in the Atlantic. The Atheneum is not your average run-of-the-mill library. In addition to boast-ing some of the most stately and beautiful architecture in Nantucket, with its white facade and soaring columns at the entrance, it also boasts one of the richest histories, as we were taught in school at a very young age. It has hosted some of this country's greatest political and literary figures. We had to memorize all of their names—and for whatever reason, they've stuck: Ralph Waldo Emerson, Henry David Thoreau, Frederick Douglass, Maria Mitchell, Lucretia Mott … oh, I could go on and on.

So Bernard made the great hall of the Atheneum, where all these luminaries spoke, his war room. He was at loggerheads with Mama and Da, and he knew he couldn't read the newspapers in front of them without causing arguments. He bought a map of the world and carried it with him at all times, marking the vari-ous skirmishes between the German, English, Dutch, and American vessels. He kept track of the losses sustained by all sides. I'm not sure what Mama and Da thought he was doing in the Atheneum, but I don't believe they knew he was secretly following the war.

Lucky for him, Mama became sidetracked by the possibility of airplanes land-ing in Nantucket. But Mama didn't call them airplanes. She called them automo-biles, because the flying machines had engines. I'm sure you think I've lost a few screws for saying that, but I swear to God it's true. Mama and Da would disagree on this regularly.

"If they did allow airplanes to land …" Da would begin.

"Automobiles," Mama would correct him. "They have engines, remember?"

On one particular instance, Da shook his head in frustration, just like always, then continued, "If they allowed them to land, they say they'd begin delivering our mail by air, which would benefit us, because we'd get it faster."

"And why is getting the mail faster such a benefit? You're always concerned about getting things and going places faster."

"It's called progress."

"Progress will ruin our way of life if it doesn't kill us first."

My nightmares were replaced with dreams of flying.

I would soar like a red-tailed hawk in my flying machine, with Sam behind me. We'd fly over the windswept shores and the blue-gray sea. We could spot seals, whales, and schools of cod swimming below. The stripers would be running, and we'd point them out to the fishermen, who would wave and cheer us on. We'd fly over town, making crazy eights between the steeples of the Congregational and Unitarian churches. Mama was always below, shaking her fist at us and yelling something we couldn't hear over the roar of our engine. I'd land the airplane on the highest point on the island, Altar Rock, so everyone could behold us. People would rush from all over, in their carriages, on horses and bicycles, to greet us, and Sam would hand over a bag of mail to the postmaster. We'd all dance around my airplane, and I'd take off into the white clouds before waking up in the early morning, feeling exhilarated and hoping beyond hope that one day, my dream would come true.

But for some reason, my pleasant dreams have always been plagued with resurfacing nightmares. Just when I thought I'd forgotten the nightmare about the German invasion of Nantucket, Sam and I passed the offices of the *Inquirer and Mirror* as they were posting the latest newspaper on the board. There it was, on the front page of the paper: "U-boats Spotted Off Nantucket." I grabbed Sam's hand. I couldn't believe my eyes. Suddenly, as if possessed, I went all sail set to the Atheneum. Sam did everything she could to keep up with me.

"Where are you going?"

"I've got to tell Bernard."

We heaved open the doors to the Atheneum and ran up the stairs to the great hall. Sam was at least three steps behind me. I flung open the door to the hall, startling the librarian on duty.

"Shhhh. Keep quiet."

"Sorry, ma'am. I'm looking for my brother."

She pointed to the corner table.

I walked over to his table. "Bernard. You're not going to believe it."

"What is it?"

Sam joined us, out of breath. People sitting at other tables cleared their throats and sighed heavily. The librarian came out of nowhere.

"Excuse me, young ladies and gentleman. The library is not a place to hold discussions. Please take your conversation outside."

This woman was getting on my nerves. After all, given the circumstances, this was big news.

But Bernard, ever so polite, acquiesced. "Yes, ma'am."

We ran out of the library and over to the *Inquirer and Mirror's* board, so he could read it for himself.

"Well?" I asked him.

"I'm as good as in the legion."

"They'll never let you do it, Bernard."

"It's my decision. I'm going."

Sam saw the terror in my eyes and held my hand, squeezing it. I thought Bernard might really go.

The story reached the New York papers, but instead of heeding our warning, they ridiculed us as greenhorns on Nantucket. We stuck to our story. If the big-city folks weren't going to listen to us, that would be their own undoing.

Our meals that spring were fraught with tension. Mama and Da were completely against Bernard becoming a legionnaire. I can remember constant arguing between the three of them. I kept out of it—not because I didn't have an opinion, because I didn't want him to go. But I understood his reasons and thought it would probably be a great adventure. While Mama was ranting and raving, I couldn't help thinking it was nice to have someone else absorb her wrath. But as usual, she pushed too hard.

"Why must you go into the legion? You know it's full of nothing but people who are running away from something."

"It is not."

"Don't think I don't know about the kind of men who join the legion, because I do. They're criminals."

"Mama, they are not."

"Oh yes, they are."

Bernard pressed her. "How would you know?"

Mama explained, "When I was living with Nanna, before I met your da, we had a few legionnaires stay at the boardinghouse. All they did was drink, smoke, and whistle at me and Nanna. We even caught them trying to steal money from Nanna's purse, and when we confronted them and asked them if all legionnaires were like them, they said yes. They were all running from the law and had found shelter in the legion. Nanna had to call my father's old friends on the police force to get them out. So I know a few things about their kind."

"That's not what it's like, Mama."

Mama tried another tack. "What are you running from, Bernard?"

"You really think I'm running from something?"

"Have you committed some kind of crime your father and I aren't aware of?"

"Are you accusing me of something?"

Da could feel the heat rising and tried to turn down the thermostat. "We aren't accusing you of anything, Bernard. We respect your convictions."

Mama just wouldn't give in. "Speak for yourself, Obed. He's running from something, and I want to know what it is."

I've never seen my brother explode the way he did that evening. He jumped out of his seat and screamed at the top of his lungs.

"You, Mama. I'm running from you!"

Da stood up to defend Mama. "Hold your tongue, boy."

Mama brought out her most potent weapon against Bernard: she burst into tears. He immediately slumped in guilt. He went over to her and held her tight.

"I'm sorry, Mama."

"I'm afraid, Bernard. I'm afraid I'll never see you again. I'm afraid you'll go over there and get yourself killed. All for a war we're not even fighting."

"I have to do this, Mama. I can't stand by and not do my part. It's just not right."

Da got up and pulled Mama away from Bernard. "Bernard, do what you've got to do."

And that was the end of it. Bernard was enlisting in the legion.

As fate would have it, that summer, Bernard also fell in love. She was the plainest Jane I'd ever laid eyes on. Abigail Smith, a summer resident from Providence, Rhode Island, pulled on the heartstrings of a wide-eyed, determined eighteen-year-old future legionnaire.

She was one year younger than Bernard and looked like a stork. She had long, skinny legs, a short trunk, a nose that was narrow and beak-like, and white hair. And she was known to have a skin disease. That alone would have motivated me to keep my distance, but not Bernard. Abigail scratched herself red and left a trail of skin flakes in her path. No lotion or potion seemed to work, and she wore long-sleeved blouses to cover her arms. She never bathed at the beach. But like Bernard, she spent most of her days in the library, which is where they met and carried out their courtship. He read every book on warfare and tactics. She spent the summer reading the Brontë sisters. Or at least that's what he told me. I guess they were reading—although I must admit, I never went to the library with them and cannot attest to that fact. For all I know, they were fornicating in the stacks.

But for the sake of my brother's reputation (and not my sordid mind), I'll give them the benefit of the doubt.

I guess I was fifteen years old at the time. I was always off with Sam, hunting for turtles, counting ospreys, clamming, and looking for Indian-head coins. Mama was beside herself because I wasn't interested in needlepoint, knitting, crocheting, teas, church bazaars, benefits, and all those hobbies I was supposed to have possessed a natural talent for. Mama was determined to be a good mother and instruct me in the art of household management and attracting eligible bachelors. This was another one of her causes.

"How are you going to attract a decent man when you act like a boy?"

"I don't want to attract someone who isn't interested in what I'm interested in."

"But it doesn't work that way, Amelia. When it comes to finding a wife, they want someone who can manage the house and provide them with homely comforts. They want someone they can be proud of when in public. They want to show you off. They're not looking for someone to go clamming."

"Then they won't be with me."

Having lost that battle, but not the war, Mama would pour herself a nip, and I'd run out of the house.

"You'll never find a husband until you learn to tend the kettle halyards …"

Her voice trailed off as I ran down the street to pick up Sam, so we could go off into the moors in search of creepy crawlers.

That's when Mama decided to dedicate her efforts to raising money for the Home Economics School for Nantucket Girls. She was determined that I would be one of its first students. I was fortunate that the project moved at a snail's pace, but it didn't save me from the weekly instructions and quizzes that she gave both Abigail and me.

"Every woman should read the names of ingredients printed on the label and know what she is using. Let's take baking powder, for instance. There are three different kinds of baking powder. Can you name them?"

Did I care? "No."

"You need to know this, Amelia, so pay attention."

I knew I had to sit through this, or I'd be beaten alive.

"Cream of tartar, alum, and phosphate of lime. Do you know what cream of tartar is derived from?"

Abigail puffed up her chest, stood upright with a big smile on her face, and delivered the correct answer. "I know, Mrs. Moorland. It's derived from grapes."

Mama's face lit up like a Christmas tree. "Very good, Abigail."

Abigail smiled and scratched her arm. I rolled my eyes, but I soon discovered Mama had found the daughter she had always wanted in Abigail. They made apple pie together, knitted, crocheted, and baked cookies for the parish priest. Mama even introduced her to bourbon—something she would later regret, as Abigail constantly invaded Mama's stash and became quite effervescent. Though Abigail professed that it was medicinal (she swore the itch went away), that first sip of bourbon created another itch that lasted her entire lifetime.

"Da! Mama! Amelia?" Bernard came storming into the parlor on a hot afternoon in July, holding a newspaper.

"What is it, son?" Da asked.

"What is all this excitement about?" Mama chimed in.

He placed the newspaper in front of Da. "Read it. Read there."

Da took the paper out of his hand and scanned it with Mama until they came upon the headline that excited Bernard.

"U-boats Off Norfolk, Virginia."

"And those know-it-all New Yorkers thought we were crazy. This vindicates us, I tell you. It vindicates us."

Mama, the proud Nantucketer that she was, offered her two cents. "The New York papers should apologize to us. It's only the right thing to do after calling us greenhorns."

Our family were united in agreement with that sentiment—in fact, all Nantucketers were. The apology, however, was not forthcoming.

We were all irritable those last days in September before Bernard left for France. Abigail moved to the island to be closer to Bernard and cried daily. Mama burned pie after pie, started needlepoint project after needlepoint project, and went through five bottles of bourbon, but she couldn't numb herself of Bernard's upcoming departure. Da tried several times to make my brother change his mind.

"You know, you don't have to do this. We're not at war."

"It's already done, Da. I'm going." Bernard kept a stiff upper lip but bit his fingernails to the skin.

I asked Sam if she thought Bernard would be all right.

"He'll come home, Amelia."

"In one piece?"

"I can't be sure."

"What do you mean, you can't be sure?"

"It's not clear to me."

When it wasn't clear to Sam, I got spooked. It wouldn't be the first or last time that she spooked me. Her uncertainty left me unsettled.

Just before Bernard left, the World Series was being played in Boston and Brooklyn. This time, it was the Red Sox against the Robins. Da, Bernard, Sam, and I congregated with the rest of the town down at Mack's. For those few days and hours, our attention was on baseball—not Bernard's upcoming departure, the war, airplanes, automobiles, or cream of tartar.

It was during the Sunday game in which Babe Ruth was pitching for the Red Sox, that our attention was forever diverted.

Mr. Mack stuck his head out of the doorway. The crowd shushed itself quiet. He barked out the latest on the game: "Hy Myers hit a home run in the first off the Babe. Brooklyn is up by one."

The crowd moaned. Mr. Mack went back into his shop.

Bernard kept our spirits up. "Wait till Hooper and the Doc get up to bat."

Sam lightly punched me on the shoulder. "That's right. We'll be back in this game in no time."

Joe the bootblack piped in. "This is going to be the battle of the lefties. You've got the Babe and Sherry Smith. I predict it's going to be a close game, with low scoring."

Mr. Wyer brought the crowd to laughter. "I'd wager a bet against you on that, Joe, but I know I wouldn't win."

Mr. Mack quickly came back into the room, looking as if he'd seen a ghost. He didn't speak. Everyone got quiet. Da tried to pry the news out of him. "What is it, Dick? Another score for the Robins?"

Mr. Mack shook his head in disbelief. "German U-boats …"

The crowd wanted nothing to do with submarines that day.

"Oh, come on, Dicky."

"We don't want news of the war today."

"Yeah. Stick to the baseball game."

"It's the World Series, for heaven's sake."

Mr. Mack raised his hand to fend off the protests. "But you don't understand."

Da moved forward to hear what Mr. Mack was trying to say. "Go on, Dick. What about German U-boats?"

And then Mr. Mack said the words I had hoped I'd never hear: "German U-boats attacked a Red Cross liner off the Nantucket Lightship."

The crowd was stunned. That one sentence struck out the joys of following the World Series.

That afternoon, the waters off Nantucket became a battleground as the Germans attacked steamers. By the end of the day, Mr. Mack interrupted the series updates six times with news of the number of steamers that had been sunk.

Nobody said it, but we were all thinking the same thing: Would these attacks escalate into attacks against the lightship? Would the Germans attack the ferries that brought supplies from the mainland to our island? What would the attacks do to our summer season? Would summer residents stay away for fear of being blown out of the water? But the question that weighed most heavily on my mind was, could the Germans take over the island?

Da, Bernard, Sam, and I stuck it out until Mr. Mack announced the final score. "Gainor pinch hit and sent Hoblitzell in for the winning run. Boston wins in the fourteenth inning."

I don't recall ever getting such great news as the Red Sox win without having the strength, energy, or will to care. That day on Nantucket, the mood wasn't particularly celebratory. That war soured everything.

The following week, on a dreary, rain-soaked day, we took Bernard to the ferry. Tears flooded my parents' eyes. Abigail was a mess. My brother embraced her, and she wouldn't let go; Da had to pry her away. It was my turn. Bernard kissed me on the cheek and gave me a hug.

"Watch out for her, will you, Amelia?"

"Of course."

He whispered into my ear, "I'm going to come back and marry her."

I looked at her birdlike appearance and still couldn't register what he saw in her. But I wasn't going to put in my two cents just yet. "You watch yourself, and come back to us."

"You know I will."

"I love you, Bernard."

"I love you too."

"Don't forget to make a wish to come back as you round the point."

And with that, he boarded the ferry.

I don't remember the first time I joined in the tradition by making a wish to return and throwing a penny as I rounded Brant Point. However, I remember running to the edge of the ferry with Bernard as children on our way to visit Nanna or when we'd go with Mama to shop in New Bedford. We'd close our eyes, wishing to come back, then drop our penny into the waters. It seemed to work, as we always returned. But that day, I especially hoped that tradition would prove itself to be true.

My parents and Abigail waved from the wharf. Sam and I ran off the wharf, over to Brant Point, to bid the ferry good-bye. There he was, on the top deck: young, energetic, passionate, and scared. Bernard held out a penny, closed his eyes in what I knew was a wish to return, and threw the penny in the water as he passed Brant Point. I watched that penny fall from his hand, through the air, until it hit the water. The penny was visible for less than a few seconds before it sank to the ocean floor.

We sat on the shore in the rain and watched the ferry disappear past the jetties and out into Nantucket Sound on its journey to America. From a steamer ferry with its black smoke trailing in the wind to a dot on the horizon, my brother's ship evaporated into the flat, wet, gray waters and fell off the horizon. Bernard was gone.

United States Coast Guard
Special Report upon the
Incident on the Steamship *Uncatena*
October 16, 1921
Excerpt, Testimonials, Captain Swain

"Tiny and Rip had brought her up to the captain's quarters. I asked if she was conscious. She was wrapped in blankets, and Rip started slapping her face, telling her to wake up. I ordered more blankets, as she appeared to be freezing. Tiny asked what in God's name she was doing out there, and I told him she's got a lot of explaining to do. She mumbled something and started to come to."

CHAPTER V

After Bernard left, Mama was almost impossible to live with. Her days were spent trying to make me a competent manager of a household, praying three times a day for Bernard's return (in church, no less), working on her various community projects, comforting Abigail (who scratched, drank too much, and sobbed all day long), and running the house. I give her credit for juggling so many responsibilities. Her resolve to remain as strong as an ox was relentless.

She was so relieved when Bernard's first letter was delivered. I took the letter from the postman and ran into the kitchen.

"Mama. Mama! It's a letter. It's a letter from Bernard."

I remember she was lining the kitchen cabinets with white shelf paper, just to keep busy. She dropped the roll of paper and plucked the letter from my hands. She and Da had agreed that if a letter came, she'd wait until we all were together before she opened it. Her anxieties, unfortunately, got the best of her, and she immediately began to tear it open.

"Mama, don't open it."

She pulled the letter out and unfolded it.

"Da wanted us to wait."

"Oh, child. I can't wait. He'll understand." She began reading.

19 November 1915

Dear Mama, Da, and Amelia,

I'm writing to you from France. I can't tell you from where, exactly, as the censors told us not to provide that information. I never imagined I would write to you from foreign soil, but here I am.

The trip over was uneventful, but I'd be lying if I didn't admit to being nervous throughout the sail about being sunk by a German U-boat. I spent part of my days looking out over the vast waters and wondering how I'd survive if we were struck. But luck must be on my side.

Speaking of which, Mama, you'll be pleased to know that I've decided not to join the legion. That doesn't mean, however, that I'm turning around and coming home. I still think it's important to fight the Germans, and I'm hoping that President Wilson will see the light of day soon.

I met a businessman in New York, and we got to talking. He happened to be scheduled on the same vessel as I was, so we had a drink or two at a pub next to the docks. His name was Westcott "Westy" Holmes. I told him that I was signing up for the French Foreign Legion. He saluted me, but told me there was something I could do that was more exciting and would be more fulfilling than holing up in some trench on the front lines. I asked what that would be, and he told me about the aviators. He told me he had signed up with the Lafayette Escadrille, which is a squadron of Americans who fly for the French, and he was going over to complete his training and begin flying missions. This sounded like the berries to me. So when I arrived, I went with him and signed up immediately. Can you believe it? I'm learning how to fly an aero plane!

Now, don't get upset, Mama. I'm being very careful. I know you don't like these machines, but there's really nothing like being able to fly. When I come back, maybe I'll take you up in one. And you too, Da and Amelia.

The weather has been cold and rainy most of the time. A lot of the guys can't get used to the dampness. I guess I'm a little more used to it, having spent so many autumns and winters on Nantucket.

The food isn't bad, but I've been craving your apple pie, Mama. I wish there were a way for you to send one over, but I'm sure it would be spoiled by the time I received it—or the mail censors would eat it before it left America.

That's it for now. I miss you all and hope that you understand why I'm here. Please keep Abigail safe and sound. And write to me when you get a chance.

All of my love, Bernard

Mama was relieved that he hadn't become a legionnaire (for whatever reasons, she had visions of escaped convicts in its ranks), but she was less than enthusiastic that he was training to fly airplanes. She was forced to lighten her indignation at the possibility of airplanes landing in Nantucket, for fear of being exposed as the mother of a son who flew one of the damn contraptions.

Sam and her mother (Mrs. Witherspoon), along with the ladies from town, made Red Cross bags, socks, cotton eye bandages, surgical shirts, and sandbags for those serving in Europe. We'd send them to the Metropolitan Chapter of the Red Cross on Newbury Street in Boston. I inventoried the supplies and packed them for shipment, as I had no talent (or interest) when it came to a needle and thread. Abigail and Mama would join us, and I endured relentless vocal abuse from Mama because I couldn't sew.

"She can place a fishhook on a line, but she can't thread a needle. Look at her, doing a man's work. I'm embarrassed that I raised such a daughter. I'm fortunate to have you, Abigail."

Abigail smiled, and all I wanted to do was slap that smirk off her face. During this time, I really didn't like her. She was always playing Little Miss Perfect with Mama, and she never made any attempts to be close to me. Not that I went out of my way, either. But I put up with Abigail, because I loved my brother. Deep down inside, I hoped he would find someone else in France or come to his senses and see her as I saw her.

Mama continued. "If you're able to get married, your husband will no doubt be on my doorstep, wanting reparations for your ineptitude."

I ignored her most of the time. Abigail would scratch and snicker. Sam looked at Mama with such contempt. The other ladies lost themselves in their work.

Sam's mother would always come to my defense. "Now, Catherine. Not all women are meant to do this kind of work. Amelia is special in other ways. Why, I've never seen someone scallop better than Amelia—man or woman. That takes talent, Catherine."

"But it doesn't ensure a husband ... or at least a good one," Mama would answer.

One day, she pushed too far. "No one will want to be with you, Amelia. You're downright worthless."

I couldn't remain silent. "If you keep talking like that, Mama, I'm likely to join a convent. Maybe they'd have me."

I had no intention of doing so, and Mama knew I was far from a good Catholic. Oh, I went to church with her and participated in all the proper rituals, but she knew I was just going through the motions. The rest of the family knew never to invoke Mama's precious Church and its traditions in any argument or debate. It was the one thing she held sacred. Her devotion was always fearfully respected—until that day.

"What did you just say?" she asked as she moved toward me.

"I said I'm likely to join a convent."

Slap. Her blow was so loud, Mrs. Witherspoon jumped out of her seat. Abigail began scratching uncontrollably, and Sam reached out to comfort me. Embarrassed, I pushed her away. There was a shuffle in the room. The other ladies began to leave.

Mrs. Witherspoon tried to inject a dose of calm. "Please don't leave, ladies."

"It's time to be getting home."

"We'll be back tomorrow."

"I work better at home, with no distractions."

Mrs. Witherspoon was beside herself. Mama forged ahead. "Don't you ever say such a thing, you ungracious heathen."

Mrs. Witherspoon attempted once more to help Mama regain control of her senses. "Catherine, please."

Her efforts, unfortunately, didn't work. "You're lucky they even let you through the front door of the church," Mama continued.

I wiped the hurt off the left side of my face and massaged my inflamed lip with my tongue.

"A convent would never have you."

Utterly powerless but grimly determined, I persevered. "The only reason I'd go to a convent is to get away from you—just like Bernard signed up."

She swung at me to the right. I caught her arm in midair. We froze. I tell you, we froze. Mama had never been countered or challenged to this degree. I think her heart stopped beating, for she turned pale, her eyes widened like an angry cat and her mouth fell open almost to the floor. I couldn't believe I had the nerve to stop her. In those days, you took what came to you. You never fought back. She couldn't believe I had the strength to defy her.

With a shaky voice, Mrs. Witherspoon desperately attempted to change the subject. "Why don't we get back to the task at hand?"

Frazzled and embarrassed (she rarely put on such displays in public—she reserved her violent tirades for the privacy of our home), Mama cleared her throat, gathered her coat, and walked out of the room, bidding Mrs. Witherspoon adieu. Abigail stopped scratching, got up, and awkwardly followed Mama, not knowing whether she should stay or go.

"Good day, Mrs. Witherspoon. Samantha."

"Good day, Abigail."

The door closed. Sam embraced me. Her mother began to fidget. "Is this how she treats you all the time?"

I tried to defuse her concern. "Not always. It's just some of the time."

Mrs. Witherspoon shook her head in disapproval. "The crosses we bear."

"She's under a lot of stress, what with Bernard and everything. Maybe I deserve it."

Sam interjected. "Don't say such a thing."

"I know how to get her wound up, and sometimes I just can't stop myself from doing it. That's how I get back at her."

Sam sat me down and held my hand. "You need to get away, Amelia."

"I wasn't serious about the convent."

"You don't have to go to the convent. Mother can get you into the Red Cross."

Mrs. Witherspoon was caught off guard. "Samantha, she's not old enough."

"But you could make it happen. You know the people who make those decisions. You could tell them she's old enough. You could sponsor her."

"They need trained nurses, not teenage girls with no credentials who are having problems at home. What could she do over there? I won't do it, Samantha. I won't."

"Your mother's right, Sam," I said glumly.

"It's the only thing that will save you, Amelia."

The hairs on the back of my head stood straight up. Sam had hit a nerve.

"Now, girls. Let's not waste any more time. We've got work to do."

They went back to their sewing, and I returned to my counting and packing, all the while replaying what Sam had said. *It's the only thing that will save you.*

Agitated, Mrs. Witherspoon finally put down her needle and thread. "Amelia, perhaps I can talk to your mother about the way she treats you."

"Please don't."

"It may help. She may not be aware of what she's doing."

"It'll only make matters worse. Please."

"But coming from another mother, another woman, she might ..."

I interrupted her. "Thank you, Mrs. Witherspoon. But I know my mama, and it's better not to say anything."

"Perhaps you're right. Samantha and I sure know not to rile the feathers of Mr. Witherspoon. But you must be careful. You've got to learn not to antagonize her."

"Yes, ma'am."

"That's how we deal with Samantha's father."

Sam's mother had never talked about Mr. Witherspoon in that way. I had known him to be stern and even had seen him hit her, but Mrs. Witherspoon always put on a happy face when I was around—at least back then. It would be later in life that we would butt heads.

Useless as it might have been, I accepted her advice as a touching gesture of concern. I knew what she was saying, but I couldn't help thinking that I was rarely the one who instigated the trouble—that fault always lay with Mama, and probably always would. Whether she knew it or not, Mama encouraged me to rebel. Sam's comment, however, stuck with me and even scared me. Was leaving my only escape from the future? But how could I leave?

Sam and I tried for months to come up with a plan for my departure. We would take long walks along Hummock Pond and plot my next move.

"If you had the money, you could just get on the ferry and leave," Sam said wistfully.

"But where would I go?"

"I don't know. You could go anywhere in America."

"And how would I live?"

"You could get a job."

"Sam, you know that won't work. Besides, I don't have money to do something like that, and my parents aren't going to give it to me."

"If only my mother would call her friends in the Red Cross."

"Well, she won't, so let's just forget it."

"But it would be perfect. You'd be safe, away from your mother, and doing something you could do for the rest of your life."

At times, just to have some fun, I offer a completely impossible plan and then tease Sam about her commitment to our friendship. "What if you called your mother's friends and pretended to be her?"

"I don't think I could do that."

"I can make a toll call. Bernard taught me how, remember?"

"It's not that I don't know how to make a call."

"Then what is it? You're my friend, right?"

"You know I'm your friend."

"And you'd do anything for me, right?"

"Amelia, I don't know those people."

"So? You know me. Aren't I the most important person in your life?"

"You know you are. But it wouldn't work. I don't sound like her."

"You can't always tell the voices over the telephone wires."

"If it ever got back to my mother, I don't think I could live with myself, especially when she's already said no to calling herself. And I don't want to think what my father would do."

I pouted. "I thought you wanted to help."

"I do. But you'd still need money to get to Boston."

And then I came up with the most ridiculous idea yet: "Couldn't you steal the money from your father?"

"He'd beat me to death."

"It wouldn't hurt that badly."

"He'd probably beat me and then throw me out of the house. I'd never cross his path. Never."

"Come on, Sam. Do it for me."

"I'm serious, Amelia. You think your mother is mean? He's worse."

"I'm just teasing you, Sam. I'd never ask you to steal anything."

She pushed me in the chest and smirked, playing along. "You need to eat a piece of mad dog if you think I'd ever do that."

I pushed her back, and she ran away from me, laughing. "How dare you say that!"

I chased her through the wild grasses.

I caught up to her and wrestled her to the ground. "Apologize for saying that."

I pinned her arms to the ground. "I'm sorry. I'm sorry!" she gasped between giggles.

We laughed as I rolled off her and onto my back. We looked up at the endless blue sky.

"The key is the Red Cross. I can feel it, Amelia."

"We'll figure it out someday."

That day finally came in April 1917, when President Wilson declared war on Germany. Men and women were joining up. Boys like Charles Chadwick, Byron Sylvaro, Walter Ramsdell, Charles Ryder, and Maurice Killen enlisted in the AEF, the American Expeditionary Force. The Red Cross pleaded for volunteers.

I'd gladly volunteer; they just wouldn't take me because of my age. So how were we going to make this happen?

"My mother said they don't think they'll have enough people to handle the wounded," Sam mused. "They're sure to take you, Amelia. Now if only we could figure out a way to get you off the island with your mother's blessings."

"I've only had her blessing to go off island once, and that was to see my nanna."

Sam grabbed me by the shoulders. "That's it, Amelia!"

We decided I would take a trip to New York. I would send a telegram to Nanna, begging to come visit her. Since I was her favorite (albeit only) grand-daughter, she would acquiesce. It was perfect: I would go to Brooklyn to see my nanna, and one day, I would venture into the Manhattan offices of the Red Cross, enlist in the Voluntary Aid Detachment, and head off to wherever I was needed (which I prayed would be far from Nantucket).

But there was one more problem. If I were to get over to America and inter-view with the Red Cross in New York, I'd have to have my birth certificate changed to reflect an older age. Fortune smiled on me, as Sam was an expert at forgery—though she only used that talent in emergencies. This was one of those emergencies.

I knew my da kept important papers in his top bureau drawer. One day, when Mama and Abigail were out at the store and Da was at work, I snuck into their room (forbidden territory), opened the drawer, and took my birth certificate. Being the curious person I am, I opened another drawer and looked at all of Da's cufflinks and timepieces. He had three of them; only two were in the drawer, as he was wearing his everyday timepiece. The other two—one from his grandfa-ther, who had willed it to Da when he died, and one Nanna gave him when he married Mama (Mama's father's timepiece)—were closed up in faded velvet boxes. Besides faded photographs of the timepieces' previous owners, those watches were the only link back to those who had come before me.

I hoped that Da would pass them on to me. I would keep them and cherish them, ensuring that they'd be passed down to the next generation of Moorlands. I held each one up to the light … and then I heard the front door open.

"Amelia?"

It was Mama. I had been in my own little world, where time passed so quickly. You'd think that looking at timepieces would have aided me in this real-ization, but they weren't set. It was as if time had stopped as I existed solely in the land of my imagination. I scrambled to get everything back into their appropriate boxes and drawers.

"Amelia? Is that you up there?"

I thought for sure I'd be caught and hung out on the line to dry. "Coming, Mama."

I double-checked to see that all the drawers were closed. I then cracked the bedroom door and looked down the stairs. The coast was clear. I had no sooner closed their door and started toward the first step that Mama appeared at the bottom of the stairs.

"There you are. Abigail and I were looking for you."

"I was just in my room."

"Are you all right?"

"I'm fine. Why?"

"Well, you look as if you've seen a ghost."

"I told Sam I'd meet her to pack up more supplies, and I'm really late."

I cautiously moved past her and then ran out the door. I had missed disaster by only a few seconds. I got to Sam's house and told her of my ordeal. She told me it served me right, and that from now on, I should stay focused when engaging in covert actions.

I gave her my birth certificate, and she began to make the necessary changes. "Where did you learn to do this?"

"I didn't exactly learn it. I'm just applying what I learned in penmanship and art classes."

"I guess I should've paid more attention in those classes." I continued, "Do you really think I can pass for twenty-one?"

"We've already gone through this, Amelia. They need women. They're not going to send a healthy, strong, and young woman back home. Now, let's practice. Name?"

"Amelia Moorland."

"Place of birth?"

I stated matter-of-factly, "Nantucket, Massachusetts."

"Date of birth."

"June 16, 1896."

"And if they look up at you, questioning your age?"

I smiled flirtatiously and batted my baby blues. Sam smiled.

Now all we had to do was wait until school let out for the summer.

The time finally came in June, and I left for a visit with Nanna just before my birthday. Mama, Da, Abigail, and Sam took me to the wharf to send me off.

"Don't give your nanna the trouble you give me," Mama commanded sternly.

"Yes, Mama. I'll behave."

"Don't overstay your welcome."

"I won't."

"Come and give me a kiss and hug."

I kissed Mama and embraced her for a long time. Tears welled up in my eyes.

"Come now, Amelia. You're only going away for a month or two."

A part of me wanted to tell her that I was going to be away until the end of the war, whenever that was, but I knew I would ruin any chance at getting away if I spilled the beans. So I held her tight. As much as I wanted to be away from her, I wanted to remember what she felt like. Despite our differences and her bullhead-edness, she was my mama, and I loved her. I knew she loved me too; we just needed to be away from each other.

"Now give your da a hug." She let go and pushed me into Da's arms.

"Good-bye, Da."

"Good-bye, sweet pea."

I closed my eyes and embraced him, filling my lungs with his scent. A rush of memories came over me. He was my protector, sympathizer, peacemaker, and teacher. He kept me on an even keel, supported my interests, and shared my enthusiasm for baseball. I wish I could have told him where I was heading. It would have to wait until I could write him with a safe distance between us.

"You'll be back before you know it."

I pulled away from Da. Abigail was next to Mama. I smiled and hugged her, looking at Sam. Our scheme was going as planned, except for my emotions. I had to keep focused. I had to leave.

I walked over to Sam and stood, nervous, looking down at the ground. I did not want to say good-bye to her. "I'm not sure I can do this."

She lifted up my chin and looked me in the eyes, just as she had when we first met. "Sure you can. You'll have a terrific time."

"Good-bye, Sam."

"Make sure you write me, Amelia."

We embraced for what seemed an eternity. She whispered in my ear, "The Bambino will be playing his last year as a Red Sox when you return."

I giggled at the preposterous comment. "When pigs fly, Sam."

"I love you, Amelia."

Mama hurried us along anxiously. "OK, girls, she's got to get on that ferry, or she'll miss it."

We pulled away from each other and kissed on the cheeks. I made my way up the plank, never looking back for fear I might abort this mission. I found a place on the upper deck and sat crying like a lost schoolchild. I had never dreamed I would be this sad. Why were these feelings so strong?

The steamer jolted as it pulled away from the dock. I remember a seagull floating above, leading the way out of the harbor. I stood up to get a final glimpse of Nantucket. I didn't want to forget it. I wanted to burn it in my memory as if it were a photograph. As the ferry came upon Brant Point, I took out a penny to drop overboard in a wish to return. I hesitated. Part of me never wanted to return. Why would I make that wish? It had taken so long to get away.

Sam's voice whispered in the wind. "You'll be back after the war."

And as I looked back at the wharf and the town behind it, I realized that despite all the hardships I'd encountered with Mama, this was my home. Though my life was taking me on a journey far from these shores, my heart was bound to this wisp of sand forever. I kissed the penny, closed my eyes, and threw it. It fell from my hands, and my eyes opened of their own accord to watch it glisten in the sunshine, then skip across the surface before disappearing.

The steamer chugged past the point, out the jetties, and into the sound as Nantucket's steeples faded slowly into the distance. I was on my way.

United States Coast Guard
Special Report upon the
Incident on the Steamship *Uncatena*
October 16, 1921
Excerpt, Testimonials, Captain Swain

"She finally came to. I asked her what her name was. She said, 'You know my name.' Tiny said, 'Just answer the questions, Amelia.' She said 'Amelia Moorland.' I asked her where she lived. She said 'Nantucket, Massachusetts.' I asked if she had a brother. She said yes. She told me his name was Bernard, and that her parents' names were Obed and Catherine. I then asked her how old she was, and she told me it was none of my business. We knew that it was Amelia."

CHAPTER VI

The train pulled into Grand Central Station and jolted to a halt. I looked out the window and saw men and women scrambling on the platform. I had come to New York with my parents many times, but as a child, I had relied on their direction and lead, missing so much of what was around me. Arriving alone, I was awestruck by the grandeur of the place. As a child, I remembered it being crowded as a sardine can. This would hold true, but this time, I was aware of an energy surrounding me. It gave me a sense of purpose—a feeling of life.

I held my bag tightly as I walked up the platform and into the main hall. Looking up at the ceiling, which depicted the stars and heavens in their splendor, and up at the sunlight streaming through those magnificent windows, I felt like a modern-day Cleopatra entering Rome. I stopped in the middle of the grand hall by the stately, gilded information booth and turned around and around, taking it all in. This temple was mine. I had arrived. I had left behind the struggles and frustrations of my childhood and was moving toward something bigger and better. I was determined to go from what I considered nothing to something.

The scream of train whistles, the bark of conductors, the chorus of people murmuring, and a tug at my sleeve brought me back to reality. I turned to see my grandmother. There she was: Nanna, a slender woman with white hair tied in a bun and steel blue eyes that pierced their way right through your soul. Her arms were wrinkled yet muscular, and her hands looked twice the age of the rest of her body from years of cooking, cleaning, scrubbing, yanking, pulling, and gripping—all in the name of hard work. By this time, Nanna had given up the boardinghouse, and to make ends meet, she worked as a cleaning lady at the Brooklyn Navy Yard's commandant's house on Evans Street.

"Nanna!"

"There's my little lass."

We exchanged hugs and kisses and made our way onto Forty-Second Street. As we walked, Nanna kept talking, but I have no idea what she was saying; New York City was at my feet. I was mesmerized by the buildings, the hustle and bustle, and the people. I jumped into this stream of humanity.

I don't know how we got there, but we made it to the Brooklyn neighborhood where Nanna lived—Vinegar Hill. The neighborhood had changed since my last visit. Oh, the Irish (like Nanna) were still there; in fact, a few years before, there had been so many Irish in the neighborhood that they started calling it Irishtown. But as we walked down Marshall Street, I couldn't believe what I saw.

"Where are all the houses?"

"They've been gone for quite some time. These factories and warehouses have been popping up all around me."

"I don't remember it like this."

"The neighborhood is changing so fast that I can't remember what was where when."

What hadn't changed was the effect of the Brooklyn Navy Yard on the neighborhood—especially the businesses, both pleasure and retail, that appealed to sailors' appetites. The streets were lined with everything from stores with uniforms and sailing gear to bars, saloons, lunchrooms, and gambling rooms (or so Nanna told me).

"I'm going to have to work every day while you're here. But I don't expect you to sit in the house all day. You're a young woman now, and you can go out and explore the city … but there are places I forbid you to go."

"I can spend the day helping you, if you wish."

"No. You need to spread your wings a bit. If I know your mother, she's had a hold on you too long. And you're going to have to learn to fend for yourself, just as I did when I was your age."

I wanted to tell her I agreed, but my instincts told me not to boast.

"But you must be careful," she continued. "There are rules."

"Of course, Nanna."

"I don't want you going down Sands Street. And you're not to talk to strangers."

"Yes, Nanna, I won't. But what's wrong with Sands Street?"

"It's no place for a lady. It's the Barbary Coast."

I had visions of pirates and sailors fighting each other to the death. Women of all ages were taken advantage of in the middle of the street. Every two seconds, you would hear a pint glass of beer break, or a whiskey bottle whisking across the street to shatter at your feet. No one refrained from drinking and smoking; every-one boozed it up twenty-four hours a day. I wondered if I could survive such an environment.

I'm sure by now you can guess that I ignored her instructions, and on my first day of spreading my wings, I sauntered down Sands Street all the way to the head of the Brooklyn Bridge and back. At the beginning of this trek, I was terrified. I got to the corner of Navy and Sands Streets, took a deep breath, and turned down the Barbary Coast with a purpose. I kept my eyes on every storefront on both sides of the street, waiting for some pirate or devil to pounce in front of me. I casually looked down at the sidewalk, occasionally turning my head ever so nonchalantly to the side and then to the back to make sure no one was following me. As I continued, I realized no one was going to hurt me. Danger wasn't behind each corner, or lurking behind storefront entrances and windows. Glasses and bottles weren't being hurled across the street, no one was fighting, and if women were being taken advantage of, it certainly wasn't out in the open. Except for the occasional civilian like me, only uniformed sailors walked the street, behaving like gentlemen.

I have to admit, I was taken by these men and their uniforms—the officers in their whites and the ensigns in their blue undress with scarves and white caps. They came and went out of bars and lunchrooms and tipped their hats out of politeness. I became much more at ease, so much so that this blonde little num-ber passed by and teased them with a smile and an occasional "hello." It seemed completely harmless. I walked down Sands Street every day during my stay with Nanna, but I never ventured there after dark.

During one of those walks, I found myself at the entrance to the Navy Yard and saw the most peculiar-looking vessel I'd ever seen. It looked like a big iron cigar.

"That's the *Intelligent Whale*."

Startled, I swung around to see a handsome, tall, and gangly young lieutenant with deep green eyes and a kind smile standing before me. I was surprised to see that his uniform didn't seem to fit; you'd think the navy could find decent tailors. His baggy shirt made him look thin as a handspike, but his smile and those vel-vety eyes had me hook, line, and sinker.

"I beg your pardon."

"It wasn't always called that. It was originally named *Halstead's Folly*."

I wasn't comprehending a word he was saying. I must have looked glazed over.

"Do you know what it is?" he continued.

"No, not really." I was amazed that I could carry on this conversation. How was I following this?

"It's one of the first submarines built."

"A U-boat?"

"Well, it wasn't called that then, and this one proved to be impracticable. But to honor her, they renamed her the *Intelligent Whale* and placed her here, so people could see her."

"With all due respect, it doesn't look like a whale."

He cocked his head, looked at the vessel, and considered that comment. "You know something about whales?"

"I know one when I see one, and this one looks more like my da's cigar than a whale. They should have called it the *Stogie*."

He chuckled. "I don't think the navy would have gone for that."

"No, I guess you're right."

"My name is Willie. Lieutenant William Carey."

"I'm not sure I should tell you my name." Butterflies fluttered in my stomach and flew up my throat; I was so nervous, I thought I might throw up.

"Well, whoever you are, I'd sure like to get to know you."

I was taken by surprise. "You would?"

"Why, sure. You're the prettiest thing I've ever laid eyes on."

My legs were shaking, and I must have turned crimson. It was everything I could do not to pass out right there in front of him. Nobody had ever talked to me like that. And there he was, smiling again. I was going into a panic.

"I guess I'll call you Stogie, then."

"My nanna wouldn't approve."

"I'm sure she wouldn't."

"No, I mean of me talking to a stranger, or a navy man, especially on Sands Street."

"I understand. I mean you no harm, ma'am. It was nice meeting you, whoever you are."

He tipped his hat and entered the yards. I don't know what possessed me, but something made me yell out my name: "It's Amelia."

He turned around, beamed me a smile, and tipped his hat yet again. "Tell you what, Amelia. I get off every day about this time. If you'd like to get to know me, why, come and meet me here someday."

I smiled. "Maybe I will."

"Good. I hope I see you around."

With that, he disappeared into one of the warehouses.

I took off like a Nantucket sleigh ride and ran back to Nanna's house. A young man had said I was pretty. He said he wanted to see me around. Could this be true? I swung open the front door and ran into the kitchen, then hugged Nanna as hard as I could. Startled, she jumped back.

"What's gotten into you, girl?"

"Thank you for having me, Nanna. I love it here. I love being with you."

"Oh, child, don't be silly. You can visit me anytime."

"You'll never know how grateful I am for this."

That night I dreamed of my sailor boy, Willie Carey. I woke the next morning determined to see him again. After Nanna left for work, I went down to the corner store on Hudson Street and picked up a Kamp Kit Pack. I don't know if you remember what those were, but they were pretty popular in those days. It was a box filled with a selection of Fig Newtons, peanut-butter sandwiches, lemon snaps, and—my favorite—Zu Zu ginger snaps. Mothers and fathers would send the kits to their boys in the service.

I then walked to the entrance of the yard and waited until I saw Willie exiting. He was surprised to see me.

"Well, if it isn't Stogie."

"I brought you these."

"What is this for?"

"It's for your kindness."

"Why, thank you. But I don't remember showing any extraordinary amount of kindness to you."

"It's for telling me the story of the *Intelligent Whale*." What a crock.

"Oh, I see."

He opened the box of biscuits and offered me one. "Care for one?"

I really wanted a Zu Zu ginger snap, but I refrained. "No, thanks."

He popped two into his mouth. "I'm going over to the Pitkin to see the new Theda Bara picture."

"I love Theda Bara." In reality, I'd only heard of her.

"I wouldn't think a woman like you would like her."

"What kind of woman do you think I am?"

"I think you're proper and kind and nice."

"Can't someone proper, kind, and nice like all the picture stars?"

"Well, I guess they could. I'm a big fan of hers and haven't missed any of her pictures. This one's *Cleopatra*."

I could relate to Cleopatra. Theda and I had something in common.

"And if you like moving pictures ..."

"I really do."

"Then they're playing Charlie Chaplin's new one, *The Immigrant*, over at the Fox. Would you like to join me?"

How could I pass this up? Theda Bara, Charlie Chaplin, and Willie Carey? I was sitting in a butter tub.

To be honest, I had never seen a Theda Bara picture before that day. I had seen photographs of her, but Da wouldn't let me see her movies when they played at The Dreamland. He said he liked Theda Bara, but he always thought her costars couldn't act, and that was why we couldn't go to see her movies.

When the lights went down, the projector illuminated the screen, and the piano music began, Theda Bara came on. I instantly understood why Willie Carey was a fan—and why Da hadn't been keen on me seeing her pictures. You see, Willie loved Theda's costumes … or should I say, the lack of costumes. I looked over at Willie, who was enthralled at the sight of her, and then I looked up at Theda, who wore something transparent. It registered immediately.

I looked back at Willie. Something about him seemed different … and it wasn't the lighting. My gaze turned to his lap. It was the first time I was aware of a man's pecker standing at full military attention. I'd never seen it before. Oh, I'd seen it on animals—you know, dogs, cats, and horses. But never on a man, and never poking up his pants like a tent pole, just begging to get out.

I thought to myself, *What should I do? Should I ignore it, or should I leave? If I leave, he'll follow, and then all of Brooklyn will see him at full mast. They'll think I was the one who caused it. They'll point their fingers at it; he'll try to cover it up and point at me, and then they'll scowl at me. They'll make me wear a scarlet P, for "pecker."*

And what if Nanna is in the crowd or finds out? She'll disown me. I'll be excommunicated from the church by the pope himself. I'll be banished from Nantucket, and I'll be burned at the stake in front of Brooklyn City Hall.

I decided to sit with my hands folded in my lap. As I continued looking at Theda, who (supposedly) played Cleopatra almost nude, I began to wonder what it looked like. Had Theda seen one? She must have seen several; she was the Vamp. How many would I see in my life? Would I see Willie's?

What was I thinking? I had to get these impure thoughts out of my mind. *It will go away, soon enough.* I occasionally looked down in his lap to see if it was still there. It didn't seem to retreat until the lights came up, and Theda had vanished from the screen.

"She is so incredible!" Willie exclaimed.

I was relieved that it was over, and I didn't know what to say. "She sure leaves little to the imagination."

"Shall we try to see *The Immigrant*?"

"I'd better get home. My nanna may start to worry."

"How about getting a bite to eat?"

"Maybe next time."

"Am I being too forward?"

"Well, I don't really know you or how old you are."

"Unless you spend time with me, you'll never get to know me."

I did know he liked Zu Zu ginger snaps (like me), was as handsome as a picture star, and appeared to have a pecker as tall as a main mast.

"I'm twenty years old," he added. "What about you?"

I couldn't tell him I had recently turned sixteen. "It's not polite to ask a lady her age."

"That's fair enough. Would you like to see me again? Get to know me better? Because I'd sure like to get to know you."

I couldn't believe this was happening. Why hadn't it happened before? What did Willie see in me? I was running before the wind. "I think that would be nice."

"Would you like to go to Coney Island with me tomorrow?"

"I've wanted to go to Coney Island all my life. I'd love to."

"Then it's a date."

He took hold of my hands, then kissed my right one. He was being such a gentleman.

"Until tomorrow."

I held onto his hands for as long as I could; I didn't want to let go. I thought that maybe he'd kiss me on the cheek, or perhaps the lips. I'd never kissed a man on the lips—only Da and Bernard on the cheek. *If he tries to kiss me, will I know what to do? How will I know that I'm doing it the correct way?* He gently pulled my hands away and smiled, and we walked down Navy Street. Outside the navy yards, he turned and kissed me on the cheek.

"Good night, Amelia."

"Good night, Lieutenant."

His kiss hadn't felt like Da's or Bernard's. Granted, it was on the cheek, but the chemistry between the two of us created a more intense reaction—a magnetic one that made me quiver. It was something special.

Something was happening to me. I think I was falling in love. I have no idea how I made it back to Nanna's house, but I got in just as she arrived, and I had to quickly pull myself together. I felt as if I had walked home in the clouds.

After work, Nanna always made herself a cup of tea. She was taking the water off the stove when I got the nerve to walk in and fib my way through the events of the day.

"What did you do today?"

"I went to the picture show."

"That's nice. What did you see?"

I couldn't tell her I had seen Theda Bara; Nanna probably knew all about her. I had to think fast. "The new Charlie Chaplin picture."

If she asked me the name of it, I'd be done.

"Oh, I like Charlie Chaplin. Was it good?"

"As good as all of them." *I'm doomed if she asks me the name.*

"Well, I'll have to try and take that in. Where'd you say it was playing?"

"The Fox." She didn't ask the name, thank God.

"Would you like a cup of tea?"

I was out of the woods. "Yes, that would be nice." Something—anything—to calm my nerves.

As we sat at the kitchen table and sipped our tea, I started to feel terrible about lying to her. She was my nanna. How could I do something so wretched? I decided that if I was going to continue seeing Willie (and I was), I had to let her know. It was the only thing to do.

"Nanna, I met someone." I waited to see if she'd come at me, like Mama. Her expression was calculating as she put her cup down slowly onto the saucer.

"Oh, you did, did you?"

"Yes, and I don't want you to get angry. It's nothing more than a companion to go about with."

Nanna looked straight at me. I felt as naked as Theda Bara. "I'm almost afraid to ask … is it a man or a woman?"

"It's a man, and he's a little older than me."

"How much older?"

"Four years. But he's really nice, and he's in the navy, and he wants to take me to Coney Island tomorrow."

She didn't take her eyes off me. I finally had to look away. Her stare could gaze too deeply, revealing too much. Could she see into my heart? I picked up my teacup and took a quick, nervous sip.

"Amelia, I've been without your grandfather for almost thirty years. I know you didn't know him, but I think you know that he was the love of my life, and that we were smitten for each other from the moment our eyes met. This new friend of yours probably seems very special to you right now."

"He does, but only as a friend." There I went, lying again.

"I remember how difficult it was for your grandfather and me to spend time together. I wasn't much older than you are right now, and our parents wouldn't allow it. We'd have to sneak around every corner to spend just a moment's time together. And despite my parents' opposition to our relationship, your grandfather and I were very much in love. I miss him so much, Amelia."

"I wish I had known him, Nanna."

She sat looking off into some faraway place. I imagine she was reliving moments, desperately holding onto his image.

"I won't tell you not to see this young man."

I was overjoyed; telling the truth hadn't backfired. "Oh, thank you, Nanna!" I embraced her.

"But I will say to mind your ways. You have a good father and a good mother, so don't do anything disgraceful."

"I won't. I promise."

"And I'd like you to bring him around, so that I can get a good look at him."

"Oh, Nanna, you'll think he's the berries."

"We'll mention none of this to your mother or father unless we have to, understood?"

This was even better than I had imagined. "Yes, Nanna. Thank you. Thank you so much."

Nanna and I met Willie the next day at our usual spot. At first, Willie was stiff as a board—in an entirely different way than he had been the day before; he could hardly get a sentence out. Nanna looked him up and down, peered into his heart and soul, and besides a cautious hello, said only one thing. "You know, I could make those clothes fit for you."

This took Willie by surprise. "I beg your pardon?"

"Your uniform. Send them by, and I'll make them fit you properly."

He loosened up and beamed that smile of his. "You will? That would be too kind of you."

"Be careful with my granddaughter, and I'll take care of your uniforms. Have fun, dearie."

With that, she kissed me and was off. I felt on top of the rain barrel. Willie looked as if he had won the jackpot. He grabbed my arm, and we took off toward the BMT station—and Coney Island.

Coney Island seemed like a city of its own, bustling with people, all having the time of their lives in what was the biggest playground I'd ever seen. We went to Luna Park and rode the Whip and the Top (both of which made me scream with such delight, I must have frightened Willie), then saw the Pawnee Bill Pioneer Days *Wild West Spectacle*. After that, I was ready for the next amusement.

"What should we do next?" I asked Willie breathlessly.

"Let's go see the Submarine Wars."

I wanted to go on a ride, not see another spectacle. "OK, but let's do the Star Ride on the way there."

I think Willie was getting tired of the rides. I was just getting started.

"You sure do like rides."

"What's the matter, sailor boy? Don't have the stomach for it?"

He grabbed my hand, and we ran to the Star Ride queue. It was a wonderful day. We stopped at Nathan's hot dog stand and each ordered one with all the fixings. I was having the time of my life with Willie.

"So, Ms. Amelia Moorland, amusement-park fanatic, you've never told me where you're from."

"Nantucket."

"Ah. You do know a thing or two about whales."

"Just what they look like when they beach themselves on our shores. What about you?"

"I'm from Chicago. I've been in the navy for three years now and have worked my way up to lieutenant."

"Will you ever have to go into battle?"

As the words left my lips, I felt like an idiot. Of course he'd have to go into battle. There was a war on.

His smile faded and he turned away. "I'd rather not talk about that."

"Why?"

"Because I'm having such a wonderful time with you, and I don't want it to end."

I didn't want it to end either, but I didn't want the conversation to become blue, so I didn't lament the changing times along with him. "Well, I'm going. I'm joining the Red Cross."

I hadn't thought about the war, my family, Sam, or the Red Cross since I arrived in New York.

"How old are you?"

I thought I'd test my skills. "I'm twenty-one."

He chuckled. "I thought ladies weren't supposed to tell their age."

"We only tell those close to our hearts."

"Well, I like that."

"But it doesn't mean I'm telling the truth." Had I opened myself up for too much scrutiny?

"You don't look a day over eighteen."

I smiled and batted my baby blues. "It's my fair skin, I'm sure."

"Whatever it is, it's beautiful."

At the end of the day, Willie got very melancholy. I wasn't sure if he was tiring of me, but something was eating him. On the train ride home, I leaned against his shoulder, as I had with Bernard on ferry rides home from America. He didn't say a word.

We made our way down the elevated tracks and out onto the street. Night was beginning to fall. I walked by his side. The only sound was our shoes against the pavement. Abruptly, Willie stopped and took hold of my hands.

"Amelia, there's something I should tell you."

"What is it?"

"I won't be able to spend time with you after tomorrow."

That hurt as badly as a blow from Mama. "Oh." I tried to mask my disappointment.

"It's not that I don't want to … but we've been put on notice. We're shipping off to Europe any day now."

How could this happen? How could someone come into my life and say the things he said, and do the things we did, and then leave so quickly? I hadn't had the chance to see if he was the real deal, but I thought I was falling for him. I didn't know what to say.

He looked away. "Bad timing, I guess."

I tightened my grip on his hands and tried to stay positive. If I only had him for one more day, then it was going to be the best damn day ever.

"We might as well make the rest of your time here the most memorable, right?"

"You don't think I'm taking advantage of you?"

"No. I've really enjoyed my time with you. You've shown me so much in so little time. I've never had so much fun."

"I'd like it if you'd go with me tomorrow night to the Hippodrome. Houdini's playing, and I'd really like to see him before I go."

"Why, of course. Yes, I'll go."

He then took me in his arms and kissed me. I tried to pull away. "I don't know …"

"What is it? You don't want—"

"No. I just don't know if I kiss well."

He smiled and pulled me toward him. We both closed our eyes and kissed. I suddenly heard that swooning music from the movies swelling in my head. We were still kissing when I opened my eyes to see exactly what was going on. I could feel that I was having the same effect on him as Theda Bara. His eyes were closed, and his soft lips were attached to mine. Our tongues danced with each other. I closed my eyes again and found that I really enjoyed this. This couldn't be considered disgraceful—it felt too good.

Then he broke away and kissed me on the forehead. "I'll remember that kiss until the day I die."

"Me, too."

That was my first French kiss, and I never forgot it.

"We'd better get you home, Stogie."

With that, he stretched out his arm and escorted me to Nanna's doorstep. "Good night, Amelia Moorland."

"Good night, Lieutenant William Carey."

He bowed and walked away, disappearing around the corner as the dim streetlights sparkled in the darkness of the evening.

I tossed and turned the entire night, and then Sam came to me.

"Have you gone to the Red Cross yet?"

"You know I haven't."

"But why?"

"I'm going to guess you know that too."

"You've met a boy."

"Yes."

"And you have feelings for him?"

"I think I do."

"You know you do."

"Yes, that's true. But it doesn't matter. He's shipping out in a couple of days."

"You can't get distracted, Amelia. Your mother and father will come and get you in New York. You've got to do as we planned."

"I wish you could see Willie."

"I have seen him."

"Isn't he beautiful? Maybe after the war …"

"Amelia, so much is going to happen in the next year or two. You'll probably forget your Willie Carey."

"How can you say that?"

"It's only natural."

"You don't understand. You don't know Willie."

"Amelia, he won't ..."

"I'll never forget him, Sam."

I awoke, breathing heavily and sweating feverishly. The tone in Sam's voice chilled me. I didn't want to know what she saw in Willie's future. I tried to convince myself that our discussion had only been a nightmare.

And how could we communicate this far away? Over a couple of blocks on the same small island, maybe. But there were hundreds of miles between us. I kept telling myself it wasn't possible. It had just been a bad dream.

Do you remember the Hippodrome? Oh, forgive me. Of course you don't. I forget that I'm ancient, and that most of you weren't even born then. I can tell you truthfully, there has never been anything like it. Walking up to the Hippodrome at night was like walking into a jewel-box fantasy. Two towers rose from either side of this enormous building. On top of the towers sat these globelike, illuminated iron structures. There must have been a million lights, because you could see the glow from several blocks away. As Willie and I neared the theater, we saw the lighted billboard over the entrance. There, in what seemed like another million lights, was the title of the show: *Cheer Up! A Musical Revue in Three Cheers.*

I remember the inside was enormous. There were circus rings, a water tank, thousands of seats, and a stage that seemed bigger than Nantucket Island. And there were people—the place was filled with people. The production billed itself as the biggest show in the world with the lowest prices, and it lived up to its word. It seemed as if every living person in Manhattan were there that evening.

Willie and I took our seats in the second balcony and got ready for the big show (my first). I thought I'd died and gone to Hyorky. I was really here, little me, sitting in this large theater in New York City next to a man who was attracted to me (and I to him) and seeing, among other things, Harry Houdini.

Willie bought a program for five cents. We studied it between glances at the people arriving and the decor of the building. Willie raised his eyebrow to a statement in the program.

"Do you believe this is true?"

I leaned in and read the sentence under his finger. Typical of the time, the notice in the program stated that every member of the Hippodrome organization had fulfilled all obligations in respect to military service. "I don't think they'd put it in the program if it weren't. I think they're just reassuring us."

The lights dimmed, and the show began. The curtain opened to an enormous set that boasted floor-to-ceiling toy soldiers, actresses dressed as butterflies flying across the stage, and what seemed like a cast of one thousand actors. In between scene changes, clowns performed and delighted the audience. And then Houdini made his entrance.

Everyone stood up and cheered for Harry Houdini. I was stunned at how small he was. The Great Houdini always conjured up visions of this great big man, but he was no taller than I was. A ten-thousand-pound elephant was brought onstage and, as God is my witness, he made the elephant disappear in front of our very eyes. People clapped and howled. Nobody could figure out how he did it. My eyes were bigger than a barn owl's; I had never seen such a thing. Maybe the Great Houdini could show me how to make Mama disappear—I would gladly volunteer her for the act.

At intermission, Willie and I went to the lounge on the first-floor balcony and had a cup of Horton's ice cream while we listened to music played by the Marconi Trio and tried to make sense of the magic we had just seen.

"It's got to be an illusion," Willie theorized. "He couldn't possibly make an elephant disappear."

I was more of a believer than Willie. "It must be magic."

"It's got to be more than magic. Where did that elephant go?"

And then I thought that if Houdini wouldn't make Mama disappear, maybe I'd volunteer and go myself. "I wonder if he could make one of us disappear," I pondered.

"I bet he could. But he'd make me very unhappy if he couldn't bring you back."

Willie gave me a quick peck on the cheek. I'm sure I blushed.

The Second Cheer was a John Philip Sousa extravaganza about America from 1492 to the present. It featured so many prominent history makers: Christopher Columbus, Captain John Smith and Pocahontas, Hendrick Hudson, George Washington, Ben Franklin, John Adams, Abraham Lincoln, and Stonewall Jackson, concluding with Teddy Roosevelt and Miss Liberty herself, played by Ethel Hopkins. Anyone ignorant about history before seeing it would have no excuse to remain so afterward, as the show seemed to cover just about everyone of importance.

Houdini came back and did his submersible, iron-bound box trick. That was the one where he was manacled and roped, then nailed into a weighted iron box, which was then lowered into the water tank. The box, riddled with holes, quickly filled with water. Women in the audience began to scream in fear that he wouldn't get out. As time seemed to be running out, some in the crowd became panicked. Although everyone knew he had done this trick so many times, it was frightening to watch, because I had no idea whether he was going to make it. Too much time seemed to be passing. Everyone in the audience spoke under their breaths, creating a disturbing, anxiety-filled mumble. I couldn't take the suspense any longer. I buried my face into Willie's shoulder.

"I can't stand this."

"He'll get out, don't worry. He's Houdini."

"Is it over?"

"It's just a trick. He'll get out."

"Can you see him?"

Nervous gasps and female screams seemed to bounce off the walls of the theater. Willie pulled me away from him.

"Look. There he is!"

I looked down at the tank and saw Houdini wading in the water, smiling and waving to the audience. The orchestra began playing, and everyone clapped and cheered. I was happy it was over.

Willie and I made our way out of the theater, along with the thousands of other spectators, and poured out onto Sixth Avenue. Willie had arranged for an after-theater supper at the Café Boulevard on Forty-First Street.

"I really enjoyed that show," I told Willie.

"Me too."

"I never dreamed I'd see something like that."

"Stick with me, kiddo—there's more where that came from." He took hold of my hand. "I know it's my duty to go. And if I have to die for my country …"

"Don't think that, Willie."

"I will."

"You can't say things like that. You might make them happen."

"I can't help thinking that I'd like to take you with me somewhere. Disappear. Escape all of this."

I knew something about escaping and disappearing; I was in the early days of just such a plan. But I couldn't tell him that. "I feel the same way, but it'll be over soon, and we'll pick up where we left off, right?" Deep down, I wasn't so sure.

"I hope so. I think you'll be the one thing that gets me through this. Just don't disappear on me, OK?"

"We'll make a pact to meet at the corner of Sands and Navy when it's all over," I offered. "The exact corner where we met the first time. And we'll write. Promise me that we'll write each other."

Sam's unfinished sentence played over and over again in my head. "Amelia, he won't …"

Come back?

Willie and I walked all the way home. We walked down Broadway, crossed the Brooklyn Bridge, and strolled back into Vinegar Hill. We didn't say much as we slowly walked arm in arm. We paused in the middle of the bridge and looked down at the frantic, glistening black currents of the East River rushing below. We didn't want the evening to end.

We made it back to Nanna's house and stood on the doorstep for what seemed like hours, caressing each other's hands and just looking at one another. We both had tears in our eyes.

He finally embraced me. "This is it, Amelia."

"Don't let go." I buried my face into his shoulder.

"I don't want to."

"Then don't."

"I'm afraid I'm going to have to."

"Not now. Just hold me. Hold me tight."

Willie's embrace shielded me for a moment from the realities of the situation. He then kissed me one last time and wiped a tear off my cheek.

"Good night, Amelia."

"Good night, Willie."

"I love you."

"I love you too."

"I'll come looking for you if I don't hear from you. So write me, you hear?"

"Every day, my love," I vowed. "Every day."

With that, he let go of me, turned his back, and walked down the street. As he vanished into the darkness, the terrible feeling that I would never see him again left me an empty shell. I tried to be optimistic, but I couldn't help thinking that there would be no reunion at Sands and Navy streets once this awful war was over. There would only be the memories and the souvenir program from the Hippodrome. I hoped those feelings would be proven wrong.

New York without Willie seemed an empty place. For a week, I moped around Nanna's house, occasionally taking a short walk over to the navy yards to see if perhaps Willie had been mistaken, and he wasn't shipped off. Disappointed, I'd walk over to the commandant's house, down the long drive and up to the white clapboard mansion, to meet Nanna after her shift. We'd stroll around the neighborhood, picking up groceries for that evening's dinner and peeking through storefront windows at the latest fashions. I tried to show some enthusiasm, but I felt as if life had been drained from every pore of my body. Nanna easily recognized that I was heartsick.

"I know you've seen the Charlie Chaplin picture, but would you like to see it again?" she asked.

Of course I hadn't seen it, but I wanted to, and Nanna was right: a little slapstick might cheer me up.

We stood in line in front of the Fox Theater. The billboard displayed that forgotten title in large letters: *The Immigrant*. We braved the long lines to see the seven o'clock show. The moment The Tramp came on the screen, I began laughing. My stomach and sides ached as I laughed watching him trying to walk on board a ship as it rolled in the waves, or attempting to eat soup on the rough voyage. I wondered if Willie would experience such comic difficulties. For that matter, would I find my sea legs when I crossed the Atlantic to work in the Red Cross?

Had I forgotten the Red Cross? After all, the Red Cross was my reason for being here. It was time.

Resigned to the fact that Willie was no longer in New York, I decided the next morning to pay a visit to the Red Cross recruiting center. How Nanna knew something was brewing, I'll never know, but she had a sixth sense about these matters.

"What do you have planned for today?"

I had to tell her another lie. "Nothing, really. I thought I'd take in Brooklyn Heights … maybe walk over the Brooklyn Bridge and down to the Battery."

"Are you sure that's all?"

I was annoyed by her powers. "Of course that's all. What else would there be?"

She looked right through me. "I think that's for you to tell me."

"Nanna, I've got to get over these blues about Willie. If I don't get out and see something else, I'm going to be stuck in the doldrums forever."

She considered this carefully but didn't seem convinced. "I let you see Willie Carey, but only because you were straight with me. Don't go hiding things from me, because if I find out, and you know I will, it will get my goat, and I'm likely to send you packing back home."

I knew Nanna and I might not get along so famously for much longer. I had to quell the inquiry. "I tell you everything. You know that."

How could I possibly tell her that I was going to enlist in the Red Cross? She'd never let me do it, and then my scheme would get back to Mama and Da, and I'd be stuck in Nantucket under Mama's thumb for good. I had to keep this from Nanna—at least until I left.

I wandered off to the Manhattan offices of the Red Cross and made my application into the Voluntary Aid Detachment (or, as we called it, the VAD). As expected, the officials were skeptical of my age. The first recruiter, a very attractive woman about Mama's age, thought I was in the wrong place.

"Are you looking for your mother or older sister, dear?"

Sam and I had never thought of that question. I was on my own now. I stood tall, met her gaze, and told her with confidence the purpose of my visit. "No. I'm here to enlist."

Her left eyebrow almost hit the ceiling; I'd never seen so much of the white of an eyeball. "Oh. And how old are you?"

"I'm twenty-one."

She smiled and looked me up and down, the eyebrow still stuck on the ceiling. "Surely you don't think I believe that."

"But it's true. I get this all the time. I'm Irish. My fair skin makes me look like a baby. It's quite a nuisance."

With that, I handed her my papers. She quickly perused them, and without looking up, she asked another question.

"And your nursing experience?"

"I have none, ma'am."

She looked up at me and seemed ready to give me the heave-ho. In those days, there was a bit of rivalry between Red Cross workers who were nurses and those who weren't. If you were a full-fledged nurse, they called you "sister." If you weren't, they called you "nurse." In truth, the sisters didn't really want the nurses around, but there was such a need for women to help at the hospitals around the front lines that the Red Cross had to accept the inexperienced.

I was ready to feel the hard point of her boot on my behind as I headed for the curb when a slightly plump, balding middle-aged man came up to the recruiter's desk. I batted my blues at him and gave him the most flirtatious smile I could muster. He immediately got that look on his face, just like Willie looking at Theda Bara—as if he were dreaming of a sexual tryst or two with me. His vacant smile suggested that he was undressing me, fondling me, and closing in for the kill. But before he could do any of that, he regained his composure when the sister nudged him back to the matter at hand.

"I'll take this one over, sister."

She rolled her eyes, and I gladly moved along to his desk.

He first made it clear to me that normally, I would have been rejected, because I had no training or experience in nursing. In fact, he said, many members of the VAD deplored the inexperienced. I guess that's why the first recruiter never warmed up to me; she and the other sisters believed I'd just be in the way. He wasn't giving me much hope, and I was beginning to feel very discouraged. I dreaded the thought of telling Sam they hadn't accepted me. She'd probably blame it on me for not going directly to the Red Cross upon my arrival in New York.

He then asked me what I thought was the most peculiar question. "Can you write letters?"

"I beg your pardon?"

"If a soldier wanted you to write a letter to his sweetheart or family, could you write that letter for him?"

"What an odd question."

He started to turn red under the collar and asked crossly, "Do you want to enlist in the VAD or not?"

"Oh, I do! Really I do."

"Then your comments are inappropriate."

I wasn't having much luck with him, either. How could I turn this to my advantage?

"Yes, sir. But I just couldn't figure out why you would ask me that."

"Some of the boys in the hospitals won't be able to write home. My asking whether you can do that for them is hardly an odd question."

"Of course I can do that."

"Under normal circumstances, we would have turned you out of this office in two seconds. But the number of wounded is overwhelming. Our sisters can't tend to the sick and dying and do the little things, like writing letters, for the boys as well. Like it or not, we need women."

The situation seemed to be changing in my favor.

"If you can write letters …"

"Oh, I can, sir. I'm a very good letter writer. I can make things up. I can make it sound nice."

He looked over my papers—and me—about twenty times. Finally, he stamped my application. "Then that is what you will do."

"You won't be sorry, sir."

"I'm hoping I won't. These boys need nice girlie girls like you to look at and take care of them before they meet their maker. God rest their souls." He sounded morbid, but I wasn't going to protest.

"Yes, sir."

"Now, you'll report next Tuesday to this office, and we'll arrange for any training and shipping over as soon as possible. Get your things in order."

"Thank you, sir."

With no experience, letter-writing or otherwise, I was to be shipped out to the western front on the next available steamer. I burst onto the avenue, overwhelmed that, despite the odds, I was now part of the war effort. Or perhaps selfishly and more to the point, I was free from the claws of my overbearing mama.

But how was I going to manage leaving Nanna?

While I mulled over how to tell Nanna I was leaving, her mind was apparently becoming heavy with something she wanted to tell me. Over dinner that evening, we were both ill at ease. I was so nervous that my throat was dry, and I couldn't keep enough liquids down to get rid of that horrible feeling, let alone swallow the roast beef and mashed potatoes she had prepared. Nanna pushed her food around her plate and bit her upper lip. She finally spoke.

"Amelia, dear. I want to have a serious discussion with you."

"Yes, Nanna."

"And I don't want this conversation to be shared with anyone. Not your father, or mother, or any of your friends. This is intended just for you."

"It sounds serious, Nanna."

"It is. And if the discussion goes beyond this house, I could be in terrible trouble. I might even be arrested."

"It won't leave this room."

"I've been following the writings and speeches of two women that I've gained a lot of respect for over the past few years."

I couldn't figure out why this was weighing so heavily on Nanna.

"Have you ever heard of Emma Goldman and Margaret Sanger?"

"I think I read about them in the *New York Times*. They speak about women's rights, don't they?"

"Yes, they do. Oh, you should have heard Emma Goldman speak in Union Square last year. It was the most inspiring speech I think I've ever heard."

"What was it about?"

"Surely you know she's an advocate for birth control."

I did not. I didn't even know what birth control was. "Birth control?"

"Yes. That's what they call it."

"But what is it?"

"They believe in the right of the child not to be born, and that a woman's body shouldn't be controlled by the government."

This countered everything I had been told by Mama. "And you believe this, Nanna?"

"I've seen too many unwanted babies in my life, too much abuse, too many young girls and women with botched abortions, and too much unhappiness— not only here in America, but in Ireland too. It breaks my heart thinking about it. It's inhumane. I think women should have the right to use birth control, and I think it's important that you understand this movement and become aware of others—like women's suffrage."

"Da is against women's suffrage. He says we don't need to vote, and that giving us the vote will be as messy as giving the Negro men voting rights after the Civil War. It makes Mama madder than a hornet's nest."

Nanna shook her head in disapproval. "And what do you think?"

I sat back in my chair, taking in this moment. Nanna was the first adult to ask me my thoughts. Was this a sign that I truly was grown up?

"I think I'd like to vote, but I don't know about birth control, Nanna. I mean, I've never … you know."

"That's fine, love. There's no rush. If you're at all interested, I have a publication I'd like you to look at. It's called *The Woman Rebel*. But you can't take it out of this house. It's illegal to have it. So promise me you won't take it out of the house, and you'll hide it away when you're not looking at it."

"I promise."

"I think it's important for you to be open to these things." With that, she handed me the pamphlet. I opened it and began to read.

I immediately understood why the journal was illegal. It discussed arousal, sex education, prostitution, unwanted and unhealthy babies, the enslavement of women in marriage, and a woman's right to know how to prevent conception. These topics may sound ho-hum today, but back then, just thinking about them could land you in prison.

At first, such naughty thoughts excited me. The mere sense of danger made me feel rebellious. I wondered if it were really possible for a woman to believe these ideas. And what were these devices and methods to prevent conception? Did Nanna know of them? Not that I'd necessarily want to use them, but what would it be like? Would it hurt, or would it make me feel good? Would I be aroused? Or was I destined to become a prostitute if I knew of these things?

I spent the next few days reading the journal over and over again, almost memorizing all of the words. I started to think about women who weren't as lucky as I was—women who didn't have a Nanna who exposed them to such things. So many of them wouldn't know what to do—or that something called birth control was out there and could perhaps change their lives.

But would I ever find the need to use it? Naturally, at some point in my life, I wanted to get married and to have children. What circumstance would make me use birth control? But whether I used it was not the issue. The issue was that I had the right to know it existed and how to use it. Men (and women) who thought otherwise were persecuting women, just as they were denying us the right to vote. My da was one of those men. I couldn't have that; I'd have to convince him otherwise. Surely he didn't know all of the facts. It became ludicrous to me that it was illegal to read this pamphlet, let alone think these thoughts.

On the way to Nanna's work one morning, I asked her, "Do you think things will ever change? Do you think it will be legal?"

"I hope so, love. It will be up to you and your generation to make it happen. Don't let public opinion dissuade you from seeing and doing things that you might think right, or that you think you should consider."

Given that advice, I wondered whether I should tell her I was leaving. She might understand. She might support my decision. But if she didn't support it, my career in the Red Cross would be short lived. I was going to be a letter writer, and Nanna would be the recipient of my first letter on the day of my departure.

When that day came, Nanna left for work as usual. Before she left, I ran down the stairs to say good-bye.

"Nanna." I was out of breath.

"What is it, dear?"

"I wanted to see you off to work today."

"Why is today any different from any other?"

"I feel as if I haven't been appreciative enough." I kissed her and embraced her.

"Careful, sweetie—you're going to break my bones!"

"You'll never know how much this time with you has meant to me."

"I enjoy having you around, but you're not leaving anytime soon, are you?"

I squeezed her harder. "No. I don't think I'll ever leave."

"Your mother might have a word or two to say about that."

"I love you, Nanna."

She pulled me away and looked into my eyes. "I don't know what this is about, Amelia, but I trust your judgment and hope that whatever it is, you'll keep safe. I couldn't live with myself if you didn't do that. I'd feel responsible. Now, I've got to get going. I'm late, and you know I don't like to be anything but on time."

"Good-bye, Nanna."

With that, she was gone. I had that same feeling in my stomach as I had when Willie left; I didn't think I'd see her again. I prayed my feelings would betray me.

I placed the letter explaining everything about the Red Cross on the kitchen table where Nanna and I had shared tea, meals, and advice. In that letter, I included my forwarding address.

I took a deep breath, taking in all the smells of Nanna's house, and left. As I walked down Navy Street, I heard a group of sailors singing, "Over There."

I was going with them.

United States Coast Guard
Special Report upon the
Incident on the Steamship *Uncatena*
October 16, 1921
Excerpt, Testimony, Captain Swain

"I asked her how she was feeling. She told me that she was very weak. And then she asked if we had found the body. I asked her, 'Whose body?'"

CHAPTER VII

Before I continue, you should know that I've never discussed my experiences during World War I with anyone—not a soul. I remained silent not out of embarrassment or shame, but out of a feeling that I had gone to hell and back. Day in and day out, I was tormented by the sounds of bombardments and gas victims' rattling lungs. I was taunted by the smells of ether and rotting flesh, and the pungency of the musty, muddy, and heavy clothing worn by the soldiers. It was torture to see the violated faces of the maimed struggling to cling to their lives that were desperately expiring. The sight of the cold, stiff, emptiness of the dead made me feel hopeless. Finally, to add salt to the wounds, the Spanish influenza ravaged so many of us. Somehow I survived.

When I returned, I thought I could erase all those memories. Even though I've never talked about them and have thought many times that the memories had faded, they suddenly appear when least expected. I've come to realize they have always been there—not in the solemn parades and memorials of annual Armistice Day celebrations, or in nightmares (although it took years for those to go away), but in the most trivial and insignificant ways. Take the smell of chicken on the barbecue: To some, it conjures up memories of past summer cookouts with friends and family. To me, it is the smell of burned flesh, and it won't go away.

My only consolation in finally divulging these untold memories is I'll never have to do so again, since I'm hours away from the inevitable. But I'm getting ahead of myself again.

I left New York for France on a mid-August day, crossing the Atlantic on the steamship *Leviathan*. The ship was packed with nurses and sisters from the Red Cross and women who were going over to work the YMCA canteens. We were all nervous, but excited to be on our way to do our part in turning back the nasty Huns.

We sailed out of New York and passed Ellis Island and the Statue of Liberty. As we approached her, everyone on board turned in her direction to get a glimpse of her. She gleamed in the morning sunshine. Her strength, beauty, and power reigned over us. I wouldn't consider myself patriotic (although I love my country), but seeing her that day brought a lump to my throat and burned an indelible image as real today as it was then.

Some on that ship had been welcomed by Lady Liberty in their voyage from Europe to America. Others stood proud of the liberties and freedoms she embodied. Although we knew some of those standing next to us would not return, we prayed that her light, lit thousands of miles away, would somehow guide us back home safely. Just to be sure, I threw a penny overboard and made a wish that I would return—alive and in one piece.

As we sailed out of New York Harbor, I kept my eyes on her. The farther we sailed, the smaller she got, until she was indistinguishable from the horizon. I wouldn't see America again for a long time; this image burned itself onto my brain.

After paratyphoid vaccinations were out of the way, my first order of business was to write Mama and Da. If I thought I could write letters for soldiers who were injured or almost ready to die, I could surely handle a letter to my family, especially since I was already many miles away. But I couldn't help thinking they would be the quintessence of furious, stewed down to half pint, when they found out I had left New York and enlisted in the VAD. My da, after thinking about it, would probably accept and support my decision, just as he had with Bernard. But Mama would probably never forgive me (and she never did). It took me about one week to figure out what to say. Years later, when she died, I was surprised to find the letter in the back of Mama's closet, in a shoe box with so many others. She had kept it, and after she died, I did the same.

August 24, 1917

Dear Mama and Da:

By now, you must have learned the news that I enlisted in the Red Cross. I hope that you are not angry with Nanna. She had no idea of my plans. Nanna and I had a wonderful visit, and it was hard for me to leave. I'm hoping that she understands why I decided to enlist and that she doesn't worry about me.

As I write this, I am crossing to France to help our boys in their efforts to end this god-awful war. I will not be able to tell you exactly of my where-abouts. Our superiors have told us that the war censors will black out any information that could compromise our efforts, or they may even destroy the letter entirely, so I am obliged to keep those details from you.

I am sure you are worried and upset, but I want you to know that I am fine and will be fine. I have met some interesting girls already, and everyone is treating me well. To pass the time on the ship, we are learning French from a woman from Gary, Indiana, whose voice is high-pitched and nasal. She makes speaking French sound like a cat trying to clear a fur ball. She has most of us in stitches and doesn't know why. Those of us who haven't been to France are hoping beyond hope that they do not sound like this. The only thing I can say so far is oui, non, merci, and bonjour. I hope my vocabulary grows with time.

This is an opportunity for me to serve a higher cause and to see other parts of the world beyond home and New York. You have always known that I want to experience everything life has to offer.

Please don't be cross with me. I will write you often and hope that you will write me. Tell Abigail I said hello, and also all of the ladies making supplies for the Red Cross. By all means, tell them to continue. We've been told supplies are scarce. I'm hoping I'll see Bernard somewhere over here, although if he's in the air, and I'm in one of the hospitals, I probably won't see him. God knows I don't want to see him in a hospital. I love you, Mama and Da, and I hope you still love me. I think of you always and of the day that I return.

Love, Amelia

The second week of the sail, the weather turned for the worse and stayed that way until the end of the voyage. For two relentless weeks, the violent seas tossed the ship as it crashed its way to France. Up and down and up and down—the ship pitched heavily and rolled from rail to rail, the decks awash with green water. It was difficult keeping your wits about you.

I'm embarrassed to say that I spent a lot of time hanging my head overboard and throwing up (like father, like daughter). But we all did. When I wasn't vom-iting, I spent my days in the dining hall, gamming with the sisters and nurses. All of our faces were flushed, and it wasn't uncommon for one of us to abruptly run out and empty our roiling stomachs. When the feeling came upon you, you looked for the nearest exit. Rarely did you have time to excuse yourself or ask someone to hold that thought until you returned.

One thing was for sure: wherever you went on the ship, you wore or carried your life preserver—even in these unpleasant instances. We were told to keep our life preservers close by in case of any emergency, and it was an order taken seriously and followed to the T.

As if the weather weren't enough, we were under constant threat of a U-boat attack; this was, of course, my greatest fear. Ship lights were always off after dark. We'd crawl into our bunks with our life belts on over all our clothes and attempt to sleep the darkness away. Every night, I heard the hush of women talking to each other.

Camilla Mansfield bunked above me. She was thin as a waif, blue-eyed and fair-skinned like me, and she had small, sensuous lips and long, auburn hair. She'd hang her head just over the bunk and whisper. I found our nighttime gams rather personal, but educational and downright titillating. You see, Camilla was experienced in the ways of men and women.

"Do you have someone special, Amelia?"

"Yes, I do."

"Have you … you know."

"Have I what?"

"Have you been with him?"

"Been with him?"

"Yes. You know. Have you had relations with him?"

"I kissed him."

"But did you …"

"That's a rather personal question, isn't it?"

"I'm just wondering."

So was I. "What about you?"

"I have."

"You have?"

"Many times."

"What was it like?"

Camilla teased me. "That's rather personal, isn't it?"

Curiosity was killing me. "Come on, Camilla. Don't keep it to yourself."

"This can only be between you and me."

"I won't tell a soul. Honest."

"You can't imagine how it feels."

"Is it awful?"

"Oh, Amelia. It's not awful at all. It feels so good."

"It does?"

"It's indescribable, and it makes you want to feel it again and again."

Butterflies began filling my stomach. No one had ever talked to me about sex like this.

"At first, it hurts a little. But you get used to it. And then, if you're not already, you start to get wet."

Pain and wetness? This was not my idea of feeling good. I looked around to see if anyone else was listening. Despite wanting to hear what she had to say, I was jittery about discussing such a taboo subject.

I wanted to ask her what she thought about birth control—you know, of the things I had read in *The Woman Rebel*—but then I remembered what Nanna had said about it being outlawed. Nanna had sworn me to secrecy; I didn't want to get her in trouble, let alone myself, so I tried to take the moral high road. "Camilla. Should we be talking about this?"

"You want to know, don't you?"

"Yes, but isn't it wrong?"

"Do you want me to stop?"

I was nervous and conflicted, but I was curious—and I didn't know who or when anyone else would discuss this with me. "No. Go on."

"After you start getting wet, the pain goes away, and then your body completely succumbs to this unimaginable feeling."

"What is it?"

"You don't want it to stop, and yet, you can feel it building to some kind of release, and then something happens."

She paused. I could hear her breathing heavily. She had me on the edge of my bunk.

"Go on."

"Your body tightens, and in that tightness ... you feel as if you're in ecstasy."

I couldn't imagine hearing such a thing. No one spoke so openly about it; it just wasn't done.

"Are we supposed to feel those things?"

"I did."

"But do you think that it's all right?" I couldn't imagine that the church, any church, would condone such feelings.

"What can be wrong with having feelings that come to you naturally?"

She had a point. If God didn't want us to feel those things, then why did he give us the opportunity to feel them? Was it temptation? Did the devil have his hand in this?

"I've just never heard anyone talk about it the way you do."

"I'm all for breaking the rules."

While I felt the same way, I didn't have the experience that Camilla had, and I didn't feel I could speak as freely as she on these subjects. As free spirited as I thought I was, I had a lot of living to do to reach her level. (It took me a while, but as you'll surmise from the rest of my story, I think I got there.)

"I hope it's that way for me."

"If you don't fight it, it will be."

"What was your man's name?"

"Johnnie."

I longed to be in Willie's arms. "You miss him?"

"Something terrible. I hope he comes back safely."

"And Willie too."

Camilla turned over with a good-night rustle, and I got melancholy thinking about Willie. Would he return? Would we pick up where we had left off, or would everything be different? Would he be my one and only love? Would I feel as if I were in ecstasy, as Camilla described it?

When I wasn't sharing these secret moments with Camilla, I was listening to the desperate prayers of Ellie Cartwright below me. Ellie was a big girl with a bigger heart from South Carolina, or Georgia, or somewhere down south. Ellie also had a special relationship with the Lord. She never missed praying in the morning, afternoon, or night. She'd probably get along with Mama.

"Please, dear Lord. Calm the seas. Make it end. Bring us safely into port, and keep the U-boats away from us. If this is not your will, then please just settle my stomach. Make my journey to you as comfortable as possible. Bless me and all the women on the ship. Bless Mother and Father, Alan, Vincent, and all of my family and friends. Most of all, dear Lord, end this war quickly. I ask this of you as your humble servant. Amen."

Unfortunately, the Lord didn't seem to be listening. Ellie continued, like the rest of us, to get sick; the seas never calmed; the war was far from over; and the U-boats remained a continuous threat. As for her family and friends, I have no idea if they were specially blessed by her prayers, but given the odds, I doubt it.

One night, Sam visited me in the deep of my sleep with news of impending danger.

"Amelia? Wake up."

"Sam?"

"Wake up, Amelia. You need to get to your lifeboat."

"But why? Are we sinking?"

"You're going to be struck. You've got to get up on deck."

"What?"

"You've got to move, Amelia. Quickly."

"Am I sleeping?"

Just then, there was a terrible, deafening, thudding boom—like an explosion.

"Amelia? Wake up. Wake up." I opened my eyes and saw Camilla shaking me. The ship quaked and moaned in the darkness. Was this a nightmare? I jumped out of my bunk.

"Ellie? Camilla?"

I looked down and saw Ellie screaming uncontrollably. Camilla took charge and slapped her across the face, and Ellie quieted down. Orders were being hurled at us left and right.

"We've been hit."

"Check your life belts."

"Get up on deck."

"Don't panic."

"Move."

"Get to your positions at the lifeboats."

Camilla, Ellie, and I ran to get up on deck. It was very hard to see in the pitch black darkness. That, coupled with panic, created pandemonium in the halls. As I reached the deck, there was another boom.

Ellie screamed out, "We're going to die!"

Camilla attempted to keep her wits about her. "Don't say that, Ellie."

We kept running. We were halfway down the deck when the ship lurched forward and knocked me off my feet. "Camilla? Ellie?"

They were nowhere to be found. I was facedown on the deck, and I couldn't move. People were scrambling all around me. I tried to will myself to get up, but I was paralyzed. Was I in shock? Why wouldn't my legs move? Why couldn't I get up? I heard screams and saw what seemed like thousands of feet trampling around me. Would I meet my maker by being crushed by this mad rush instead of being blown to kingdom come by the U-boat?

Suddenly a woman grabbed my coat and pulled me up by my shoulders. "You've got to get to your boat."

I was stunned and couldn't comprehend what she was saying.

"Don't you understand? You've got to get to your lifeboat!"

I must have looked dazed, because the next thing I knew, she was shaking me. I could feel her fingernails driving into my arms.

"Go to your boat!"

I regained my senses and shook free, running to my lifeboat to rejoin Camilla and Ellie. We hugged each other and were all relieved to be together again. The other women were shaking and holding on tightly. I joined them. As we looked out at the water, we saw nothing but the murky slate black of the sky and watery horizon.

"Quiet down. Quiet down."

No one said a word. We heard the clapping of the water against the ship, the creaking of the steel hull, the murmur of the ship's engines, and the muted sobbing of the inconsolable. We stood at our lifeboats, courting fate and staring out at black for what seemed like hours, until the black brightened in increasingly lighter shades of gray. Whatever had struck us appeared to be gone.

In the early morning, we were ordered back to our bunks: "All right, ladies, there's no detectable damage."

We moved slowly and stoically through the halls. We had been so consumed with the thought of being sunk by a U-boat that we had no idea how cold we were until we got back in our bunks and the damp chill surrounded us. I pulled my blanket up over my eyes, trying to get warm. It was difficult getting any sleep between the chattering of teeth and the discussion of the near miss with the U-boat.

Ellie was the only skeptical one: "I don't think it was a U-boat."

Camilla poked her head over the side of her bunk. "What else could it have been?"

"A whale?"

I conjured this image of Moby Dick ramming the *Leviathan*, and I chuckled.

Ellie took offense. "You don't think it could have been a whale?"

I couldn't stop giggling. "It's the *Leviathan*. Not the *Pequod* or the *Essex*."

Camilla began laughing as well. Ellie was completely mortified.

"The Pea what?"

"The *Pequod*. Did you ever read *Moby Dick*?"

"I haven't gotten to that one yet."

I stopped laughing and tried to convince her. "It wasn't a whale, Ellie. It was a U-boat."

She turned over as if to pout. "It had to be a whale. A U-boat would have sunk us."

How I wished she was right that it hadn't been a U-boat.

Ellie pressed me. "Explain why we weren't sunk, then."

"Luck, I guess."

The truth is, I couldn't explain it, but I hoped that the U-boat wouldn't be back. I was scared to death that it or another would return to finish us off.

That day, the crew got rid of all of the electric lightbulbs, blanketed all of the portholes in the hallways, and hung canvas in front of all of the doors leading to the decks. They were going to make sure that no telltale glow escaped from the ship.

I spent the next few days with my eyes weather-peeled to the sea, my knees constantly crashing together.

"Your knees are going to be black-and-blue by the time we arrive in France if you keep shaking like that."

I turned around and saw a tall, thin, attractive woman smoking a cigarette. She had a long, angular face. Her black hair was pulled up in a bun, and her eyes hid behind a pair of wire-rimmed glasses. She was older than me (who wasn't on that ship?) and had a wild look about her that seemed to spell trouble ... and we know how much I love trouble.

"I've been watching you staring out there. Do you really think spotting a U-boat barreling down on us is going to make any difference? I mean, if we're going to go up in smoke, we're going to go up in smoke."

Defensively, I turned away from her. "I'm not looking for U-boats."

"Then what are you looking at?"

"I'm whale watching."

How could she believe that? I certainly knew it was a crock. I could feel her eyes looking me up and down as she took a long drag from her cigarette. She exhaled the smoke and held the cigarette out.

"You want a drag?"

I had never been offered a cigarette and hadn't really seen too many women smoking (it wasn't socially accepted in those days), but I was attracted to it, because it seemed daring.

"It might calm your nerves," she said, extending her arm farther. "It sure takes care of mine."

I reluctantly took the cigarette (only to calm my nerves, mind you) and placed it in my mouth.

"I hate it that they won't let us smoke at night. I get anxious until daybreak." She suddenly got short with me. "Don't just stand there dangling it from your mouth. Inhale!"

I inhaled and swallowed the smoke, then suddenly spit it back out in an uncontrollable, hacking cough.

The woman laughed. "A novice." She took the cigarette out of my hand. "Here. Watch. Slowly inhale, but don't let the smoke go farther than your lungs." She blew the smoke out. "You try."

I took the cigarette and did as she told.

"You like it?"

In all honesty, I didn't, but I wasn't going to admit it. I forced a smile. "It's aces."

"I'm Vera. Vera Guest."

"Amelia Moorland."

"What are you in for?"

"I'm in the VAD. And you?"

"YMCA. I'm entertaining our doughboys."

"That's nice. What kind of entertaining?"

She winked and vamped. "Any kind of entertainment they need."

"You must be talented."

"I am, sweetheart. After this war is over, I'm going to be in moving pictures— maybe star in one or two. Maybe even fall in love with my leading man. Or marry and divorce him."

"You sure have the looks to be a picture star."

"Thanks, kid."

She took another drag from her cigarette and handed it to me. "Here. Finish it off."

I held the cigarette as I watched her walk down the deck. Before entering the cabin, she turned and waved. I waved back and took a drag, but didn't inhale. When she was gone, I blew the smoke out of my mouth and threw the cigarette overboard. Smoking was not in the cards for me—at least not then.

After three weeks, the *Leviathan* finally pulled into Brest. As we entered the harbor, the crew stayed on guard for mines and U-boats. We all stood on deck, looking out over the water and praying that we would make it to the shore, which seemed to be within our grasp. The ship proceeded slowly, and it seemed as if another day passed before the ship settled into its berth. We breathed a collective sigh of relief when we set foot on land; we had made it.

Brest was full of activity; a constant stream of supplies, men, and women poured off the boats. We stayed in Brest for a couple of days to shake out our legs and get acquainted with being on land again. We'd wake to the sounds of regiments being readied by drill sergeants for their journey to the front.

One morning, I was awakened by bugles. I walked out of my tent to see hundreds of men lined up in perfect formation in the drill field.

"There's no excuse for failure."

"No, sir."

"No man is ever so tired that he cannot take one step forward."

"We'll always move forward, sir."

"The best way to take machine guns is to go and take them from the Boche."

"We'll take them all from the Boche, sir."

"Always press forward. Never go back."

"Yes, sir."

"To the front! To the front we go!"

A loud cheer went up, and the men moved en masse toward the trains. They were loaded and packed in with very little room to move, like cattle, then were sent off to the front.

We were told that we would be transferred by train to Paris. Three days later, we were to go on to Compiègne, where we would receive our training. Most of us had no idea where Compiègne was located, but the head sister told us that it was a short train ride from Paris: "Only about sixty miles, so you won't be cramped for too long."

The Red Cross and YMCA girls left with little fanfare. We were given a little more room than the soldiers, but that didn't stop some from moaning. I was too excited and terrified to notice. I was going to see Paris for the first time, but I was also going into training to work close to the front lines. Could I cut the mustard?

With every movement, from Nantucket to New York to Brest and on to Paris, I was getting closer to the center of the war. On the train to Paris, I looked around at all of the women, wondering which of us might not make it. Would I live to tell of my experiences, or would I die?

I had to keep such thoughts out of my mind. I had to survive.

United States Coast Guard
Special Report upon the
Incident on the Steamship *Uncatena*
October 16, 1921
Excerpt, Testimony, Captain Swain

"She was not making sense. She kept mumbling and looked very agitated. I told her I was sorry for not understanding her, but I had to know whose body she was referring to. She said she followed her and saw her jump. I asked her again, 'Who did you see jump?'"

CHAPTER VIII

The idea you conjure up in your mind of Paris—a magnificent, romantic city of lights—is true. I must admit that I was taken with it instantly. How can you not be? The wide boulevards, monuments like the Arc de Triomphe and Eiffel Tower, the parks, the energy and enormity of Les Halles (I had never seen a market quite like it and haven't to this day), the rippling Seine making its way through the heart of the city, the blinding white steeples of Sacre Coeur on a sunny day ... all have a way of casting a spell over you.

But the joie de vivre was missing when I arrived in 1917. It seemed everyone was dressed in black. There simply was no other color—not even gray. Only black. As I walked the Champs Elysses among these Parisiennes, it occurred to me that they were mourning. This war had been going on far too long, taken so many men, and displaced the lives of the survivors.

The citizens weren't, however, completely demoralized. There was a flame of hope there, even if only a dim one that you had to cup between your hands, to lighten this blackness. It could be found in the quiet bonjours and tips of hats and murmurings of *"Merci, mademoiselle,"* *"Merci, les Etats Unis,"* as I passed them by.

Yet most of the men on the streets were gray-haired and wrinkled. They had been left home, too old to fight. Those who hadn't stayed home limped, fumbled blindly, struggled to compensate for missing limbs, or breathed laboriously from the aftereffects of gassing. Though they tried to blend into the sides of buildings, sidewalks, and the backs of cafés, you couldn't help but notice them. But you knew not to approach them to offer sympathy. They didn't need any reminders of what they had lost; the weight of their scars already pushed their heads and shoulders down. Their service in the war was over, but their fight to survive and function in society was just beginning.

The women had been left to keep some semblance of order in their households. They walked with a purpose to the markets, keeping their children closely in tow. They allowed little time for nonsense. Their faces showed concern for their loved ones still at the front, longing for those who had died, and fear of what fate might throw at them later that day or the next day or the next. But through all of this, I found a sound resolve in the stiffness of their jaws and the pursing of their lips. They would survive and triumph, come hell or high water.

As I walked the streets of Paris and took all of this in, my secret desire for chocolate pastry slowly made me feel quite blue. I had always heard so much about French pastry (you know, "let them eat cake"), and it was the only treat I wanted while in Paris. A chocolate tart would quench my desire. But looking at these people, and passing closed patisserie after closed patisserie, I couldn't help but feel down in the dumps.

Fermé ... Closed. How could this be? This was Paris, after all. I had always thought it was a country of pastry and bread. It must have been some kind of holiday. I stopped and asked several passers by why they were closed. Of course, no one understood my broken French.

"*Qui est non patisserie fermé pas?*"

They all looked at me as if I were spouting off some primitive language (clearly, I was).

After several attempts, I was ready to give up. A robust woman dressed in a long coat and oversized hat that looked like a basket, and her dark, slim, exotic-looking friend were making their way down the sidewalk toward me. They were carrying boxes that appeared to hold medical supplies. I decided to give it one last try. "*Qui est non patisserie fermé pas?*"

The larger of the two women continued walking, then set her boxes down in front of a Ford truck that was parked on the side of the street. "You must be American."

"Yes. And are you?"

She shuddered. "I was born in the States but live in Paris now."

She opened the back of the truck, and the women began loading the boxes. "You know, they're happy you're here, although they wish you had come sooner. But just the same, don't destroy their language."

I replied earnestly, "I'm actually trying to learn the language."

Both women stopped what they were doing and smiled. "Isn't that polite? Americans are so polite. Polite, polite, polite."

I couldn't tell whether they were mocking me. They continued to organize the boxes. The large woman was clearly in command as she ordered the other one around.

"Put those bandages on top of the gauze, Birdie."

"Yes, Mr. Cuddle-Wuddle."

Birdie and Mr. Cuddle-Wuddle? What kind of names were those, and who would use them? And why was the little one calling the larger Mister? Despite their queerness, these women were my only hope of finding out why Paris wasn't afloat in pastries.

I piped up. "Can you tell me why the patisseries are closed?"

The stout woman called back to me with authority. "Today is Wednesday. Nobody eats sweets on Tuesday or Wednesday. Rations, you know."

"Oh, I see."

The exotic woman fluttered around the big woman like a hummingbird. She chirped in, "You must know that sugar is scarce. You have to have tickets to buy it."

"What about chocolate?"

Mr. Cuddle-Wuddle's eyes seemed to pop out of her head. "Are you related to J. P. Morgan?"

I didn't understand the relevance of the question, but I answered politely. "No."

"Then I'd assume you can't afford the dollar-a-pound price."

"No, I can't."

"Of course you can't. Now, if you'll excuse us, my boss and I have supplies to deliver." She patted the hood of the Ford. "Auntie is loaded and ready to go."

Not only did the women have queer names, but they had named the truck as well. With that, the two women got into Auntie—Mr. Cuddle-Wuddle at the wheel and Birdie, the boss, at her side. Auntie turned over, and they were off. Other automobiles swerved out of their way. Mr. Cuddle-Wuddle was a bit reckless in her driving.

Just as they turned the corner, a woman dressed in a Red Cross uniform came running down the street, carrying a box packed much like those in the Ford. She called out, "Alice! Gertrude!"

She stopped running and came up to me, out of breath. "Did you see two ladies drive off in a Ford?"

"Yes. As a matter of fact, I spoke to them before they left."

"They forgot this box. Oh, well. They'll be back."

She started walking back to the storefront. I couldn't let her go without inquiring about the women's names; I was just too curious.

"Pardon me, ma'am, but who were they? I mean, they have such queer names."

"You mean Ms. Stein and Ms. Toklas? They're the strangest Americans I know, but they're doing a lot of good work for us, so we don't question them. If you don't know already, Paris is full of eccentrics and artists … and most of the time, the two are the same."

The two of them were such oddballs, but they really seemed to enjoy themselves. Their friendship reminded me of mine with Sam, and I wrote to her and told her so.

October 13, 1917

Dear Sam:

I'm sitting in a café on the Boulevard St. Germain in Paris, having a tea and thinking of you. Paris is as wonderful as it can be, given the war. I must look like a kid in a candy store, taking in everything as I walk down the streets. I haven't mastered the language just yet, but I'm getting by as best I can.

I met two women today who reminded me of the two of us. They were much older than we are, but they gave the impression that they did almost everything together. I could picture us in the future looking just like them. But it made me sad, as I wish you were here with me. I'd really like to experience this with someone. I don't know exactly what I'm getting into, going off to the front. I sometimes think I might be in over my head. I'd sure like to have you next to me, telling me we'll be fine.

I'm wondering what you're doing. The World Series must be playing soon. You're probably going down to Mack's to get the scores. Write me and tell me who is playing and who won. I hope it's the Red Sox.

I miss you, Sam. Write to me as often as I think of you.

Fondly, Amelia

It wasn't until later in life, when I was burning my bra for the women's-liberation movement in the seventies, that I figured out who Gertrude Stein and Alice Toklas were. I picked up a copy of *The Autobiography of Alice B. Toklas* at Mitchell's Book

Corner and read it from cover to cover in one night. When I finished the book, I kicked myself. I wish I had known who they were when I met them. I would have tried to secure an invitation to dinner or drinks, or to one of their soirées. I might have met Picasso. I would have liked to have gotten to know them, but it wasn't in the stars.

The morning we left Paris for Compiègne, where we were to begin our training, word of Mata Hari's demise spread across the boulevards. Newspapers declared, "Mata Hari est Morte." It was all the talk on the train out of Paris. You couldn't help but overhear the conservations on the platforms and throughout the train.

"She got what she deserved. The traitor."

"But what if she was innocent? What if it was a setup?"

"Anyone who would work for the Huns should be dragged through the streets and shot—no questions asked."

"It's a bit extreme, isn't it? Especially for a woman."

"A sympathizer, are you?"

"Do you really think she could have been a double agent?"

"She was a whore. She'd do anything for money, including betraying France."

The sister sitting next to me nudged me below the ribs. "Let this be a lesson to you."

"I beg your pardon?"

"Don't be caught making eyes with any of the Huns. The French are liable to shoot you for it. And rightly so."

"Yes, rightly so. I'll remember that."

I didn't fancy myself the Mata Hari type. While I was adventurous, I had no intention of flirting with the other side. I hated them and wanted them driven back, along with all the nonsense that had accounted for this war. We had been warned that we'd most likely come upon wounded German soldiers, and even though we didn't like it, we were to assist them medically. But we were never to get close to them. After all, they were prisoners of war—the enemy.

As we passed through the French countryside on that chilly October day, my thoughts switched from Mata Hari to what lay ahead. I wasn't sure what kind of training I would receive as a letter writer. Were they going to give us grammar lessons? Or penmanship lessons? It seemed far too late to be doing that. Perhaps there were stock phrases and words they wanted us to use, or subjects to avoid because of security—or even psychological reasons. Or maybe training would focus more on logistics: how to order more paper or pencils (not pens, because ink was scarce) and things like that. Little did I know that my letter-writing skills would be rarely called upon in my service with the Red Cross.

Upon arrival in Compiègne, we were separated into two groups: the sisters and the nurses. Head Nurse Victoria Fairmont—a short, stout, middle-aged woman who was as bullying and combative as a blue jay—was in charge of the nurses. She immediately put us to work rolling bandages, stocking medical kits, inventorying supplies, and knitting socks. I, of course, couldn't knit to save my life, and did everything I could to avoid that duty. I'd make my way to the back of the line, or hide behind other nurses, or immediately move toward the inventorying group. This worked for the first month or so. But it was inevitable that my turn would come up.

Head Nurse Fairmont barked out the orders. "Today, Moorland, I want you on knitting duty."

I panicked. My stomach felt like a can of worms crawling all over each other. I had to think fast and try to save face. "If you don't mind, Head Nurse, I'd rather roll bandages, ma'am."

She swung around quickly and with such force, I thought she might hit me. "And I'd rather be having tea at the Ritz, but that's not something that's happening anytime soon."

"But I don't know how."

Her eyes widened. She spoke methodically and quietly. "You don't know how, missy?"

The other nurses giggled. I could feel my face turning pink and then red. "No, ma'am. You see, I was enlisted to be a letter writer."

"If you haven't figured it out by now, Moorland, you'll not only write letters. You'll do as you're told. You understand?"

"Yes, ma'am, but ..."

"You'll empty bedpans, pick cooties out of the wounded, sterilize medical equipment, clean outhouses, roll bandages, whatever is asked of you. Do you understand?"

"I understand, ma'am."

"How in the Lord's name you got out of your house and into the VAD without learning to knit is beyond me. What's wrong with your mother?"

While there were several things wrong with Mama, it was I who needed to take the blame this time. "It's my fault, ma'am. I'm sorry."

She frowned and put her hands on her waist. "Well, if you can't knit, you can't knit. We'll find something else for you to do."

I was relieved. In an instant, the red went out of my cheeks, and I was back to feeling normal. "Thank you, Head Nurse. I do appreciate it."

Without a smile or recognition of my gratitude, she yelled across the room. "Nurse Fielding?"

A very petite woman with blonde hair and a perpetual smile came up to us. She was humming under her breath.

"Hummum ... Yes, Head Nurse. Humm ..." She hummed constantly.

"Show this greenhorn how to clean an outhouse."

I was taken aback. "Outhouses? But ..."

"No buts, missy. Move your pithy ass."

I hopped to, trying to get away from this wretched woman. I moved quickly to Fielding's side.

"Humm. Yes, ma'am. Hummm."

It wasn't as if she were humming a particular tune. She just hummed. "Humm. What's your name? Hummm ..."

"Amelia."

"Humm. I'm Helen. Come on. Hummm ..."

With that, I was relegated to the worst job, but I was determined to show the head nurse that she couldn't break me. Every day, she would enter the hut and bark out orders.

"Morton, medical supply duty. Dunn, bandages. Moorland, outhouses. Berry, bandages. Fielding, outhouses."

My bunk mates—Elaine Morton, Harriet Dunn, and Morgan Berry—took bets every day that Fielding and I would get outhouses. After two weeks I stopped wagering, having lost every day. My fate seemed sealed. However, day in and day out, I muckled away, cleaning outhouses and hoping that their spotlessness would get me assigned another task the next day.

I'm not sure which was worse: wiping piss off toilet seats or listening to that human hummingbird. Fielding just wouldn't stop humming that bizarre non-tune. Her tic was driving me mad. I wondered if I was cut out for this. Was it better to be here or at home with Mama? How could I have such thoughts? Of course this was better ... wasn't it? If I had stayed at home, Mama would have continued her abuse. In no time, I would have started fighting back, and that would have only perpetuated our struggle. We needed some space between us. But as they say, distance makes the heart grow fonder—occasionally making it forget why it had needed to be free in the first place.

I had come so far. But in the hardship of the lowest of the lowest tasks, I suddenly became homesick.

I missed my da calling me sweet pea every morning. I missed walking the moors on a foggy morning with Sam, looking for snapping turtles and pheasants. I missed Willie "some awful," as they said on Nantucket. I wrote to him several times, but I hadn't heard back from him since we said good-bye in New York. I told myself that was because he was on the seas and couldn't send letters to me easily. I missed my nanna and New York. And believe it or not, I missed Mama—for the first time in my nearly six-month absence. Every time I wrote to her, I told her I missed her, but she never wrote back. Da had written several times, as well as Nanna, but I heard not a word from Mama. Da always said she told him to give me her love, but I had a feeling he was just being nice. I began to wonder if she missed me and decided to try to break the long silence.

January 8, 1918

Dearest Mama:

I'm ready to turn in after a long day's work, and I'm missing you something terrible. I'd give anything to hear your voice, but, absent that, a note from you would sure brighten my day. I'm hard-pressed not to admit that volunteering for the Red Cross wasn't what I thought it would be. I knew it would be hard work, but until you get here and see what has to be done, you can't imagine what these women are doing for the war effort. I'm honored to serve with them, but it's not easy. Don't worry, though—I'm trudging on.

I got a letter from Da last week. I read it about fifteen times. Any news from Nantucket is always a welcome relief. Have you heard from Bernard? Nanna wrote to me and said she got a letter from him. I pray for his safe return, as I'm sure you do, every night.

Mama, I know that I don't always act the way you wished a daughter would act. I'm sorry for all of the bad things I've done to you. You'll get some satisfaction in knowing that I was singled out because I couldn't knit. It was terribly embarrassing for me. While it was happening, I kept telling myself, "I should have paid attention when Mama was trying to teach me." I guess there will be plenty of those kinds of lessons as I grow older.

In my heart of hearts, Mama, I hope that when I return, we can figure out some way to act more like friends than adversaries.

Give my love to Da, and if you get the chance, please write.

Your loving daughter, Amelia

She never wrote back.

To add more water to the already wet blanket of my disposition, the weather was purely dreadful. The world was seemed made of nothing but rain, gray, and mud. Everything was soaked; our huts, our clothing, our boots, the trees, the leaves, the landscape, and even our souls felt waterlogged in the cold damp. Each night, we'd fall asleep praying for sunshine, then wake to rain—or at best, gray clouds.

I was slipping deeper and deeper into the mollygrumps when I received a letter from Nanna. I always looked forward to her letters. I remember her first letters were filled with feelings of disappointment and nervousness about my safety, but she always concluded by saying she was proud of me and couldn't wait to hear about my exploits. Her letters always made me feel happier, but this letter, from the moment I touched the envelope, seemed different.

On the back of the envelope, Nanna had written, "Make sure to read this with someone." I thought that terribly weird and ignored it. I tore the envelope open, fell back on my bunk, and began to read.

My dearest Amelia:

I hope this letter finds you safe and in good health. As you know from my previous letters, I have been terribly worried about you ever since you left. Your mother refuses to talk to me and blames me for your going. She'll forgive me one day, I'm sure. I just hope I didn't push you to spread your wings too far.

I received some very terrible news, and I don't know how to tell you, but I guess I'll have to just come out and state it. Your navy boy, Lieutenant William Carey—Willie—of Chicago, Illinois, died in action. His boat was torpedoed and sunk off the coast of Brittany. There were few survivors. The news came through at the commandant's house. I saw his name on the list of the dead. I remembered you said he was from Chicago, and it listed him as such, so I'm sure there is no mistaking it. I am so sorry and feel so helpless because I'm not there to hug you and comfort you.

After a while, you'll see that you were blessed with your time with him, even though that time was short. He was a good man, Amelia, as you are a most beautiful and wonderful young woman.

I hope someone is near you now who can embrace you. I love you so much, am so proud of your courage, and I pray every day for your safe return. Write to me, darling Amelia.

All my love, Nanna

I lay in bed, listening to the rain plunk on the tin roof of our hut, sobbing uncontrollably. I put my head in my pillow to soften the noise. How could this be possible? My body convulsed as I heaved, trying to breathe through the sobs. I felt as if I'd been hit in the stomach and then hit there again, and again, and again. My Willie was gone.

"Amelia?"

I heard my name but continued to bury my face in my pillow.

"I wanted to tell you, Amelia, but I knew it would hurt you so."

It was Sam. She had heard my cries three thousand miles away. I didn't acknowledge her.

"Amelia? I know you can hear me. Say something."

"You should have told me."

"I just couldn't."

"I could have at least prepared for this. Maybe I could have stopped him from going."

"It wasn't like that, Amelia. It was a feeling—a god-awful feeling—and I prayed that it was wrong."

"You're never wrong, Sam, and you know it. How could you?"

"How do you tell your closest, dearest friend that kind of news?"

"I feel betrayed."

"I wish I were there for you, Amelia. I wish I could shoulder some of your pain."

"Well, you can't."

"Do you think it was easy for me, knowing that what I had envisioned was going to come true?"

"He was everything I had to look forward to after this war. And now he's gone!" I was furious and hurt. "I never want to speak to you again."

"Amelia, I know you're hurt. But I'll always be here, and if you don't respond, I'll continue to pester you until you do."

I refused to speak to her, but my resistance was useless; she kept reading my mind.

Sam tried to reason with me. "It's not as if I knew months ago."

She was probably right about that, but that didn't change the fact that she didn't tell me.

"There's nothing you or I could have done to change what happened," she continued. "It's like the Barnes's fire. Remember?"

How could I forget? I was done with sages. I didn't need Sam anymore.

"I love you, Amelia. And I know you love me."

I didn't respond. I continued to sob. I felt hands on my shoulders. I was being lifted up. I wanted to resist but felt too weak to try.

"Amelia?"

I turned around and saw Head Nurse Fairmont with the letter in her hand and tears in her eyes.

"I am truly sorry, Amelia. Really I am."

I buried my head in her arms and continued to cry.

"There, there. You need to be strong. You need to have courage, as he did. He died a brave man, I'm sure, and for the right cause. We must fight on, Amelia. We must."

She cradled me for what seemed like hours. This tough-as-nails woman had a soft and kind heart after all. Elaine, Harriet, Morgan, and even Fielding the hummingbird surrounded me, tears in their eyes, each embracing me and telling me they were sorry. They all had sweethearts, and they feared the news I had just received.

That night, we were closer than ever before. It got me through the night, but it would not last forever, as we were soon assigned to different hospitals along the front.

I spent the rest of my time at Compiègne in a fog. I didn't sleep well. I trudged along, doing whatever I was told. I attempted to fake a smile, pretending that I was all right. But I was numb. I didn't really care whether I lived or died.

I thought about telling Head Nurse Fairmont that I'd volunteer for the most dangerous tasks—anything to get out of this camp. "Send me to the front. You've given me outhouse duty. What could possibly be worse?"

I was game, and in my mind, I had nothing else to lose. Finally, the day of my assignment arrived. I was on my hands and knees, scrubbing the toilet, when the head nurse barged in like a pack of wild horses.

"Moorland?"

"Yes, Head Nurse."

In the split second after she barked my name, I couldn't think what I did wrong. I didn't know what to think. She had never burst into the outhouse before.

"It's time for you to ship out."

"Yes, ma'am."

She looked down at a piece of paper and then up at me. "You're off to Evacuation Hospital Number 114 in Fleury-sur-Aire."

I had no idea where that was, but I was on my way to the front.

"Godspeed, Moorland. Godspeed."

"Thank you, ma'am."

On our last night in Compiègne, Elaine, Harriet, Morgan, and I couldn't sleep. We were anxious about our assignments and what lay ahead for us. I was content to sit around the stove, keeping warm and quiet, but the rest of them were jittery and needed to talk. We gripped our tin cups of coffee to keep our hands warm.

Morgan piped in. "What do you think it'll be like?"

Elaine took a sip of her coffee. She made a face at the bitter taste, then spit it out onto the floor before answering back. "It ain't going to be pretty, that's for sure."

"I'm scared. Are you scared?" Harriet surveyed our faces, hoping we agreed with her.

"I'm scared to death," said Morgan.

Elaine, always the tough one, interjected, "What are you scared of?"

Harriet answered back. "I've never seen someone wounded before. I'm scared that I might not be able to take it … you know, I might faint."

"Aww, you'll get used to it. I've seen plenty of blood, what with all the accidents that happened down on our farm … hands caught in plows, you name it. I've seen it."

Morgan pressed Elaine. "But what about the dead?"

"They ain't going to bite you."

"I've just never seen someone who just died."

"Dead is dead."

"But doesn't it frighten you to think that you might be there the moment someone fades away?"

"It don't make no difference how long they've been dead. They're dead."

Morgan began to pace as her emotions rose. Tears formed in her eyes. "That seems so unfeeling."

"It's just the way of the world. You'll see so much of it, you'll just get used to it."

Deep down, I wanted to believe that I could mourn with every person who died in my care. I didn't want it to become normal. I finally spoke up. "I hope that's not true, Elaine."

Elaine sat up in her chair. "She finally speaks."

"It frightens me too, Morgan," I added.

"After you see a few of them, it'll be just like the passing of another day."

Elaine was right in a way. Just as the doughboys had to get used to war and killing, we had to get used to the sight of the wounded, the smell of death hovering over those who might or might not make it, and the horror of the dead.

United States Coast Guard
Special Report upon the
Incident on the Steamship *Uncatena*
October 16, 1921
Excerpt, Testimony, Ms. Amelia Moorland and Deputy Officer William B.
Madden

"Thank you for coming in."

"It's the least I can do, Officer."

"You know you have the right to have an attorney present?"

"I don't need a lawyer. I've nothing to hide."

"For the record, you're waiving your right to an attorney?"

"Yes."

"Are you feeling any better?"

"I'm still a little weak, but not chilled to the bone, like when I was fished out of the water."

"You know I hate to ask you the questions that I'm going to have to ask you. It's just my job. Do you understand?"

"I understand. I'll do my best to answer all of them."

"Shall we begin?"

CHAPTER IX

Evacuation Hospital Number 114 in Fleury-sur-Aire had twelve hundred beds and served the slightly to seriously wounded. It was always filled to capacity and then some, and the day I arrived, I had no sooner put my bags down than I was placed on duty.

The night before, hundreds of seriously wounded soldiers—or *grand blesses*, as we called them—were evacuated to our hospital. Some died, others had required surgery and were just coming out of their anesthetized state, and still others waited to go into the operating room. Everything smelled of ether, mud, and rotted flesh. I found myself holding my breath as much as possible.

Sister Elizabeth Brighton showed me around the hospital, then gave me my orders: "Your job right now is to comfort them."

"Comfort them?"

"Yes, comfort them. Just make them comfortable."

Sister Brighton was in charge of the nurses and the sisters. She had dark circles under her eyes and pale skin, and walked as if she were a sewing machine in need of oiling. The other sisters were in similar shape, but they forged ahead, determined to do their duty. I would soon mirror that same look.

I entered the ward with pencil and paper in hand, thinking perhaps the men would like to write letters to their sweethearts. I saw bed after bed after bed filled with maimed soldiers. The sisters buzzed around them, settling them into their beds, doing everything to make them feel comfortable, all the while knowing that when the morphine ran out, they would hear horrible cries and whimpers from these men who had fought heroically, but whose bodies and souls were left stripped of everything that defined them as men.

They were boys, damn it—boys! A few years older than Sam and me. Willie's age. Bernard's age.

I was overwhelmed. I couldn't believe what I was seeing: Men bandaged up from head to toe, legs and arms (if they were left) up in slings. Limbs cut off. The blood-soaked bandages serving as a vivid reminder that an arm or a leg used to be there. Would that bloodstain ever go away?

How could I possibly comfort these boys? How would they ever convalesce? If I was called upon to write a letter to their sweetheart, or mother, or father, or brother, how was I to sit with a smile on my face, knowing that any dreams they had prior to the war had been ripped away by the bomb that exploded next to them, or the machine-gun fire that riddled their bodies, or the gases that blinded them (or worse, ate their lungs away)?

"Sister?"

The soldier to my right groggily called out for a sister. I looked at him. If he had a chest once, it didn't appear to be there anymore. "Sister?"

I looked around, trying to find a sister who wasn't attending someone else. There wasn't a free sister in the place. I ran down the aisle to the nearest one and tugged at her sleeve. "That man over there, in the first bed, is calling for a sister."

"Go and attend to him. I'll be there in a moment."

"But he sounds as if he needs someone now."

"They all need someone now, nurse. Go to him, please? I'll be right there."

I slowly walked back to the front of his bed.

"Sister? Please. Please. Come here."

Apprehensive, I reached his bedside. "Yes, soldier?"

"Please. Please call me Harry."

"Yes, Harry."

"Am I dead or alive?"

"Why you're alive, Harry. Alive."

He moved his hand over to mine. "Oh God ..."

His face tensed up in enormous pain. I took his hand. "Don't let me die, sister."

I looked around for the sister I had spoken to, but she was gone.

"I'm not a sister. I'm a nurse. And I'll do everything I can—as will the sisters—to keep you alive. You should rest now."

"I'm afraid."

"Afraid of what?"

"Afraid of sleep. I'm afraid of sleep. I'm ... I'm afraid ..."

His eyes rolled back in his head. Was he dead? Was the first man I attended to really going to die on my watch? I placed my finger under his nose, as I was scared he had passed away. He must have smelled my hand cream, for he smiled and whispered something I couldn't make out.

"What was that, Harry?"

"Roses. Sweet roses. Hands are roses."

His hand went limp in mine as he dozed off. I tucked him in as best I could, then kissed my hand and placed it on his forehead. "Rest now, Harry."

As I took my hand away, an explosion boomed through the hospital, followed by another and then another. I was thrown to the floor. Any item that wasn't bolted down fell to the floor. The beds pulsed up and down. A few men moaned. It seemed as if the cannons were right outside the door to the hospital. I thought my world was coming to an end. I curled myself into a ball with my hands over my head. Sister Violet Williamson ran over to me and helped me to my feet. "Are you all right?"

"Are we under attack?"

"It's the big cannons at the front."

The noise continued. It was deafening. I couldn't hear what she was saying. "What?"

She screamed at the top of her lungs. "It's at the front."

Just then, Head Sister Brighton grabbed my shoulder and turned me around. "We're going to have a lot of new boys coming in. I need you to work the admitting station with Sister Agnes Billings. Go down and report to her."

"Yes, sister."

The admitting area was lined with what seemed like thousands of cots. At present, they were all empty. It was located right next to the operating areas. In between the constant pounding of the cannons and the firing of guns, doctors and sisters prepared the area for the next set of arrivals. I asked where I could find Sister Agnes.

"Over there, by the stove."

"Sister Agnes?"

A big, burly woman with round, rose-colored cheeks turned around. "Yes?" She had a gravelly voice.

"The head sister said I should report to you. I'm Nurse Moorland."

"Yes, of course."

She was all about business—very serious. "You'll work with me for the first part of the evening until I need to go off and join the surgical *equipes* in the operating area. Then you're on your own. We rarely give this duty to a nurse, but we're so short staffed, we have no other option."

"Yes, ma'am."

Over the roar and thudding of the cannon fire, she gave me my orders: "You'll learn to look at the men and decide which ones can wait, which ones need to be operated on immediately, and which ones won't make it."

My heart sank. How could I do that?

"Are you up to the task?"

Another big explosion rocked me off my feet. I fell to my knees. "I ... I don't think I can ..."

She helped me up. "On your feet! There's no time for apprehension, Moorland. Men are dying. They're being wounded. We have to work together to save those that we can."

"Yes, sister."

"The ambulances drop them outside, in that area. The stretcher bearers will bring them in here. We'll stand at the entrance and make quick decisions on what sections they'll be taken to. The operable will be placed as close to the operating area as possible. Those who can wait will go in the middle, and those who are beyond our help will go over there."

I was so afraid that I would make a mistake, mislabel one of the boys who should have been operated on immediately. I imagined that after the war, his family would track me down and blame me for their loved one's death: "How could you have been so stupid as to not see that he could have lived? Why did you take our son from us? You're a murderer, Amelia—a murderer!"

My heart raced and my muscles tensed as I did everything I could to hide the sheer panic I was feeling. "What if I make a mistake?"

"You do your best, Moorland, and don't worry about that. There are plenty of sisters and nurses who'll be attending those areas and can immediately reassess the situation."

What a relief. I wasn't looking forward to doing this, but I took comfort in knowing that I wasn't expected to play God.

The earth shook once again, but this time, I regained my balance. We heard trucks pulling up. Everyone got into place, awaiting the stretcher bearers and the casualties.

I stood next to Sister Agnes as they were brought in. She barked orders. "Over there!" She pointed to the area farthest from the operating room. I looked down at a man covered in blood and mud who appeared to have lost half his face, an arm, his stomach, and a leg. I gagged at the sight; I'd never seen anything so awful. Sister Agnes reprimanded me.

"Pull yourself together, Moorland. It's bad for morale."

I shook it off. One of the stretcher bearers, a gray-haired old Frenchman, looked at me and shrugged as he moved the soldier past us.

"*Que voulez-vous? C'est la guerre.*"

I smiled (or at least I thought I smiled), not knowing what he said. I must have had a blank stare on my face, because Sister Agnes translated for me: "What do you expect? It's the war."

"I beg your pardon?"

"He said, 'What do you expect? It's the war.'"

Another wounded man was brought in front of us.

"Take him there," Sister Agnes commanded.

After the first ambulance had been unloaded, Sister Agnes left me to the task. I felt sick to my stomach. I thought I was going to faint on the spot. I clenched my fists and willed myself to overcome the light-headedness.

"Place him over there," I said, hoping I didn't sound as shaky as I felt.

Steady streams of the wounded flowed in throughout the night, covered in a mix of blood and mud. Some were conscious; others were not. They panted or choked, bodies heaving in pain. Their moans and whimpers occasionally broke through the constant pounding of the cannon fire.

As I looked across the admitting station, I could see shadows of nurses and sisters attending to the hundreds of men brought in. Close to the operating area, nurses hurried in and out of the sterilizing rooms, carrying big, shiny metal boxes and enameled trays into the operating area. The smell of ether permeated the air.

At some point during the night, I was reassigned to digging éclat out of wounds. That's what they called all the shrapnel, bone splinters, and other objects that festered. It was an awful job, but it had to be done. The wounds looked horrible and smelled something terrible. One of the sisters trained me quickly, then left me on my own. Row upon row of soldiers needed my attention. Some had been hit days ago and were just getting to our hospital for care.

When I came upon my first patient, he was writhing in pain. His pant leg was bloodied and caked with mud. The first thing I had to do was cut his pant leg.

"Don't hurt me," he pleaded.

"I'll try not to."

I began cutting the fabric. I got to the area where his wound began, and he tensed up. I cut a little, watching his face to make sure he wasn't in too much pain. As I began to pull the stiff, damp, muddied fabric away from his wounds, he bit down on his lower lip. I looked down at the leg. His skin looked shredded. I could see splinters and fragments of artillery shells stuck in the flesh. Using tweezers, I slowly pulled these pieces out of his leg, placing the fragments in a metal bowl. Each time I dug a piece out, it clanked in the bowl, reassuring me that I had one less piece to remove.

"I'm not going to lose the leg, am I? Please tell me I'm not going to lose it."

I couldn't exactly tell him that, as I didn't know. I had never seen anything like this; even if he kept it, I wondered if he'd ever have use of it once it healed. I also couldn't tell him that I had never done this before, as I'm sure that would have sent him reeling. I responded tenderly, "I'm going to do everything I can to make you better."

I had a washbasin next to me, and as I pulled the éclat out of his leg, I dabbed the ravaged limb with water to help clean the wound. Though I knew he was in pain, he treated me with kindness, and I could tell by his manner that he appreciated that I was doing all I could for him.

But I had to resist fainting several times. I had to breathe through my mouth, for the smell of blood and rotted flesh was almost as powerful as a beached whale slowly dying on the shores of Nantucket. I couldn't let this man down.

I pulled the last fragment out and looked over his wounds again to ensure I had gotten it all. I was finished; the sisters could now dress the wound.

"Thank you, Nurse."

"Get well, soldier."

I went on to the next soldier. And the next. And the next, until daybreak—I stopped counting after ten men. By dawn, the sounds of the bombardment didn't faze me.

A new crew of doctors, sisters, and nurses came in and took over at about eight in the morning. I had been on duty for over sixteen hours. I knew I had to keep up and maintain composure, especially after seeing all those boys who had given a part of themselves for this cause.

I went into my hut and collapsed. Only then did I realize the bombardment had stopped, replaced by birdsong—primarily of skylarks. I was lulled to sleep by their sweet voices. I could only imagine that they were chirping away at each other, asking themselves what all the noise was about, and why we were wreaking havoc and destruction on ourselves and this land.

I went into a very deep sleep and didn't awaken until the bombardment started again, just after sundown.

I was still angry at Sam and tried to rid my mind of her, but I couldn't stop thinking about her. When her letter arrived, I hated to admit it, but deep down inside, I was thrilled.

March 4, 1918

Dear Amelia,

I can't sleep knowing that you are angry with me. You are the most important person in my life and the closest friend that I have. You have to know
that it was impossible for me to tell you about the feeling I had about
Willie. You and I have these feelings. Sometimes they're right, and sometimes we have to hope that we're wrong, or we have to try to believe that
they won't come true. That's how I felt about Willie. But we have no control over these feelings—or the outcome.

We used to say these feelings were a gift, but it's times like these that I
think it is a curse, especially when it comes between the two of us. Let's
not allow this to break apart our friendship.

I pray for your safe return every day, and I know you're thinking of me as I
am of you.

Until I see you again, I remain

Fondly yours, Sam

I knew she was right: we had no control, and she couldn't have told me. If the
tables were turned, and I knew something terrible was going to happen to one of
her loved ones, I couldn't tell her. But I was being stubborn; I wasn't ready to forgive her just yet.

You must think that this period of my life was filled with nothing but darkness. The truth is, the darkness reigned, but even life in the war wasn't without its
good times. Luckily, there were YMCA and Salvation Army camps around us.
They afforded us recreation. They organized everything from musical revues to
baseball games. In fact, I think there was some sort of ball game every day for
those soldiers on leave from the front lines. On my days off, I'd watch the baseball games, then duck into the tent to be entertained by a variety of music-hall
performers.

On one of those days, I spotted Vera Guest performing for the troops. She was
such a coquette as she danced on the stage while a tall and lanky pianist sang,
"Oui Oui, Marie."

The men hooted and hollered as Vera raised her eyebrows, winked at the boys,
and pretended to scratch like a cat. She sure knew how to get them all riled up.

When the song ended, everyone stood up and applauded. Vera absolutely glowed in the limelight. She blew everyone a kiss and danced off the stage into the crowd. She was immediately surrounded by soldiers; she kissed every one of them on the cheek. What a flirt. I often envied her ability to command a room.

"Vera?"

She turned around and surveyed me with a blank stare. She had no idea who I was.

"It's me. Remember? On the ship over?" I pretended to smoke a cigarette, inhaling and then exhaling with a loud cough, as if choking on the smoke. Her face immediately became alive.

"Yes, of course. How are you?"

"Fine. You were terrific."

"Thank you. I'm so terribly thirsty after the performance. Let's get something to drink."

"Sure."

We walked over to the canteen and ordered soda water. Alcohol wasn't allowed.

"Are you stationed around here?" Vera asked.

"Yes. And you?"

"Good heavens, no. I travel around to all of the YMCA camps, doing a little bit of this and a whole lot of that."

"You're a natural on the stage."

"I hate modesty, so I'll agree with you. You work in the hospital, right?"

"Yes."

"And are you surviving?"

"I'm managing. It's very hard work, but someone's got to do it."

"I imagine. I've yet to visit any of the hospitals. There's talk about sending us around to some of them to try to cheer the men up. But I'd really like to go up to the front."

"You would?"

"Of course. Aren't you interested in seeing what it's like?"

"Before I was assigned, I thought so. Then I heard the bombardments. Have you heard them?"

"Only in the distance."

"I think if you ever heard them up close, you'd want to stay well away."

Just then, a Tommy came up to our table. "She's right, you know," the British soldier said. "The front's no place for ladies—especially ladies as beautiful as the two of you."

Vera took out a cigarette, placed it in her mouth, and looked him right in his eyes. He immediately searched for his briquette. He pulled it out and lit her cigarette.

"Thank you, Casanova."

"I couldn't help but overhear your conversation."

She slowly blew the smoke out of her mouth. "You're so very proper. Just like all the English."

He blushed. "Chester Winifred."

"Vera Guest—"

He interrupted. "Yes, I know. I've seen you many times."

"Hopefully it's provided you some pleasure."

He smiled and winked at her. "Every time."

"And this is Ameliahhhhhhhhh ..." She couldn't remember my last name.

I broke the long sound as she fished for my name. "Moorland."

He bowed. "How do you do?"

Vera cut me off before I could answer. "If it's no place for ladies, what's it like?"

He pulled out the chair next to Vera. "May I?"

"Please do."

"Well ... where to begin? The trenches always have six inches of water in the bottom of them, and they're dark as a pocket."

"What's it like when you're under attack?"

"The attacks usually happen at night. The blackness is interrupted by rockets that go up, and you hear them explode like fireworks. Then, the sky turns bright red or green. That's when you raise your gun and get ready for bloody hell to happen."

Vera and I were enthralled.

"Suddenly, shells start whining. You think they're coming toward you. You can't see them. You just hear them, and you crouch down, hoping to holy heaven that one doesn't strike next to you, because if it does, they'll be playing taps for you. And the sound becomes deafening when the big guns start bombarding on both sides. It's almost impossible to hear orders being screamed at the tops of lungs. And the bullets whiz by you. You'll be standing next to someone, and in an instant, your mate is fallen to the ground, either dead or wounded. Then there are the gassings ... they're the worst. But you can usually tell if a shell is loaded with gas."

"How do you do that?" Vera asked.

"If it's a regular shell, it bursts and destroys nearly everything near it. If it's a gas shell, it explodes with a pop, like a champagne bottle."

"Then what do you do?"

"You stop breathing and put your gas mask on, adjust it, continue fighting, and hope you weren't exposed. I tell you, if I'm going to be pushing daisies up in skeleton park, I'd rather be shot or hit with an explosive shell than die by gassing."

I had seen some of the gas victims—blinded, wheezing, their lungs rattling with impending death. "We've had some cases in the hospital. It's horrible to see."

Vera snubbed out her cigarette in the ashtray and looked up at Chester. She took both her hands and placed them on his cheeks. She pulled him close to her and kissed him on the lips. "You're a brave man, Chester Winifred."

With that, Vera stood up and quickly left the table. Chester didn't have time to get up and see her off; he half stood, then sank back into his chair. I didn't know whether to stay with Chester or go after Vera. She was out of sight before I could run after her.

Chester smiled at me. "She's quite something."

"Yes, she is."

"My talk of the front didn't disturb you, did it?"

"The whole war is disturbing."

"You're quite right about that."

"Have you been fighting around these parts?"

"Truth be told, I haven't been on the lines fighting in quite some time. You see, I'm charged with taking dignitaries, civilians, and reporters as close to the front as possible."

"I can't figure out why anyone would want to go up there and see it."

"It's human nature, I believe. There's some deep-seated desire in humans to see death and destruction."

"Perhaps you're right."

"I'm taking around an artist right now; he's American, actually. He's been asked by the British Minister of Information to paint a picture of British and American troops working together."

"It sounds admirable, but I can't imagine why anyone would want a painting of war."

"He's actually quite famous in his own right. Have you heard of John Singer Sargent?"

I had to admit I hadn't. At that time, I wasn't interested in art or artists and certainly hadn't spent any time in museums or galleries. I felt like a country bumpkin. "No."

"You'll have to search out his work. His paintings are really something to see."

I felt quite the imbecile and very much the clodhopper. "You must think I'm Polpisy."

"I beg your pardon?"

I laughed. A little bit of my da and old Nantucket had crept back into my speech. Of course he had no idea of what I was saying. "It's what my da used to say when someone wasn't as informed as they should be."

"That's an odd phrase, but I like it."

"It's named after Polpis."

"And who was he?"

"It's not a person. It's an area on Nantucket, where I'm from, that is outside of town. People who lived there were farmers who didn't get into town often, so they weren't in the know. It's quite a beautiful place, though: ponds, moors, and rolling hills spread across the landscape—and the distant views on top of the highest hills of Nantucket Sound and the Atlantic all around you."

Thinking about Polpis made me homesick. Despite my anger at Sam, I ached with memories of running through the moors with her; lying on our backs and watching blackbirds chase red-tailed hawks across the endless blue sky; in the spring and summer, hunting for peepers in the wetlands and ponds and marveling at their mating call, which sounded like sleigh bells; and watching evening sky change from blue to orange, to red, violet, purple, deep purple, and then black, studded with sequins as the stars and moon began to glow. It was all so far away, yet so close in my heart.

These memories were making me melancholy. I decided it was time to leave. "Well, Chester, I'd best be getting back."

"May I walk you back to the hospital?"

"You don't have to do that."

He placed his hand on my knee. "It would be my pleasure."

He moved toward me and kissed me. Willie had been the last man I kissed or touched; I'd forgotten what it felt like. I felt a warmth I hadn't felt in months. He began caressing my knee, and then he put his hand under my dress, sliding it up my leg. I grabbed his hand to stop him.

"I can't."

"Sure you can."

He kissed me again; this time, our tongues intertwined in a tender play. My heart began to race.

"I just met you."

"So? What if tomorrow, we're not here? What if tonight is our last night? Don't you want to … you know?"

He came toward me to kiss me again. He closed his eyes. Mine remained open; all I could see was Willie. I wasn't prepared for this.

"I've got to go. Really."

I jumped up. It startled him, and he stood up and pressed his hands against his shirt and pants, trying to regain composure.

"I'm sorry, Amelia. I was too forward. I wasn't thinking."

I could feel tears welling up in my eyes. I tried to fight them back, but began to cry. Embarrassed, I ran out as quickly as I could.

"Amelia?"

That night, I couldn't get the sensation of Chester's caresses and kisses out of my mind. I should never have left so abruptly. I wanted more; the thought of his touch sent quivers up and down my body. I didn't want him to stop. Camilla had said I shouldn't fight it, but I had. Was I wrong to have such feelings? I needed more. And then Willie appeared.

How could I be with another man so soon after Willie died? Was it a slap in his face? Was I dishonoring him?

I was being silly. It wasn't as if Willie and I had ever made love or had a serious relationship. Ours was a summer affair, interrupted by duty. He went his way, and I mine. But I wanted more, damn it. Deep down, I wanted Willie—something I couldn't have.

I needed to be held, caressed, and kissed. I needed someone.

That someone entered my life at the end of the summer of 1918. James Furie was nineteen years old and from Boston. He was an ambulance driver—clipper built and some handsome with dark hair, blue eyes, and olive skin. He volunteered during his freshman year at Harvard before the United States officially entered the war. He trained in France and then went to Italy and Serbia before returning to France to be stationed at Fleury-sur-Aire.

He made eyes at me several times before he got the nerve to strike up a conversation. He'd drive up in his ambulance, which was nothing more than a Ford truck refitted to transport the injured. It was always filled to capacity. James would always help the old French stretcher bearers carry the wounded in. He would pass me and smile. I'd nod in recognition and continue with whatever task

I had that shift. Of course, he made several trips when the bombardments were going on. It was always the same: he gave me a smile, and I gave him a nod.

Then one day, he spoke. "Aren't you ever going to return the smile?"

It took me by surprise. "I beg your pardon?"

"I've been coming in here for I don't know how long and smiling at you, and you've yet to return the smile. A poor ambulance driver like me needs a little sunshine to get me through the day."

I blushed and smiled.

"Ah, there it is. There's my sunshine." He winked and smiled back at me.

From that moment on, I couldn't stop thinking about him. I felt as if my life were finally better weathering it. I did everything I could to see him every day. I felt as if I were running before the wind again. I listened for the screeching brakes and the gurgle of engines as the ambulances pulled up. I'd run to the entrance and look for James. He'd smile, and my heart would sing.

We had to be careful, though, as the sisters and nurses were discouraged from fraternizing with soldiers and doctors—or any man, for that matter. However, most rules like that were meant to be broken, and few obeyed that order.

James and I were fortunate to work the same shifts and to have the same time off together. One afternoon, during a half day off, I met him down at the Salvation Army tent. He had just received a package from home. His parents had sent him a Kodak Brownie camera. You see, James loved photography. He'd pose me in every possible situation. We went down to the river, where he posed me on a rock. Then we went out in the forest, and he leaned me against a tree. Next, we went out to some ruins of a bombed village. He made me feel like a moving-picture star.

He also let me take pictures of him. I snapped one of him in front of his ambulance, standing proud as a peacock, one of him helping the stretcher bearers carry a man out, and yet another of him standing next to a crashed German plane with his foot on the debris, as if he were responsible for its demise.

James also took a lot of pictures of the boys up at the front. Those were the most disturbing to me: Men huddled in the muddy trenches, seeking relief from the constant rain. Standing in water up to their knees. Embedded in the dirt walls with looks of fear, exhaustion … utterly beaten down. Oh, there were some of the men fooling around, dancing a jig, or smoking cigarettes and singing. I didn't mind those. But the ones taken in battle haunted me.

Getting the photographs developed was "none easy." Luckily, James had a friend of a friend of a friend (he went to Harvard, remember?) who was a war photographer, and he developed them for James in exchange for cigarettes, chocolates, and a few dollars. James placed them in a leather-bound scrapbook and presented them to me.

The day James gave me that scrapbook, we took a ride to Reims. It took almost four hours to get there, but James wanted to take some photographs of the cathedral, which had been ruined by German bombardments earlier in the war. The city, for that matter, was badly wrecked over the course of four years of bombardment. We made our way up to the cathedral, through the Place de St. Rémi. Debris was piled everywhere. Buildings around the cathedral had been hit, and we saw little sign of life, save for those weary-eyed people who had battened down the hatches in their determination to weather the storm or be killed doing so.

It was an enormous cathedral, but it had been ripped a part. All that was left was an empty shell of a building with collapsed stone walls, crushed stained-glass windows, and exposed insides laid bare to the elements.

I couldn't imagine how anyone could hit such a building. While I wasn't religious, I certainly had reverence for places of worship. Although Mama wouldn't set foot in any church that wasn't Catholic, I enjoyed discovering other sanctuaries when mass or services weren't going on. Sam and I would go to the Congregational Church on Centre Street and climb up the steep stairs to the steeple to look out over Nantucket Harbor. On our way down, we'd look out over all the pews and listen to all the creaks and noises ricocheting off the walls. Or we'd go into St. Paul's Episcopal Church and look at the Tiffany stained-glass windows, with their beautiful landscapes and flowers. The churches were always so eerily quiet, as if they were immune to what was going on in the outside world.

Tears welled up in my eyes. James took me in his arms.

"It's painful to look at," I said in a quavery voice.

"I know, Sunshine. Imagine how the French feel. This was the site of the coronations of French kings. It's so much a part of their history, their identity."

"I can't imagine what it's like for them, especially those who live here. It must be awful to see the heart and soul of their city blown to kingdom come."

It was in front of the cathedral that James presented me with the scrapbook. He had included all the photographs he had taken, as well as those that I had taken of him.

"We have to remember not only the awfulness of all this, but the good times we've shared as well. Promise to keep adding to this until it's over, even if I don't make it."

I slapped him. "Don't say such things."

"I don't want to think it, but anything's possible. Will you promise?"

"If you promise not to leave me."

"I'll do my best."

From that day forward, I kept all the photographs he and I took in that book. At the time, I wanted to keep my memories of him, and those around us, intact. It wasn't until after the war that I abandoned those memories to the outer reaches of my mind, dumping them in a box under a heap of other boxes and God knows what else up there in the attic.

The scrapbook still exists. But I'm jumping ahead again.

That night, on the way back to Fleury-sur-Aire, James pulled the truck over to the side of the road. At the end of a very large field stood the beginnings of the forest. It was a beautiful September evening; the stars lit up the sky, and for what seemed like the first night in a long time, the sky was clear, and we didn't hear bombardments in the distance.

James turned to me and kissed me.

"What's that for?"

"It's for being the best thing that's ever happened to me."

He kissed me again, this time for longer. I played with his hair.

"I wouldn't ask you to do anything you didn't want to do, Sunshine."

"I know that."

He put his hand on my breast and looked me in the eye. He started caressing it. "Tell me if you want me to stop."

He kissed me again and started unbuttoning my blouse. He brushed up against my nipple, then lightly pinched it. Although I was trembling, I did everything to keep my composure. I had decided before this moment that James was the one. I wasn't going to let the chance go by, as I had with Willie. James would be my first.

He stopped kissing me and looked at me for a long minute. Then he grabbled my hand and opened the door.

"Come on," he said.

He took a blanket out of the back of the truck, and we walked hand in hand through the field. We stopped in the middle of it and looked around. We were alone. We laid out the blanket and knelt down on it, then kissed and fell to the ground in an embrace. He began to undo his pants. It was all moving so fast ... I wanted him, but I was nervous. I had no idea what to expect or what exactly to do. I pulled his face away from mine.

"James. I want to. I really do. But you should know that this is ... that this is ... my ..."

I was embarrassed to finish the sentence. I looked away. He turned my face toward his and smiled.

"Me too."

We both chuckled. He lay on top of me, and we kissed. He hiked up my dress and undid my undergarments, then eased himself into me. I felt a quick, sharp pain. He pulled back, but I pulled him toward me again. He slowly moved in, and then almost out. In, then almost out. In, then all the way out.

James fumbled around, trying to get back into the rhythm. "Damn."

I reassured him. "It's OK."

He tried to pop it back in. He had the worst time doing that. "I guess my inexperience shows."

We kissed. He continued, with no success. Finally, I had to guide him back in. "There."

He relaxed, relieved. "Oh, yes."

I started feeling as if electric shocks were going through my body. "Does it feel good?"

James let out soft moans. "Oh, yes. Yes."

I closed my eyes and kissed him. Our breathing became heavy. His body tightened, and he thrust himself into me more forcefully, then froze. He let out a loud moan and collapsed on top of me.

I looked up in the sky, and everything seemed clearer, crisper. I could smell the rampaged earth, the leaves on the trees, the pines … and James. I could hear the distant, lazily rolling water of a river, lapping against rocks and shore. I felt the firm, yet velvety soft touch of the man I loved on top of me and inside me. I kissed him.

He rolled over, and we looked at the millions of stars in the sky, saying nothing for hours. It was one of the most peaceful memories I have of the war. I wanted James even more.

It wasn't until about four in the morning that I got back to my hut. I had been given a new hut mate, as my previous mate had been reassigned to a hospital in Verdun. I was a bit apprehensive to enter the room so late, so I went into the hospital to see if they needed any help with the excuse that I couldn't sleep. I stood over a spirit lamp and disinfected needles.

Now that I was no longer a virgin, I started to think again about birth control and *The Woman Rebel*, whose relevance had increased dramatically. I certainly didn't want to get pregnant while out on the front—and more importantly, while unmarried. But after a night of making love with James, I couldn't imagine not having sex with him as much as was humanly possible.

I kept thinking about one line from that pamphlet: "A woman's body belongs to herself alone." That was going to be my mantra. I felt it was my responsibility, at least to myself, to make sure I didn't get pregnant. I couldn't fathom buying one of those birth-control devices referred to in the pamphlet. One of them looked like something you'd find in a torture chamber. It was a wishbone looking device, and it was made of metal. The cap at the top resembled a large head of a tack. It had a long, coiled mid-section and jetted out like a wishbone at the bottom. It simply looked painful. Then there were mushroom-like cervical caps made of metal, but the thought of inserting one made me uncomfortable, as I couldn't imagine having a piece of metal inside me.

But even if I could talk myself into using one of these devices, I had no idea where I would purchase one. The only other option was the natural way: the withdrawal method. It didn't sound like the greatest choice, but it was certainly the most practical. The compromise seemed well worth it. I felt that not dealing with an unwanted pregnancy was a fair trade-off for any loss of intimacy.

I thought about this until the sun rose, then returned to my hut to wash up and meet my new mate.

I slipped in the door. She was still sleeping. I emptied the hot-water bottle I had placed in my bed before leaving with James, using that water to wash my face. You see, there was no hot running water, so the water bottle offered the only bathing water that was at least room temperature.

She stirred. I finished drying my face and lay down on my bunk. I had just closed my eyes and dozed off when I suddenly heard an angelic voice.

"Who is he?"

I sat up and saw Lena DeWitt sitting on the side of her bed. She looked a couple of years older than me. She had a twinkle in her eye, a beaming smile, and a slightly plump frame. Her cheeks were rosy red, and despite the abrupt question, she had the personality of a teddy bear—all you wanted to do was give her a big hug.

"Who is who?"

"They told me I'd meet you last night, so when you didn't come in, I assumed you were out with a sweetheart."

Her assumptions were correct, but I couldn't admit that to her. "I couldn't sleep and didn't want to disturb you."

She smiled and winked. "You know, you're glowing."

I became self-conscious and put my hand on my cheek. "I am?"

"Yes. There's definitely a glow about you. You must be in love."

I blushed and got out of bed, trying to disguise my emotions. I attempted a change of subject. "Is this your first assignment?"

She turned away from me and busied herself making her bed. "I served in Belgium for about two years before coming down here. I lost my husband about three years ago. He came over just after the war started and fought with the French."

"I'm so sorry."

"We had no children, so I thought I'd do something—anything—to ease the pain I was feeling."

There was a knock on the door.

"Sunshine?"

It was James. My heart sank. Lena turned to me and smiled.

"Coming." I walked quickly to the door and exited. "What are you doing here?" I whispered.

"I can't get you out of my mind."

He grabbed me and kissed me. As much as I wanted him, I had to be careful. I pushed him away. "Me, too, but it's dangerous for you to be showing up at my hut like this."

"I don't care."

Just as he was about to finish his sentence, Lena walked out of the hut.

He blurted out, "I'm in love!"

She smiled at us. "Congratulations."

James was taken by surprise. He had forgotten that I had a new mate.

"Lena DeWitt." My hut mate offered her hand. "And you are?"

"James Furie."

"Your secret is safe with me."

Lena walked toward the hospital. I hoped beyond hope that she wouldn't tell everyone.

"Smile!"

Lena and I stood in front of our hut while James took our photo together. She was true to her word, never discussing my relationship with anyone—including me, unless I brought the subject up first.

At times, I felt that my older hut mate was living vicariously through James and me. She missed her husband. Her grief was a reminder to cherish what I had with James, for it might be taken away at any moment. And unfortunately, sometimes our happiness was a reminder to her of what she used to have, but had no more. While this would normally ignite jealousy in most people, it made her melancholy.

One night, I came into the hut after a long shift. Lena was in bed. I could hear her sniffling as she turned away from the door.

"Lena? Are you all right?"

"I'm fine."

"Is there something I can do?"

"No."

She wept harder. I went to her bed and held her in my arms. She grabbed onto me and sobbed uncontrollably.

"I see all of these wounded men and the dead, and it makes me think of Freddie and what a lonely death he must have experienced. I don't know if anyone was there for him. Did anyone comfort him, or was he instantly killed? Did they try to operate on him, or was he relegated, like so many here, to the lost-cause area?"

"They didn't tell you anything about his death?"

"The only thing I got was a telegram in French that said they regret to inform me of the death of my husband on February 5, 1915, while serving in the trenches near Perthes."

"He must have been thinking of you at the time. I'm sure he'd have wanted you to go on."

"It's something I'll never know. I hate the Huns for this. I feel as if I could kill them … and that scares me even more."

I didn't know what to say, so I just rocked her back and forth. After a while, she pushed me away.

"I'm sorry you have to hear this. It just got to me today. I'll be all right." She wiped the tears away and beamed that smile again. I straightened her hair and hugged her tight.

James had given me a bottle of wine (which, of course, was forbidden), which I hid in a space between the wall and the roof, behind a piece of canvas. I took it out, pulled the cork, and offered her a drink.

We sat and drank the bottle in silence. After we took one final swig, Lena put her head on my shoulder. "Thanks."

"I'm sure you'd do the same for me."

In late September and early October of 1918, a lot of doctors, sisters, and nurses came to our area in a flurry of troop movements. A lot more ambulances and drivers arrived on the hospital doorstep as well. It didn't take a genius to realize that something big was about to happen.

Head Sister Brighton called all of the sisters and nurses together. We lined up and stood at attention in the yard outside the hospital. I remember feeling ill. I had a sore throat and a headache, but did everything I could to get through Sister Brighton's bellowing. Her words seemed to bounce off the stone walls.

"I'd like to welcome all the recent arrivals of both sisters and nurses to our hospital. I'm sure you're all wondering why so many of you have been stationed here. Although I can't tell you the specifics, we're expecting a big offensive soon. And you've all been called here to handle the wounded from such an offensive. I don't know when or where it will occur. And I've been asked by the war censors to order you not to write about it or to talk about it among yourselves."

Gilbert, an old, wine-soaked Frenchman with very few teeth who served as a janitor, stuck his head out of one of the windows and pointed to the sky. "*Regarder en haut! Hiver les yeux! C'est le saucisson!*"

We all looked up and saw a large German observation balloon floating overhead. As the balloon floated across the hospital and out of sight, we suddenly heard the faint buzzing of an engine. It grew louder and louder … two, three, four buzzing engines.

"It's a dogfight. Take cover."

We all scrambled to the sides of the yard. Some ran into the hospital. Others ran to their huts. Lena and I huddled in a corner of the yard.

Two great birds roared over the hospital. As they passed, I pulled on Lena's arm. "Are they ours?"

"Yes. They've got American markings. See the white star surrounded by blue? That's the doughboys."

Another two planes flew over the yard in pursuit of the Americans. Lena screamed out, "It's the Boche!"

Still another two planes flew over. "I think they're French."

After the planes flew over, we started to hear the sounds of machine-gun fire. The American planes flew straight up, the Germans following, and the French behind them, chasing each other across the sky. I heard the machine guns firing from the planes. A collision would seem imminent, but then one would pull up. To think Bernard was up there somewhere, doing something like that. Who knew? Maybe he was one of these aces.

The planes whined and roared as they maneuvered up and down, to the left and right. In circles. Upside-down. On their sides. The Americans tried to outrun the Germans as the French tried to catch up.

Then one of the American planes dropped nosefirst toward the ground, a German plane on its tail. It gained speed, and the engines shrieked. Was it going to crash? What on earth was happening?

We screamed, "Pull up! Pull up!"

We lost sight of it. Just as it seemed as if it were going to crash, it pulled up and quickly rose back into view. The German plane, trying to follow, couldn't recover. It hit the ground with a thunderous boom, and smoke billowed in the distance.

At this point, the French and American planes were going after the remaining German plane. The German plane tried to retreat, but to no avail. It descended and looped around, maneuvering behind one of the American planes. The riddle-rattle of the machine guns mixed with the throbbing sounds of the airplane engines. And then, one of the American planes burst into flames and fell from the sky.

Lena cried out, "They got one of us!"

I looked over at the ambulance brigade; James was running toward his truck. He quickly cranked the engine, got in, and took off in the direction of the crash. Three other ambulances followed suit.

The two French planes intercepted the German plane and charged it, firing round after round. The German pilot lost control. The plane turned upside down and flew crazy eights, headfirst toward the earth. We lost sight of it, but heard a loud crash and saw black smoke.

Everyone ran out to the middle of the yard and cheered the aces. They flew over the yard, just above the rooftops, and waved to us.

Later that afternoon, James brought back what was left of the American aviator and the Germans. The American was, of course, dead, and so badly burned that a blanket covered his body from head to toe.

Lying next to him was one of the German aces. He was alive … or, I should say, not quite dead. It was difficult caring for the Germans, but because we were an evacuation hospital, we were obliged to care for them. Seeing the dead American next to this Hun made me angry. He should be dead, not the American. He was out there trying to shoot down and kill our men. His squadron was probably trying to shoot down Bernard.

Bernard … what if the American lying under that blanket was Bernard? Was it possible? I had no idea where Bernard was stationed at the time, so of course it was possible. I suddenly became convinced that the dead American was Bernard. If it was him, I would kill the Hun.

I ran up to the American corpse. James stood close by.

"Is it Bernard?" I asked. Speaking the question aloud only made me more frantic.

James tried to pull me back.

"Bernard?"

I pushed him aside. "My brother, Bernard. Is it him?"

I ripped the blanket off the body. Half the man's face was charred black. Most of his hair was singed off. His one eye hung out of his head. The other, baked into his skull, was unrecognizable. Half his lower jaw was where his nose should be, and his nose began just at the tip of his eye socket.

I turned away and gagged, then ran. James ran after me. I was crying. He grabbed ahold of my shoulder and turned me around.

"Is it him?"

I couldn't speak and gagged once more.

"Amelia. Is it your brother?"

I shook my head, still gagging. "No."

He held me tight and didn't let go.

Seeing that dogfight, and the fight to death, I couldn't help but pray that Bernard was safe. And I longed to hold him in my arms. I missed Bernard. I missed my family. I missed Sam.

James kissed me on my forehead, then placed his hand on my cheek. "You're burning up, Sunshine."

I felt light-headed and faint. "What?"

"You're feverish."

The air turned still and silent. The hairs on the back of my neck stood straight up.

"Is that you, Sam?"

Everything went black.

United States Coast Guard
Special Report upon the
Incident on the Steamship *Uncatena*
October 16, 1921
Excerpt, Testimony, Ms. Amelia Moorland questioned by
Deputy Officer William B. Madden

"I know we've been over this several times, and it must be very hard for you to keep playing this over and over again in your head."

"It is."

"We're not here to make this nightmare continue. We're here to get to the truth—the truth of what happened that night—so that you can get on with your life."

"I realize that."

"Now, then. Before we go through it one more time—and this time, I don't want you to leave out any details—can I get you anything? A glass of water? A cigarette?"

"A glass of water, please. Thank you."

"I'll be but a moment. You just try to remember what happened."

CHAPTER X

"Amelia? Amelia, you have to wake up."

"I'm awake, Sam."

"No, Amelia. You're not. You're asleep."

Why did Sam think I was sleeping? She had to know better. Were her powers failing her? Couldn't she see I was digging a hole in the floor of my hut? Didn't she realize I was trying to get out?

I had to leave this place. I dug with my bare hands through layers of earth. I came upon worms, cockroaches, beetles, larvae, ants, and other creepy crawlers. None of them bothered me; I was determined to get out.

Suddenly, there was an enormous explosion. The earth shook. Dirt caved in around me. I was almost buried alive. I wheezed for air; the dirt pressed hard against my chest and lungs. It felt as if someone were standing on me. My chest was tight as a knot and getting tighter. I couldn't breathe.

The earth shook again. More dirt and debris fell on me. My body tensed up in panic. I was frozen still. My heart raced as I choked. The air became heavy. My lungs were getting tighter and tighter. I was unable to relax; I couldn't catch my breath. Everything kept pressing in around me. I knew that if I didn't do something, I would be a goner.

I pushed my arms away from my sides, loosening the earth around me. I began making angels, waving my arms and legs back and forth. At first, it was a struggle; I could only push the dirt back so far. If I hadn't been possessed to move on, I would have given up at that moment. With one more push, I managed some traction. Finally, I had enough room at my sides to continue digging. I was making progress. I was getting away. The farther away, the better.

And then, blackness came again.

I heard the deafening noise of constant bombardment. My ears burned. I couldn't get the sound out of my head. It kept reverberating from one side of my head to the other. I was afraid that I would lose my hearing—or worse, that I wouldn't. I screamed to see if I could hear myself, but I couldn't. How was I going to get away from this? I began digging again. I had to distance myself ... continents, countries, miles, days, nights, hours, and seconds away from this war.

My fingers came upon a layer of rocks, stones, and broken shards of pottery used by women long since past. The shards spliced open my fingers, drawing blood. I looked down at my hands. They were covered in earth. My fingers throbbed and shook uncontrollably. I held them up to my eyes. I saw deep, dark blood oozing from the dirt-filled cuts.

Blood curdled into blackness.

I was cocooned in mud; I couldn't seem to get through it. It oozed from my mouth. My body was turning into mud. It was folding into the earth. I looked down at my legs and saw nothing but black mud.

I was digging again. My left hand pulled up the face of a man. It was the corpse of a doughboy. He was bloated and rotting. His eyes still intact, he stared at me in disbelief at his fate. He had a smirk on his face, as if he had taken bets that I would be next. I was determined to prove him wrong.

His lower lip was frozen midquiver, silently begging me to do something to change the course of history. I couldn't bear to look at him; there was nothing I could do. He was gone, God rest his soul. As for me, I had to fight to stay alive. But he was in my way.

I gritted my teeth and held my breath. With my bloodied, banged-up, and bruised fingers, I tore open his stomach. Maggots spilled out like boiled-over milk on a stove. I winced but couldn't be deterred. I crawled through his stomach, digging as quickly as I could to get away from him.

But underneath him, the soil turned to clay—hard, mineral, chalky. All I wanted to do was to distance myself from the doughboy, but the clay wouldn't give way. I continued to struggle. I couldn't hold my breath any longer. The smell of him and the earth had me in its grip.

I gagged and then gagged again. My stomach heaved. I tried to fight off the sensation of vomiting, but I couldn't stop the violent dry heaves. It felt as if my innards were being pulled out of me. Pain shot through my stomach to my head.

I looked back to see if I was well away from him. Everything was black.

"I'm afraid she's got it."
Got what? Who is speaking? Who is she? What does she have?

"We're going to have to get her out of here."
Get who out of where? Why? I couldn't help but think that if they followed me, I could get them out of this war, out of this country. *Let me lead the way.*

I heard the sound of a railroad car clanking down the tracks. It beat with the rhythm of my heart: "Ba-doom ba-doom. Ba-doom ba-doom. Ba-doom ba-doom."

Moans and screams filled the air. I couldn't make out what people were saying, nor did I have any idea who these people were. I didn't have any inkling why they were in such pain, but their cries were unbearable.

I concentrated on the sound of the railroad car and my heart. "Ba-doom ba-doom. Ba-doom ba-doom. Ba-doom ba-doom."

It lulled me to sleep.

There was a flash of white light, and I was digging again. I struck something hard. I pulled up one hand and then the other. I was holding a rib cage and a finger bone. I grabbed another handful. This time I pulled up a foot with one hand and a shoulder blade with the other. I placed both of my hands into the earth and pulled an entire skeleton out.

As I kept digging, I ripped skeletons apart trying to get through this layer. There were too many of them. I stopped and looked at all of the skulls I had uncovered. They peered at me and made me feel guilty. They wished I had come sooner. It's possible that I may have known who they were. I could have told their stories. I could have kept them alive.

But it was too late for that. They were in my way. I was swimming in a hole of human bones; I was about to drown in them. My heart raced faster than before, and my chest and lungs were being crushed by the millions and millions of bones.

As I dug through the bones, they prodded my every organ and intestine. Were they searching for some life to cling onto? I felt as if I were being pricked to death. The bones seemed sharp as knives.

And then I came upon the mouth of a skull. I brushed up against it, teeth to teeth. I shuddered. I looked into its eye sockets and saw black.

"She's not responding."

I felt warmth on my hand. It was soft and caressing. I felt the moist, firm grip of someone. Was it a man? Did I know this person? Then I felt the wetness of a tear just shed on my face, but I couldn't recognize the touch or the voice. I thought I cried out.

"Who's there?"

"Sunshine? Can you hear me? Surely you can hear me."

Before I could answer, a hand caressed my brow. The touch was familiar. But who was it?

I was completely submerged in water. I couldn't tell if I was breathing, but I wasn't struggling. I was floating. It took no effort.

The cold water was turning warmer. The water became lukewarm, then warm. I could feel my body warm up.

"It's over, Sunshine. It's over."

Whoever that was, he sure had it wrong. It wasn't over. I tried to tell him that I would get us out of here. I would show him the way; all he had to do was to keep following me.

I turned around and barked out an order. "Stay close." But I couldn't see him.

"It's me, Sunshine. It's James."

James? Why can't I remember James? Why are you following me, James?

"I wish you could have heard the cheers. It all ended the eleventh hour, of the eleventh day, in the eleventh month. We all cried with joy."

I had no idea what he was talking about. What ended?

"Amelia? Come back to me."

Come back? But the way is through here. You've got to stay close.

The speed at which I moved in the water accelerated. I was being pulled down in a whirlpool. I let the circular tide pull me down. Resisting would have been pointless.

I tumbled head over heels, round and round, until my body was sucked out of the whirlpool and into a cave.

I opened my eyes and looked up.

The ceiling was a dull, cracking plaster. I took a breath of air. Ether. Vomit. Phlegm. Blood. You never forget that combined smell. It is disease. It is death.

I closed my eyes and was shrouded in a blanket of black.

I opened my eyes and looked down at my feet. I was in a bed. How had I gotten there?

"Sister. Her eyes are open."

I asked the nurse several questions. "Who are you? Why are all these women in beds around me? Why are they groaning?"

She didn't answer me. Couldn't she hear me? I spoke louder and felt my throat burn.

"Where am I?"

"She spoke, sister. She spoke."

I heard the scrape of a chair on the floor and the pitter-patter of two feet running.

"Hello, Amelia."

"Hello."

"Do you know who I am?"

"Hmm?"

"It's me, Lena."

"Yes, it's you, Lena. So nice to see you … again."

"Likewise."

Who is Lena?

"Amelia? Amelia?"

"Looks like we lost her again."

I can't fathom why they think I'm lost when they're looking directly at me.

"Amelia? You've got to come back."

Was that a cloth someone took off my forehead? I felt the faint brush of coolness passing over my face. My eyes must have been closed. I couldn't open them. I couldn't see any light.

"The fever has broken."

"She's coming to again."

I was back in the cave—in the bed in the cave. But as I looked around, it wasn't a cave at all. It was a hospital ward. A nurse was holding my hand tightly and wouldn't let go.

"Amelia?"

The nurse knew my name, but I had no idea who she was, nor did I know how I had gotten in a hospital ward. I was completely disoriented. Had I missed my reckoning?

"What is your name?"

"Amelia … Moorland."

"When were you born?"

"I don't remember."

"Do you remember where?"

I searched my memory, but nothing would connect. "No."

"Can you remember anything other than your name?"

"I remember digging."

The nurse looked puzzled. "Digging? Do you remember the hospital at Fleury-sur-Aire?"

"No."

"Do you remember serving in the Red Cross?"

"No."

"Or the Great War?"

"No."

"What about your brother. Your brother, Bernard?"

"I have a brother?"

"And you don't know who I am?"

"I'm afraid I don't."

"It's me, Amelia. Lena."

She looked terribly distressed. I should have known her, but it was as if I were seeing her for the first time.

"Don't worry. Your memory will come back."

She patted my forehead and walked away.

It was then that I realized I must have been sick, but I had no idea from what. I wished Sam could tell me what had happened.

I yelled out to her, "Sam. I remember Sam!"

She looked more confused than before.

"You look nice today, Amelia."

"Thank you."

"It's me, Lena. Remember?"

"Of course I remember."

Who is this person?

"You're being treated properly, aren't you?"

"Yes."

"Today's your special day, do you know that?"

"My birthday?"

"We're so excited for you."

Why is she talking so loudly?

"You know who I am?"

"Lena."

"Yes, that's right."

She's treating me like I'm a moron. This woman is driving me crazy.

"Do you remember James?"

"James?"

"He gave you this scrapbook. Do you remember?"

"No."

"He'll be coming to Paris."

"James?"

"Yes. You're one of the lucky ones, Amelia. Most of the others who got *la grippe* didn't make it."

"*La grippe?*"

"Yes. The Spanish flu."

I survived the Spanish flu? When did I get it? How did I contract it?

"Have you been looking at your scrapbook?" Lena sounded liked a grade-school teacher.

"I beg your pardon?"

"Your scrapbook. Is that your scrapbook?"

"You've told me as much."

"Am I in it?"

"What?"

"Do you have any pictures of me in your book?"

Why would I have pictures of you?

Lena continued, "You've never shared your scrapbook with me."

I've never shared my scrapbook with anyone.

"Will you let me see it today?"

"Today?"

"Yes. Today is your birthday. It's me …"

"I know who you are." *You've told me at least five hundred times.*

"Will you share your pictures with me on your birthday?"

"I'm not sure this is my scrapbook."

"Sure, it's your scrapbook. That's you there, isn't it?"

"Yes. But who are these people?"

Lena placed her hand on my forehead. "You've got to start remembering, Amelia. You can't stay in this state forever. You've got to pull yourself up by the bootstraps."

What does she know of pulling yourself up by the bootstraps? She's irritating me. She sounds like a beached whale. Will she ever stop?

"Where am I?"

"You're just outside Paris. You were brought here right before the war ended. You've been here ever since. After the war ended, I requested a transfer to this hospital, so that I could watch over you. It's me, Amelia. It's Lena."

"Of course."

"You still don't remember?"

"No."

"What about James? Do you remember James?"

He stood next to Lena. He forced a smile, but was fidgety.

"You've told me he gave me the scrapbook."

"Yes, I did, Sunshine."

"But I can't seem to remember."

Lena took hold of James's hand.

"I'm sorry. I just can't remember."

"When you do remember, James has so many things to say to you."

James turned away.

"Like what? What does he have to say?"

Lena pulled the covers up to my chin. "It can wait."

James turned around and smiled at me, but he seemed bewildered.

"There's someone here to see you."

"I don't want to see anyone. I want to get out of here."

"Amelia? It's me. Bernard."

I looked into his eyes. I had seen him before and thought I knew him, but I didn't know why or from where. He came up to me and gave me a big hug. His arms felt familiar. He kissed me on the cheek.

"Mama and Da have been worried sick about you."

"Mama and Da?"

"Yes."

I had a sudden vision of a woman slapping me across the face.

"I can't believe you were over here. Nanna wrote and told me you'd joined the Red Cross, but I was stationed close to the Belgium border and then did some time in Italy. If it wasn't for your friend Lena, we'd have had a devil of a time tracking you down."

"You're Bernard?"

"Yes. Your brother. Do you remember?"

He looked so desperate; I had to give him some assurance.

"Yes, of course."

He wasn't convinced. Lena whispered something into his ear. He began to weep.

"What is it?"

Lena tucked the sheets in around my bed.

Bernard forced a smile. "Nothing, Amelia. Nothing. You've got to remember. Please. Please remember."

It was awful. It seemed I couldn't remember anything. These people seemed nice, but I kept disappointing them. Every day was the same: they'd come and see me, hoping that I would suddenly know something other than their names and some of the times they claimed we shared together. But it was as if they were recounting another person's life.

It was all so frustrating. My memory must be somewhere ... but where? And how was I going to get it back?

Psychiatrists were brought in, and they attempted to ease my mind. "Don't worry, Amelia. It will all come back to you eventually. Don't get discouraged. It may only hinder your recovery."

I'd stay up all night, trying to jog my memory, but the only thing I could remember was Sam. I would whisper and cry myself to sleep.

"Where are you, Sam? You've got to help me through this. You've got to help me remember, so that I can have my life back. Please, Sam. Find me."

"Amelia? Wake up, Amelia."

I opened my eyes, and there she was. She smiled.

"Can you believe I'm here?"

"Is it really you, Sam?"

"Yes."

I touched her arm. I pulled her down to me and kissed her cheek, embracing her. I began to cry. "I must look terrible."

"You look beautiful, Amelia."

"I can't imagine that I do."

"You're alive. That's what matters."

I took her face in my hands. "You've changed so. You're grown up."

"So have you."

"How did you get here?"

"Bernard sent a telegram, and I begged my mother and father to send me over to be with you. I would have stolen the money if they hadn't agreed. Nothing was going to keep me from coming to be with you."

I turned away. "I'm sorry, Sam."

"What are you sorry about? Getting ill? There's nothing you could do about that."

"No, I'm sorry …"

"Sorry about what?"

"I'm sorry I got angry with you about Willie."

Her eyes lit up, and she smiled. "Who?"

"You know, Willie?"

Sam squeezed my hand. "You remember Willie?"

"Don't be silly, Sam. Of course I …" I remembered Willie. And in that moment, memories flooded back. Of Mama and Da. Nanna. James and Lena and Vera Guest. Bernard. Bernard!

"Is Bernard here?"

"He's coming by later this afternoon."

I cried out, looking down the ward. "Lena? Lena?"

I couldn't see her, but nurses and sisters were scrambling down the corridor.

"What about James?"

"They're both here."

As Sam said that, Lena came running toward my bed.

"Amelia?"

"Lena."

We embraced. I didn't want to let go. I asked her how I had gotten there. I asked how the war ended, and how I survived. Sam turned away. I thought she might be jealous of the attention I was paying to Lena.

Later that day, I asked Sam why she was so cold to Lena.

"I'm grateful to her for watching out for you. But she's taken something from you that I don't think is right."

"I don't have anything to steal."

"Don't mind me, Amelia."

"It's hard not to mind you, Sam. What is it? What has she taken from me?"

Just then, one of the nurses came up to my bed and told Sam it was time for her to leave.

"You'll tell me in the morning, won't you?"

Sam smiled and walked away.

I woke to a kiss on my cheek. It was James.

"Morning, Sunshine."

"James."

"It's music to my ears, hearing you say my name and knowing it is me."

He helped me out of my bed and took me for a walk through the hospital grounds. We walked arm in arm. The air was filled with the smell of freshly cut grass, new leaves on the trees, heather, boxwood, and peonies. The overload of the bouquet made me sneeze. But I didn't mind. In fact, I wanted more.

"I didn't think you'd ever come back," James said.

"I didn't know I was gone."

"It's been so long … seven months. Think what's happened in those seven months."

"It scares me to think where I was during that time."

"I thought I'd lost you, Sunshine."

"I'm ashamed that I didn't recognize you when I came out of it."

"The truth is, I didn't think you'd ever recover."

"It must have been terrifying to see me in that state."

"It was a very long time."

"I was so oblivious to time. I was completely out of it."

"After a while, Lena doubted you'd ever come back to us."

"I'm forever indebted to her for watching over me and finding Bernard. And also to you, for being there."

"Honestly, we gave up hope."

James stopped walking and embraced me. I could feel tears on my shoulder. I pulled back and wiped the tears away from his cheek.

"It's all right, James. I'm here. I'm back."

"I have to tell you something, Sunshine, and I don't know how to say it."

"Before you go into that, have you met Sam?"

"I really …"

"She's the one who helped bring me back. She's more than a sister—"

He interrupted me. "I have to tell you something."

"What is it?"

He wouldn't look me in the eye. He was like a small child, fessing up to breaking a knickknack in the parlor.

"Look at me, James. Tell me."

He made eye contact for a split second, and I knew I had lost him.

"During your illness, when it seemed that there was no hope, Lena and I … we comforted each other. And in doing so, over time, we fell …"

It was my time to interrupt. "Please, James. Please don't say it."

"We fell in love, and we're engaged to be married."

How could he kick me, stomp on me, extinguish my newly found joy and happiness? How could Lena take care of me, then turn around and take the one I loved away from me?

I had been robbed. Sam was right again.

Lena avoided me for most of that day. When she finally got the courage to approach me, she walked up to my bed as if she were testing the depth of a sandbar, wondering with every step when she'd fall into deep waters.

"Are you all right?"

"I'm jumping over the apple barrel. What do you think?"

"We're all a bit shell-shocked about this."

She moved toward me, trying to place her hand on my forehead. I turned away abruptly.

"Don't you touch me."

She jumped back as if avoiding a punch. "It's difficult for us as well."

"You don't know what difficult is. I've lost seven months of my life, my lover, and my friend, and you think you have it difficult?"

"You haven't lost a friend, Amelia."

"You knew how much I loved him."

"Watching you struggle for so many months with no signs of hope became too much to bear."

"So you moved right in on him."

"How can I make you understand? It wasn't planned. It just happened."

"With no conscience or thought to how I would feel?"

Lena was turning bright red. Tears streamed down her cheeks. With hands clenched she yelled out, "You were as good as dead, Amelia! Everyone around you was dying. We thought we lost you. Seven months, with little to no response. That's a lifetime in these times."

"I'm so angry and frustrated, I could scream. You keep making excuses and blaming it on me … on my illness. I loved him, damn you! I loved him."

I began to cry. She started toward me again, as if to comfort me. I lashed out, grabbing the vase of flowers next to my bed and hurling it at her. "Get away from me."

She took off running down the corridor, weeping. I heard her sobs over a flurry of footsteps as a group of nurses began picking up the shattered glass, broken flowers, and puddles of water on the floor—the aftermath of my rage.

I sank back into my bed, defeated.

Lena avoided me for days. It was probably for the best. I didn't want to talk to anyone, not even Sam or Bernard. They came day after day and stood looking at me for about a half an hour, making small talk. I wasn't in the mood. I'd finally speak up and tell them to leave.

"I appreciate the both of you coming, but really, I need to be alone right now."

Alone again, I brooded. I lay there hoping that this was a bad dream, and that I was going to wake up to my old life. But I knew that was plain foolishness. The war was over; the world had changed. My world had changed forever.

James never came back to see me. Given the circumstances, I'm not sure why he would. He was engaged and beginning a life with Lena.

Lena would pass my bed and look at me out of the corner of her eye. I think she was terrified of what I might do. Hit her in a rage? Embrace her? Congratulate her? Rip her throat out?

And I'm not sure what I expected her to do. What could she say? Was there anything that could dull the sting of this revelation? She had come to this hospital because of me. She had said she'd take care of me, and she had. She had brought Bernard. Her heart was in the right place, wasn't it?

I loved James and believed he loved me, but I could see how my condition had changed that. The truth is, the war made us all impatient. Despite the feeling that we were part of a greater cause, we wanted to get back to our lives. How could I fault the two of them for wanting that? I had brought them together. Shouldn't I find joy in that?

I had given myself too freely to him—a mistake. I should have gone about my business at the hospital, never speaking to him. It would have saved me this hurt. While being intimate with him had fulfilled my needs and desires, it ultimately left me feeling empty. Or was I just thinking this to ease the rejection?

As usual, Sam was my savior. She got me through this terrible time and helped me sort out my feelings and find myself again.

"You've got to stop feeling sorry for yourself, Amelia."

"What would you know about losing a love, Sam? You've never been in love."

Sam turned away. "You're not the only one who has lost someone during this war."

"You've lost someone?"

Sam grabbed my hand. "I thought I lost you."

"That's not the same. You didn't lose me."

"I'm not so sure, the way you've been acting."

"People change, Sam."

"They may change, but what makes them good or bad or indifferent stays the same. Let me ask you: would it have been better if James were killed in action?"

"Damn right, it would."

"That's just what I mean, Amelia. You're being cruel and self-centered, and that's not the Amelia I knew."

She was right. I was being self-centered. It was all about me and my hurt. James's death wouldn't have been better. It was childish and cruel to even say such a thing.

He occupied a special moment in my life. At eighteen, I had become a woman with him. He was gone, but not like Willie. There would never be a chance again with Willie. If it were in the fates' plans, I might see James again. We might fall in love again. But for now, there would be others, if I didn't give up—and I didn't.

I had to convalesce. It was the only way to get out of this ward and onto a ship headed for America—and Nantucket.

On the day of my release, right before Sam and Bernard came to pick me up, I sat in the garden, thinking about how we might spend our last days in Paris. Perhaps I'd finally have my Parisian chocolate patisserie.

While I was daydreaming, Lena came out of nowhere and walked right up to me. I had hoped to leave without seeing her, but I guess she finally had the nerve to confront me one last time. I stood up to ensure equal footing. Her eyes were bloodshot, and her nose was running. She had been crying.

"I hope you know that I never meant this to happen."

"I know, but you must know that doesn't make it any easier."

"James and I wouldn't be together if it weren't for you."

"If it weren't for the Spanish flu."

"We both care so much for you."

"Think of me as just another casualty of the war."

"Will we see you again?"

"I don't know, Lena. I just don't see how that will be possible."

"Here." She handed me a letter. "I want you to have this. It explains everything that happened. Perhaps in time, you'll understand, and you'll find it in your heart to forgive us."

I took the letter and stared down at it. She awkwardly kissed me on the cheek and embraced me. I slowly raised my arms to return the embrace.

"I'll be going now," she said. "You take care."

"You too Lena."

"I'll miss you."

I couldn't tell her that I'd miss her too. She sensed there would be no response and turned and walked purposefully back into the hospital.

I sat down and looked at the envelope, contemplating whether to open it and read it. But whatever she had to say wasn't going to change the situation. We had been very close friends once. We helped each other through the war. We shared secrets, crying and laughing together. We ended up sharing the love of the same man ... only he was hers now.

Deep down, the part of me that Sam knew didn't hate Lena. Nor did I hate James. One thousand apologies wasn't going to change that. But I wasn't about to subject myself to seeing the two of them together.

Sam and Bernard entered the courtyard and called me to join them. I got up, placed the note on the chair, and walked away.

Whatever she wrote didn't matter.

The trip back to America was less eventful than the trip over to France. This time, there were no U-boats to fear. The men and women drank and danced and told each other their war stories, each story trying to best the one told before. This activity would inevitably continue once we got home, and veterans started recounting stories to their families and loved ones. But as I've told you earlier, I shut all of those memories away and recounted nothing until today.

Sam and Bernard accompanied me on the journey back. It was a comfort to have them there with me. During the voyage, I spoke to Sam about what she had or hadn't known would happen before I left for the war.

"It's not like telling someone's future. It's more of a feeling."

"But did you know that Willie would die?"

"Somehow, I'm able to connect with your feelings, Amelia ... and in doing so, with those who are around you. And from them, I get a feeling, and I sense what's going to happen to them. I can't describe it."

"Have you ever been wrong?"

She turned away. "I hope so."

"What about us? What do you see happening to us?"

Sam became squeamish and jittery. "I don't like to talk about it, Amelia."

"Oh, come on. You can tell me."

She frowned and rolled her eyes. "We'll be best friends forever."

"You can do better than that."

And then she got really serious. "When it comes to you and me, I refuse to analyze the feelings. I never will."

I felt a chill in the air and wanted to lighten the mood. "Well, here's what I see. We'll both get married. Our husbands will be best friends. We'll have kids that will be friends for life. We'll go on trips together. We're going to grow old together. Our husbands will die before us. That will be sad, but we'll have each other. And at very ripe old ages, we'll die together. What do you think of that?"

"I thought you gave this up years ago."

"It's how I see it, Sam. Truth be told."

Truth be told, I had made it all up. But it's what I hoped would happen. I think she knew that. I also think she knew what was really going to happen, but couldn't bring herself to tell me. But I'll get to all of that in due time. I'm jumping ahead again … I told you to stop me if I did that.

Mama and Da met the ship in New York Harbor. It had been a little over two years since I had seen them; for Bernard, it had been almost three years. As I walked down the plank and met them at the bottom, they were both shedding tears. My da grabbed me and held me so tight. Bernard took Mama in his arms. She melted with joy and began kissing him to death.

Da let go of me and embraced Bernard. I looked at Mama. She was crying hysterically. I knew I must have caused them a fright, but with everything Mama and I had been through, I didn't think she would miss me as much as she appeared to have missed me that day. I opened my arms to embrace her. She came toward me with open arms … and then, just as she got close to me, she slapped me across the face.

"Don't you ever—ever—do something like this again. Do you hear me?"

I was furious. "Mama, how could you?" I began to cry.

With that, she embraced me for what seemed like an eternity.

But something—or rather, someone—was missing. Why hadn't Nanna come to meet us? She must be cooking up a storm. She wouldn't miss our homecoming for anything in the world.

"Where's Nanna?"

Mama looked at Da and began weeping again. My da embraced Mama and told us the news.

"Nanna passed away in her sleep last week."

I fell to the ground as if hit by a squall. I looked up at Sam. Her eyes were clouded with guilt; she couldn't bear to look at me. She turned her head away and walked off the dock alone.

I was numb. I kept wondering what I had done to deserve all of this sorrow. Was I a terrible person? What would I have to do to make it stop? Would it ever stop?

We finished packing up Nanna's house, taking the things we wanted, giving away the valuable things we didn't want, and trashing all the rest. The house was so empty. Everything that had given it life was tied to Nanna, and all of that was gone.

Before we left New York, we visited the cemetery. I stood in front of her tombstone, unable to cry but raw with emotion. My last good-bye to her had been the day I left for the war. And the feeling in my stomach had been right: it was the last time I saw her. At least I remember saying "I love you."

Like so many others who came back from the war, I was exhausted. But I survived.

United States Coast Guard
Special Report upon the
Incident on the Steamship *Uncatena*
October 16, 1921
Excerpt, Testimony, Ms. Amelia Moorland questioned by
Deputy Officer William B. Madden

"Let's take it from the beginning."

"The beginning. Yes. I saw her standing at the edge of the bow."

"What day was it?"

"It was October 16, 1921."

"You were on the ferry, going to the mainland."

"Yes. Back to America."

"Go on."

"She was standing on the edge of the bow, and suddenly, she picked up her suitcase, and she jumped overboard."

"She jumped overboard?"

"Yes, I saw her."

"And what happened to the suitcase?"

"She tied herself to it before jumping and held onto it."

"You're sure."

"Yes."

"You're absolutely positive that she was tied to the suitcase when she went overboard."

"Yes."

"What happened next?"

"I ran to the edge of the ferry to see if I could see where she had gone. When I got there, I couldn't see anything. Then I heard the crewman yell, 'Man overboard.' The next thing I knew, I was in the water."

"You were in the water?"

"I guess I instinctively jumped in after her."

"How was the weather that afternoon?"

"It was brisk. Cold."

"And the seas?"

"The seas were choppy."

"And you never took these conditions into consideration before jumping in?"

"I wasn't thinking about the conditions. I was thinking about her."

"Ms. Moorland."

"Yes?"

"Ms. Moorland, I'm sure you understand that you're not the only person we've interviewed in this investigation."

"I'm sure I'm not."

"You must realize that we've talked extensively to the crew and the captain who pulled you out of those cold waters that terrible day."

"They were brave. They saved my life."

"And you know them, do you not?"

"It's a small island. Everyone knows everyone."

"Yes. Allow me to share their testimony with you … and I'm summarizing when I say this: no one saw anyone but you jump in."

"How can that be?"

"No one. Not Captain Swain. Not Tiny. Not Rip. No one."

"But she jumped in first."

"No one saw two people jump in."

"That's impossible."

"They only saw you."

CHAPTER XI

I'm so accustomed to the sound of the noon bells coming from the Unitarian Church on Orange Street. Can you hear them? They make you stop what you're doing and resonate, if only for a brief moment, with their angelic tone. They've been ringing every day since I can remember from my childhood, through today—my last day. Well, except the days when they were doing maintenance. And on those days, the silence made me uneasy; I intuitively knew something was amiss. At first, I'd blame it on a bad night's sleep, or something I ate, or perhaps the position of the moon, or high tide. But in a day or two, when they chimed again, I instantly knew the source of my problem. They'd chime and right the world again. All was back to normal.

I find great comfort in knowing that some things never change (good God, I sound like Mama). In that moment, when the last ring slowly fades into air, just as it's about to do any second now, I hold my head up as high as possible and listen until the sound has evaporated into the rustling wind, or the cry of a gull, or the creak of an attic floorboard. I long for it to stay forever, but trust that it will return tomorrow, so that I can do the same thing all over again. I'm a creature of habit.

I want my last memory to be the bells chiming. I want to take my last breath as their music fades away with the last bdong. I'm not being morbid. If I have to go, I hope to go on the hour. Of course, it's wishful thinking.

Shh. I believe this one's twelve. Yes, there it is. Now it's gone. That can only mean Planter's Punch.

You see, when I was in Aspen—this was after the Second World War, and after Da passed away—I ran into my lost love, James Furie. I went to Aspen to get away from Nantucket. Da had died, and I needed to clear my head, so I took a job as a nurse at the hospital.

The day I ran into him, I was meeting some of my friends, who were chambermaids at the Hotel Jerome. We were going to meet in front of the hotel after their shift to go to dinner or drinks or something like that. As I stood waiting, a taxi pulled up, and he got out and stood there, looking at me. I was stunned. I thought, "Could it really be James?" He looked the same, except his hair was graying, and he had put on a few pounds.

We stood looking at each other until he finally broke the silence. "Is that you, Amelia?"

"James?"

Instinctively, we embraced.

"My God, it's been how many years? Over thirty?"

I smiled. "Yes ... almost a lifetime." I had forgiven but not forgotten what happened between us. I tensed up. "How's Lena?"

His smile faded. "Lena passed away about ten years ago."

I placed my hand on his shoulder. "I'm sorry to hear that."

"Cancer. I never remarried and have been working like a madman ever since as a photographer for *Life* magazine."

"How wonderful that you're doing what you've always loved."

"What about you? What have you been doing? Are you married?"

"I was married for a short time—a very short time. I'm divorced. I've tried to erase it from memory."

"I'm sorry to hear that."

I continued, "I was stationed in England during the war and worked again with the Red Cross. Now I'm a nurse and working at the hospital here in Aspen."

His face turned serious. "I've missed you, Amelia. Lena and I always felt terrible about how things were left. After she died, I thought about looking you up. I don't know how many times I thought about booking a ticket on the ferry to Nantucket to see if I could track you down."

"I've thought about the two of you as well."

He took hold of my hands. "This may be a bit forward, but do you think there's a chance we could pick up where we left off?"

I took a step back. I wasn't prepared to see him, let alone consider a reconciliation. "James, I ..."

He interrupted. "I'm sorry. It's just that I've been so lonely. I need someone, Amelia. Someone like you."

"But you don't know me. So much has happened in those thirty years."

"Then let's get to know each other again. What do you say?"

The truth is, I didn't know what to say. I stood there, dumbfounded.

He pulled something out of his pocket and handed it to me. "Amelia, here's my room key. Room 323. You think about it, and if you want to come up—just to talk, to get to know each other again, and to see if we should pursue it further—I'd be most pleased."

He kissed my cheek awkwardly. "I'm here until tomorrow, and I hope you'll come by. Please."

He turned and walked away. I stood looking at the key. I needed a drink.

I immediately went into the bar in the hotel and ordered a Planter's Punch. I gulped it down in two seconds and ordered another one. And another.

What was I to do? I was tempted; perhaps the fates were bringing us together again. I was lonely too. I had come out to Aspen hoping to find a husband, but I was having very little luck doing so. I was almost fifty, and my prospects of finding someone to share the rest of my life with were dimming. I held the key to his room tightly in my hand and then looked at it: room 323. And then I ordered another Planter's Punch and made my decision.

I paid for my drinks, placed his room key in my purse, and walked out of the hotel. I walked home, and I didn't go back that evening or the next day.

You see, we might have been able to pick up where we left off, but no matter how hard we tried, Lena would always be there, and I couldn't live with that. Unfortunately, Lena had been where we left off.

I credit my clear thinking that day to the Planter's Punch; almost every day since, I've had a little Planter's Punch pick-me-up before lunch. It doesn't matter whether I'm going out to lunch or eating at home or skipping lunch. Noon means Planter's Punch.

How can I resist a lot of rum, a little pineapple juice, lemon juice, orange juice, and a big splash of dark rum on top? Well, not a big splash, but a long pour … a really long pour. Oh yes, Daddy-o.

That's where most bartenders get it wrong. The secret is the dark rum, and a lot of it. I'm notorious for sending it back to the bar if I'm not swimming in dark rum. It's why I'm happiest doing it myself. Looking back, that always seems to be the way with me. If you want it done right, do it yourself.

So what should I drink to? Good heavens, not my health; this rickety old thing is being decommissioned in less than twelve hours. No, let's drink to making it to the end of the day. Cheers! Oh, that's good. If that's not the taste of mother's milk.

Now then, where was I? Oh yes, of course—the bells.

I was in such a fog when I returned to Nantucket after the war. I functioned, but felt completely anesthetized—ten sheets to the wind. I have no recollection of how many days passed before I regained my short-term memory; perhaps it was months. But my first conscious memory was the sound of the bells tolling. The moment I registered their sound, I felt reborn. I knew I was home again.

It was the autumn of 1919, and Sam and I were planting jonquil bulbs in her backyard when I heard the first ring. As if possessed, I grabbed her arm.

"Come on."

We ran across Fair Street, through the narrow dirt path on the side of the church, out onto Orange Street, and in front of the church to get as close to the sound as possible.

"Don't you just love them?"

"You're crazy, Amelia."

I took Sam's hands and began turning us round and round at the sound of the bells. Sam let go and dizzily sat down on the bench at the bottom of the steps, laughing at me. I grabbed at the air as each bell tolled. Passers-by frowned in embarrassment or picked up their step and ignored me, as if I were the village idiot, but some smiled at my joy.

When all went silent, I stood on the sidewalk, looking up at the great and tall tower of the church, with its large clock and its gilded gold top visible for the town to see. A wisp of white clouds hovered above it with a backdrop of crystal blue sky. I took a deep breath, filling my lungs with that blessed salty air, and held it in. Tears welled up in my eyes. *Thank God I'm home. Thank God I'm back in my Nantucket.* I exhaled.

Sam tugged my arm. "I hope this is something you don't intend on doing every day."

"And if it is?"

"They might lock you up and throw away the key."

I promised this was a onetime event, and with that, we strolled down to Main Street.

Having been gone for a little over two years, I expected not to recognize the town. Perhaps it was because I walked through so many ruined towns during the war. I always thought that those returning townspeople surely wouldn't recognize the rubble of the corner café or the remains of the bombed-out church.

I was relieved to recognize everything. Sure, there were some new stores and businesses, but the buildings were all the same. Some stores had new signs, or had recently spruced themselves up—like Cady's Food Store, which glistened in the sunlight, showing off its recent coat of fresh red paint. The shimmering exterior caught my eye and beckoned me in to have my favorite soda.

"What's your pleasure, Ms. Moorland?"

"I'll take a Simpson Spring Ginger Ale, Mr. Cady."

"Right away." He went back to the cooler and pulled a bottle out, opened it, and handed it to me.

Before taking a swig, I recited the soda's advertisement from the newspaper. "It's chock-full of zest-zig-z-z."

Sam and I laughed. Mr. Cady wiped his hands on his apron and gave me a crusty frown. "Zest-zig-z-z indeed."

We walked out of Cady's and turned down Federal Street to browse at the Charles Wing Company. They had Columbia and Victor phonographs in the window. I knew Da had probably tried every one of them and most likely wanted to purchase the most modern of models, but his sense of duty to give any extra income to the Victory Liberty Loan made him get by with what we had.

"Somebody's got to pay for this war." Every time he'd say that, I couldn't help but think our family had done its duty and then some. He should have bought the Victor he wanted.

While so much was familiar, so much had changed. Automobiles lined the streets. In fact, Main Street was a two-way street at the time (something that's hard to fathom today).

I was sad to see that old Mack's was gone. Unlike me, Mr. Mack had succumbed to the Spanish flu the year before. There would be no more listening to the baseball scores or darting in to say a quick hello and get the latest gossip and news.

We walked down to the Easy Street Basin. What used to be train tracks was now just sandy ground cover.

"They got rid of the train?"

"Why, yes, don't you remember? I wrote to you about that."

"Oh, yes, of course."

I was in no mood to argue, but to my knowledge, I hadn't received such sad news. Perhaps I never received that letter.

"They tore up the tracks last year," Sam explained wistfully.

Sam and I had so much fun taking the train out to Siasconset and Surfside. It didn't matter how old we were; taking the train was an endearing part of growing up on Nantucket. Like everyone, we loved it. We'd hang our heads out the window as it passed through town, the wind and sea breezes blowing through our hair. We'd take it just for the ride, but most people took it out to the beaches for their holidays. And before automobiles, it was the best way to get to and from Siasconset.

"Why'd they let it go?"

"They didn't make enough money to keep it running."

Deep down inside, I had known the answer. The train's profitability was a problem always talked about, well before I was born. But we never took it seriously. We never dreamed the train would someday not be there.

"And nobody tried to save it?"

"Everyone was upset to see it go, but nobody could figure out how to save it."

Another piece of history had ended up on the scrap heap.

"At least they allow automobiles," Sam added.

"I know. You couldn't get out to Siasconset without one."

"You'll get a big laugh when you hear what your mother's prediction of the future is now that the railroad is gone."

"I'm afraid to hear."

"We were darning socks and rolling bandages the day they started tearing up the tracks. So she says that with all the evil progress going on in the world, she wouldn't be surprised if you and Bernard didn't see the day when you'd be flying in an airplane out to Siasconset and back into town."

"It would sure be quicker."

"That's what I told her. But she just scowled at me and said, 'You youngsters need to slow down.'"

"She'll never change."

"At least she's consistent."

Well, maybe.

By now, it must be clear to you that Mama had a fear of the future and of progress. Time always dragged her forward kicking and screaming. Not only was she old-fashioned, she was set in her ways.

Two social issues had changed significantly upon my return, and Mama was adamant about both in a way that countered her traditionalist mind-set: women's suffrage and booze. Mama wanted the right to vote and, contrary to my da's feelings about it (he was dead set against it), she worked tirelessly with other like-minded women on the island to help win that right. Having lived with Nanna in New York for that short time before the war, I have to believe that it was Nanna's influence on Mama that made it so important to her. Nanna certainly had had an impact on how I viewed women's rights.

Mama was one of the first women to register on the island in 1920, and despite the fact that I was not old enough to vote (you had to be twenty-one, and I was only nineteen at the time, my forged birth certificate notwithstanding) she took me with her to register. We got dressed up in our Sunday best and went down to the town hall. The voting registrar was Warren Coffin. He was a plump, disheveled but good-natured man who always had dirt under his fingernails and food stains on his lapels. But he took his office seriously and presided over voting registration in the most official way, as if he drew a lot of water.

Mama and I went up to his table.

"Hello, Warren."

A warm smile came to his face. "Why, Catherine, I haven't seen you in a long time. How are you? How's Obed?"

"We're fine."

"What can I do for you?"

"I'm here to register to vote."

"OK, then."

He cleared his throat and put on his spectacles, his smile turning serious in a split second. He blew himself up all important-like. "Raise your right hand. Do you solemnly swear to answer truthfully all questions asked during this hearing?"

Mama answered loudly and with conviction. "I swear."

"Now, then, where was your husband born?"

"You know he was born here."

"Where have you lived since the first of April 1920?"

"Warren, please. You know the answer to that."

Mr. Coffin's serious expression deepened into a frown as he dropped his shoulders. "Answer the question, Catherine. I have to ask it, and you have to answer it, if you want to be registered."

He stiffened up again.

"Nantucket, Massachusetts," Mama said in resignation.

"How long have you lived in the state?"

"Let me see, now. I married Obed in ninety-three, so that would be ..."

I knew she had a difficult time with numbers, so I interrupted with the answer. "Twenty-seven."

Mama looked at me, relieved. "Yes, that would be twenty-seven years."

"And how long have you lived in this town?"

"Why, twenty-seven. It only makes sense."

Mr. Coffin took a piece of paper out of a file and placed it at the end of the table facing Mama. "Please sign here."

Mama bent down and signed the paper. He then turned the paper around and began reading from it.

"OK. Now, then—how old are you?"

Mama backed away, offended. "I don't think that's any of your business."

"It isn't my business. It's the United States government's business, if you want to register to vote."

In a very hushed tone, Mama told him her age. "Forty-five."

"That's forty-five years old."

"Do you have to announce it to the whole world?"

"Where were you born?"

"Brooklyn, New York."

"What is your occupation?"

"I'm a wife and a mother."

"Housewife. Where is your place of occupation?"

"You just said I was a housewife, so where do you think my place of occupation is?"

"I've told you that I'm required to ask these questions. I didn't write them, Catherine. The government did."

"My place of occupation is my home on Pleasant Street."

"Where are you living at the present time?"

"34A Pleasant Street."

Mr. Coffin gestured toward a box on the registration table. "Please take one of those cards and read it aloud."

"Why do I have to do that?"

"We have to verify that you're literate, so you have to read a few lines from the Constitution."

She shook her head in disapproval, took a card, and read aloud: "After one year from the ratification of this article the manufacture, sale, or transportation of intoxicating liquors within, the importation thereof into, or the exportation thereof from the United States and all territory subject to the jurisdiction thereof for beverage purposes is hereby prohibited."

She placed the card back in the box and straightened her blouse and skirt. Mr. Coffin then concluded the registration.

"Catherine Moorland, who resides at 34A Pleasant Street, Nantucket, Massachusetts, is hereby registered to vote."

"Is that it?"

"That's it."

"Good day, Mr. Coffin."

Mama grabbed my arm, and we swiftly left the town hall. I thought she'd be elated, but all she could think about was the stupid questions and the conspiracy and scandal of having to read from the Eighteenth Amendment.

"This town must know my thoughts on prohibition to make me read it. They're always trying to find some way to turn the screws on me."

There was only one evil in the world Mama condoned, and that was booze. By the time I came back, prohibition was the law of the land—a law that many around the country felt compelled to break. This illustrious group included Mama and Da. I mean, really. Do you think she could live without her bourbon?

Her cause was the antiprohibition movement. But to be in that cause, you had to be discreet, avoiding the notice of the police. So Mama's protests never included speeches at town meetings, marches down Main Street, or candlelight vigils. They were limited to sneaking a nip here or there and to singing songs as she prepared our meals or worked around the house. Her favorite was "The Alcoholic Blues."

The first time I heard it was at breakfast sometime during the first weeks that I returned home. Bernard and I couldn't help but chuckle.

"You think it's funny?" Mama asked. "It's a terrible law. It's unpatriotic."

Bernard and I immediately stopped laughing and sat up straight in our chairs. *Here we go again.*

Da piped in. "To think we asked our young men to go off to war and—"

I interrupted. "And women, Da. Don't forget women." I was not going to let the contributions of women go unnoticed.

"To think we asked our young men and women to go off to war and come back and not have the simple pleasures of a little nip here and there."

Mama sang on. Though I wasn't a big drinker at the time, nor was Bernard, we felt compelled to fill out the chorus and had a good laugh afterward.

It was up to my da to stock up on the bug juice. Being thirty miles out at sea made it fairly easy to rendezvous with the rumrunners and smuggle the refreshments back to shore. But you had to find ways of avoiding capture by the Nantucket police and the United States Coast Guard patrols.

My da and his friends always pretended they were going fishing. Now, everyone knew that Da had a weak stomach for fishing, so he brought me along, since I had a reputation as an excellent clammer, scalloper, and fisher. We would tell anyone who asked that Da was passing on a family tradition. Besides, what law-abiding, drought-ridden father would drag his daughter into a scheme to purchase bug juice? No man in uniform would ever consider such a thing, and if they did, I had my baby blue eyes that could distract them.

Da and I would park the Maxwell down by Monomoy and walk back to the docks. We tried to go out early on foggy evenings, and we'd meet Billy, Eddie, and Homer, who waited in Jimmy's swordfish catboat.

Off we'd go out into the harbor, into the sound, and out past the three-mile line into no man's land, shrouded in fog. Da always stayed up front, making sure we didn't run aground or crash into any ships or boats.

We were quite conniving. Just in case someone wanted to check our goods, we had a dozen codfish, blue fish, or striper that Jimmy and Homer caught earlier in the day under a tarp for our return.

On one particular night, as we crossed the three-mile line, we saw the bow of a boat slowly come into focus. We went around to the stern and saw its name. It was the booze ship *Arethusa*. There were three boats parked at her side (other liquor-seeking craft).

Da yelled out, "We've hit the jackpot, boys."

The men all laughed and patted each other on the shoulder. Da raised his eyebrow and winked at me as if I were in on a joke. But I had no idea what was so great about this boat in particular.

"What's so special about the *Arethusa*?"

He raised his eyebrow even higher and smiled. "Bill McCoy."

I racked my brain, trying to make some kind of connection. Had I met this man? Had I read about him somewhere? "I don't know who he is."

"Your mother and I always talk about him, especially when we have a nip. You still don't recognize the name?"

"I'm really sorry, Da, but I don't."

"He's known for not watering down his hooch and asking a fair price. It's the real McCoy."

Despite having the "alcoholic blues" for thirteen years, we kept ourselves in stock and never wanted for more. It was during that time, however, that my consumption increased, although it certainly wasn't up to its current levels. Everything comes with age.

United States Coast Guard
Special Report upon the
Incident on the Steamship *Uncatena*
October 16, 1921
Excerpt, Testimony, Ms. Amelia Moorland questioned by
Deputy Officer William B. Madden

"Someone must know that she was on that boat."

"We've talked to the ticket agent, to the crew, and to the other passengers."

"And?"

"The crew vaguely remembers her."

"Vaguely remembers?"

"And the ticket agent thinks he remembers selling a ticket to her father the day before. As for the passengers, some of them said they saw her on the ferry."

"You see?"

"Ms. Moorland. They also think they saw her get off the ferry in New Bedford."

"That can't be."

"We've had no luck locating her."

"There's no one to locate, because I saw her jump. What will it take for you to believe me?"

"A body. A suitcase. A piece of clothing. Anything to place her at the scene."

"Are you dredging?"

"We've been doing so for days, but with no luck. We've found nothing."

"I didn't make this up."

"Are you sure about that?"

CHAPTER XII

One of my favorite pieces in my Asian art collection is a pear-shaped bottle from the Sung dynasty. It's quite simple in design, but I've always admired the oil-spot pattern with metallic flecks in the center. When the sun hits it just right, it catches your eye.

But it's not my favorite piece because I think it's the most beautiful. On the contrary—I have many others that surpass it. Knowing my love of libation, you might be inclined to think my affection results from the vessel's ability to pour wine, but you would be only partly correct. It's really the circumstances surrounding its purchase that makes it my favorite.

You see, I was in Hong Kong in 1963. The former British colony, along with mainland China were among the first stops on a tour of several Asian countries, including Japan, Singapore (which was still part of Malaysia at the time), and Thailand. I adored Hong Kong; it had such an energy about it. I used to love getting lost on the city streets. And one day, while lost, I turned down a street whose merchants were all antique and rug dealers. As I came upon the window of one shop, I heard a voice coming from across the street.

"Hey, missus. No good antique there. Come over here."

I turned around and saw an old, bald, heavyset Chinese man with a long, silky gray beard and black pearl eyes waving to me to cross the street.

I crossed the street, and he continued to berate the other shop owner.

"He doesn't know antique from hole in the ground. He sell you something made last week, charge you as if it were made one thousand years ago."

"Is that so."

"I steer you in the right direction. I take care of you."

He ushered me into his shop and turned on the lights and ceiling fan. The shop was full of glass cases with what appeared to be museum-quality ceramics—some dating back thousands of years. We came upon a case that housed the pear-shaped bottle. He raised his eyebrow and smiled. "You like?"

"Yes, very much."

"This very simple but happy piece. Used for many parties and celebrations throughout the years."

"Is it for sale?"

He laughed. "This one priceless."

"Oh." I started walking away from the case.

"I only joking. You funny, missus—believing everything I say. You want a drink?"

It was almost time for my daily indulgence. "Yes … what do you have?"

"Well, if you buy this piece, I make you Singapore Sling and serve it to you from bottle. If not, I make you some tea while you look around the shop."

I laughed. He continued, "I'm not joking."

So I paid him for the bottle, and he made me a Singapore Sling. As promise, he served the drink from my recent purchase.

I raised my glass. "To my first piece of Chinese ceramic art."

"This your first? We make big celebration."

I can't tell you how many Singapore Slings he made and served in that bottle. During the course of our celebration, I asked him if the bottle was authentic. He replied, "As authentic as I am."

I was dubious, but I thought, "What the hell? I'm swimming in Singapore Slings. How bad can that be?"

When I got back to the States, I had a dealer from Boston who summered on Nantucket take a look at it, and he vouched for it.

I have to admit that over the years, I've served up cocktails in it. But I reserved it only for big celebrations, like birthdays or holiday parties. And since today is my last birthday, I pour myself another drink from that bottle and taste the memories distilled from years of celebration.

But I wasn't always keen on marking momentous occasions. The last thing I wanted to do when I returned from the war was to celebrate.

One evening after dinner, Bernard, Abigail, and I sat in front of the fireplace in the parlor, having an after-dinner nip of sherry. Bernard had taken up smoking a pipe and was filling his pipe with Tuxedo tobacco. He struck a match, lit up, and he puffed the chocolate tobacco scent into the room. As he smoked, he looked at Abigail, who was fidgeting in her chair and biting her upper lip. There was some unspoken language going on between them, and with a jerk of Abigail's head toward me, Bernard took the pipe out of his mouth and nonchalantly addressed me.

"I got you a ticket."

I took a sip of sherry and stared into the fire. I knew exactly what he was talking about. I could see out of the corner of my eye that Abigail was straining to weigh my demeanor.

"I appreciate that, Bernard, but I just don't think that I want to go."

"Why? It'll give you a chance to reconnect with everyone."

"After being home almost five months now, I'm not sure there are that many people who are interested in reconnecting with me. And those who are have already done so."

"The whole town is going to be there. It'll be fun."

In November 1919, the Wauwinet Tribe of Red Men gave those who served in the war a royal welcome-home party at their hall on South Water Street. I wasn't sure I wanted to attend; I wanted to distance myself from the war as much as possible. But Bernard and Abigail were keen on me going and did everything they could to persuade me.

"Can I be honest with you, Bernard? I want to forget everything about the war."

Abigail mustered the courage to enter the discussion. "I know you won't admit it, but you're just feeling a little blue on account of what happened with James and Lena."

"I am not."

Bernard pressed further. "You've been moping around ever since I came to see you in Paris. Now you've got to get on with your life, Amelia."

I was upset. "You don't think I'm trying to do just that?"

Bernard pushed his case. "Do you regret those experiences?"

"No. But I don't want to look back."

Abigail quietly interjected. "I envy you, Amelia."

"Don't say that, Abigail."

"I do. Look what you did—what you accomplished. How you helped in the effort. It makes the little I did safely tucked away on Nantucket pale in comparison."

"My service was no more important than yours."

"You know that's not true."

Of course I knew it wasn't true. Being close to the front lines was one hundred times more stressful than congregating with women back home in Nantucket, but it wasn't something worth gloating about.

Bernard knelt down in front of me and took both of my hands in his. "We can't deny that these experiences were a part of our lives."

"I don't deny them. I just don't want to remember anything about it for the rest of my life. And if I go to this event, it will only keep those memories alive."

"It's a celebration. That's all it is. Come with us. Please?"

They weren't going to give up, so I reluctantly gave in, if only to please them. Luckily, Sam was able to secure a ticket (I'm not sure how) and came with me.

As we entered the hall, almost all of the seats were taken. I immediately saw a lot of familiar faces I hadn't seen in the two years I was away. I recognized everyone in the orchestra. Harriet Hussey played the piano. Marion Norcross was on coronet. Mr. Barrett played the violin. There was Merlin Crocker on drums, and Herbert Brownell played the ukulele.

"Please rise to sing the national anthem."

Everyone stood, placed their right hands on their hearts, and sang as the curtain rose. The stage was decorated with many American flags and a big banner across the top that read "Our Heroes, Welcome Home." Lumps formed in my throat. I did not want to cry. I tried thinking of something else—sunsets over Hummock Pond, or the burnished red moors in autumn. The lump remained. Then Hazel Thomas came out holding a flag, dressed as a Red Cross nurse. George Furber came in after her, dressed in his army khakis. Gordon Chase came round her right side, dressed in his naval uniform. They all saluted the flag. When we finished singing, the hall got quiet, and from behind a curtain, a coronet began playing taps. The lump grew to a sniffle, and then tears began flowing.

Luckily, I wasn't the only one crying. There wasn't a dry eye in the audience. I was beginning to regret coming to this event. While I understood the dead should never be forgotten, I wanted it all forgotten. Selfishly, I wanted to flee such a solemn occasion.

I turned to Sam, who took my hand and squeezed it. She whispered in my ear, "It will be over soon. And then the vaudeville will begin."

The last note was played, and there was a moment of silence. All you heard were sniffles and noses being blown, a cough here and there, the hushed sounds of heavy breathing, and the creaking wood floor of people shifting weight back and forth, back and forth.

The orchestra struck up a very upbeat tune, and the mood immediately changed (thank God). A rotund woman with dark eyes and a very long nose took center stage. She was dressed in a black dress and gave the appearance of an over-weight seal, except for the large feathered hat she wore slightly angled off her head. She waited for the audience to quiet down and then began whistling. She whistled so loud, I thought the windows were going to crack. She sounded like a bird in distress, but the crowd seemed to enjoy her. She finished her act with "Yankee Doodle Dandee," parading around the stage as she whistled. A group of men in the audience began singing. She finished whistling, bowed, and exited the stage.

Next up was a woman who played a banjo and sang, "How Ya Gonna Keep 'Em Down on the Farm After They've Seen Paree." Everyone in the audience began clapping and laughing.

She stopped singing for a moment, but kept playing. "Sing with me."

With that little encouragement, the hall erupted in song. We all stood up and joined arms, swaying to the music.

Bernard and Abigail sat on the aisle. Toward the end of the song, he made a joke, yelling out at the top of his lungs: "Bonjour Madame Cow. Do you live in Paris?" He answered his question in a high falsetto voice. "No. I live in Moooooo-gens."

Everyone laughed. The banjo lady couldn't stop howling. People around Bernard were slapping his shoulder. Once we settled down, she finished the song.

The applause was deafening. Some peopled started yelling "bravo." As she left the stage, a young man dressed in full Scottish regalia took the stage and recited the Robert Burns poem "Scottish Drink" to jeers from some and the consternation of others. He then called all of the players up on the stage, and they sang "Auld Lang Syne." We joined him, swaying arm in arm in the aisles. It was quite a bang-up performance.

There was a big cheer and applause. The players came out and took their bows, and when the curtain went down, we all retired upstairs for some refreshments (there was no bug juice) and dancing.

Rip Lawton took a sheet and placed it over the clock in the hall. "There's no need to worry about the time. Tonight's all about celebrating—and honoring all those who served."

The crowd cheered, the orchestra began playing "I Want to Be the Leader of the Band," and men and women rushed to the dance floor. Sam and I started toward the side of the room, but Bernard pulled me by my waist from behind and forced me up on the dance floor. "How about it, sis?"

I smiled and placed my hand on his shoulder, and he whirled me around the dance floor. We circled the entire floor, waving to those we knew, occasionally bumping into someone on our way, and stepping on a toe or two. When the song finished, we all applauded. Abigail came out of nowhere and tapped me on the shoulder.

"May I?"

I bowed, let her take over, and walked over to the back wall, where Sam had planted herself.

"Your brother is the best dancer on the floor."

"Would you like to dance with him?"

"No. He never pays me any attention."

"He'd dance with you if I asked him."

"I'm not that desperate, Amelia."

"I didn't mean it that way. I meant if you want to dance …"

She interrupted me. "I don't want to dance. I just made an observation. Besides, he and Abigail dance beautifully together."

I could tell that Sam wanted to dance. I grabbed her by the arm and dragged her onto the dance floor, and we danced together to "Yaddie Kaddie Kiddie Kaddie Koo." Toward the end of the song, someone tapped me on the shoulder.

I turned around, and standing before me was a man who looked a little older than me. He had black hair, hazel eyes, and was built like an ox. Quite honestly, he took my breath away.

The song ended, and the orchestra immediately started playing "Me and My Girl." He half bowed to me. "May I?"

He caught me off guard. "I'm with my friend." I turned around; Sam was nowhere to be seen.

"Your friend?"

I looked around for Sam. "I don't know where she went off to. Sam?"

"You can always find her after a dance. Please, miss?"

I looked around the room but couldn't locate her. "I'm sorry. I should find her."

He looked disappointed as I walked off the floor. I turned and yelled toward him. "Maybe later. Thank you."

Maybe I should have stayed and danced at least one dance with him. That wouldn't have hurt.

Where had Sam run off to? I looked everywhere, and as I looked, I kept thinking about that man. He was quite the looker. *I should have stayed. I should have had just one dance. Maybe I should go back and find him.* As I made my way to the staircase, I saw Sam walking down the stairs.

"Are you leaving?"

"Yes. It's late, and I'm exhausted."

"I'll come with you."

"There's no need. Go ahead. Find that young man. Enjoy yourself, Amelia."

I thought to myself, *Well, why not?* "Good night, Sam."

I went back upstairs but had no luck finding him. It was as if he disappeared. I checked along the walls, in the seated area, and over by the refreshments table. I even walked across the dance floor, looking at all the couples dancing. Some of them looked at me as if I'd gone mad or was out to steal their honey.

Perhaps he wasn't real. I'd never seen him before; I didn't know his name. I started doubting whether I remembered exactly what he looked like.

Disappointed, I stood against the back wall of the hall. The crowd was thinning out. I had no idea what time it was when the orchestra leader announced the final number. Those who were truly couples gathered on the dance floor, and the singles and "just friends" couples gathered their belongings and filed out.

The music started. I spotted Bernard and Abigail on the floor. I don't know if it was the music or seeing them dance, or both, but I suddenly became melancholy. Was there anyone out there for me? Would I love again? If so, would people look at me and my man dancing as I looked at Bernard and Abigail and say, "What a beautiful pair?"

The sight of them softened my feelings toward Abigail. She wasn't a bad person, despite how annoying she had been to me in the past. Since my return, she seemed less catty toward me. And there was no question that she made Bernard happy. The most important thing was that she loved Bernard, and I had no doubt in my mind about that.

I left before the song was over. It was a chilly, starlit night. The wind whispered through the trees lining Main Street. All the shops were closed, and a few stragglers coming from the celebration moved quickly to their homes. Most of the houses were shuttered and dark.

When I reached our house, I noticed a light on in the parlor. I climbed the stairs, opened the front door, and closed it behind me quietly. Just as I was about to walk upstairs, I heard a stir in the parlor. It was Mama.

"Where have you been?"

"You know where I've been."

"Do you know what time it is?"

For the first time that evening, I looked at my wristwatch. "I guess the time got away from me."

"I don't believe you."

"Everyone was out late. Ask Bernard."

"It's two thirty in the morning."

"So it is."

"Is that all you have to say for yourself?"

"Good night, Mama."

"Don't be fresh with me. You've never in your entire life walked through that door at this hour. Do you know what kind of woman does such a thing?"

"I'm sure you're going to tell me harlots and whores."

"Amelia, I'm warning you. I'm very upset at this behavior."

"I'm not a child anymore, Mama. I can make decisions on my own, and I don't need to abide by any curfew you intend to impose."

"You will follow the rules of this house so long as you live under this roof."

"For God's sake, Mama. I was in the war. I worked through the night, sometimes never going to sleep. I saw a lot of horrible things. I know how to handle myself and what's right and wrong. How can you expect me to follow some silly curfew?"

"You're still my child, Amelia, and you will show respect, do you understand? You will not come through that door after ten thirty from this day forward so long as you live in this house. I'll lock the door at that time, and you're on your own if you want to stay out like a stray cat and wander the streets."

It was pointless. She didn't understand, and she wasn't going to budge from her point of view. She couldn't accept that her little girl had grown into a woman during the war. I was too tired to argue and dreaded coming months of push and pull. I was not going to abide by such silly rules, and if she locked the door, that would mean sleeping in Sam's father's "Hotel Chevrolet" parked in front of their house.

"Are you finished, Mama? I'd like to go to bed now." I went over to her and kissed her on the cheek.

"It'll take a little getting used to, Amelia, but it's for your own good."

The only way to deal with her was to ignore her. "Good night, Mama."

I went upstairs and into my room, undressed, and slid into my bed. What a luxury this bed had become since the cots and bunks I had laid on during the war. I stared out the window at the glowing stars in the sky and hummed myself to sleep to the tune of "How Ya Gonna Keep 'Em Down on the Farm After They've Seen Paree."

United States Coast Guard
Special Report upon the
Incident on the Steamship *Uncatena*
October 16, 1921
Excerpt, Testimony, Mr. Obed Moorland questioned by
Deputy Officer William B. Madden

"It's just so hard for me to imagine this. That my sweet pea, my Amelia, could have done such a thing."

"Do you have any idea why she would contrive such a story?"

"I have no idea. Really, I don't."

"She has no mental trouble or health-related problems?"

"She's never gone mad, if that's what you're asking. She's strong, I tell you. Strong. She survived the Spanish flu."

"Would she concoct a story if she were embarrassed?"

"Wouldn't any of us? But that doesn't make us crazy."

"I didn't say that it did."

"She served in the Red Cross, you know. She's working on becoming a nurse. I can't believe she would have jumped if she weren't trying to save someone."

"So you think she's telling the truth?"

"Yes."

CHAPTER XIII

I hear footsteps. Someone is coming up the porch stairs. What time is it? Oh, yes, it's four thirty. Then it must be the mailman.

As a child, I would run to get the mail. It was never for me, but I always raced to the door to meet the postman. Now, I sometimes let it sit in the box for weeks. They say as you get older, you revert back to the habits of your childhood. In this instance, I'm afraid that theory doesn't hold water. But I'll empty out the box today, so that when they figure out I'm gone, they'll automatically stop my mail.

I'm sure my mailbox holds invitations to all sorts of events, from art openings to cocktail parties, yacht-club openings, and fund-raisers. Once it hits the papers that I'm dead, they'll all revise their catering numbers.

Look at this one. It's for a wedding. I've been to so many throughout the years, but never to my own. Well, to some people, that's not an entirely true statement. There was an incident in my life with a fellow just after World War II, but that's all it was—an incident. An unfortunate set of circumstances that I've put out of my mind. It really didn't count as a wedding or a marriage. If anyone tells you anything different, they don't know what they're talking about.

You see, right after the war, I spent some time in London. I had befriended a couple of Red Cross women who were my age (forty-five at the time) and British. One of them, Eunice Henningsworth, invited me to stay with her in her London home. Well, Eunice had a dashingly handsome brother named Edward. He was a couple of years older than I was, and he had a full head of black, curly hair, a tan complexion, and brown eyes. And boy, did he have charisma. When he walked into a room, all eyes turned to him. He was physically magnetic, and he had a personality that matched. He could charm the clothes off you without you even knowing it. I was immediately smitten.

He was a bachelor (or so he said), a banker, and a polo player who had graduated from Oxford—a fine pedigree. If anything made me melt, it was his proper English accent. We wined and dined, went to the family country estate just outside of Bath, had tea with his "mum" and aunties, took afternoon walks in Regents Park, and made love two or three times a day.

When he asked me to marry him, I was over the moon.

We decided that a big wedding, with all of the bells and whistles, was a bit much for people our age. We also decided not to tell anyone. We agreed to surprise everyone after we were married and have a big party. So we went to the Chelsea town hall and had a civil ceremony. Afterward, we took a room at the Ritz. We drank champagne and ate caviar and foie gras. It seemed as if happiness and good fortune had finally come my way. But I couldn't have that too long, now could I?

As we crawled into bed, he casually turned to me, kissed me sumptuously, and dropped the bomb. "It wouldn't bother you, would it, darling, if I had two other wives?"

I giggled. "You're joking, Edward."

"No, I'm not. I've got a wife in Italy and one in Switzerland. And a child."

I pushed him away. "But you've divorced them, right?"

"Afraid not. I support them, and I only see them a few times a year, but I do care about them."

I couldn't believe this was happening to me. "Well, I won't be part of your harem!"

I jumped out of bed and started to get dressed. He tried to calm me down. "Oh lovies, it's not like that."

"Does your family know about them?"

"No. It's not their business."

"How could you do this? How could you think that I would be willing to go along with this?"

He tried to embrace me, but I backed away. "Don't you touch me."

"Amelia, I love you."

"And I thought I loved you too."

I gathered my things and exited, slamming the door behind me. I was so humiliated.

Thank God we had never told anyone we were married. How awful that would have been to explain. Can you imagine what it would have been like to tell Mama? She would have thought I was off my nut again.

A few days later, Edward begged me to reconsider, but I would have none of it. I finally convinced him that we had to annul the marriage. I never saw or spoke to him again.

That was the last time I accepted a marriage proposal and the closest I got to walking down the aisle. But I'm getting ahead of myself again.

What was I talking about? Oh, yes—weddings.

Bernard kept his promise and wasted little time getting engaged to and marrying Abigail. I knew Mama would soon start in again about my attracting a husband.

The truth is, I just wasn't ready for any kind of romance, let alone a marriage. Sure, I was intrigued by the gentleman who had asked me to dance, and at times, I felt alone and longed for someone. Occasionally, I even thought I was going to end up an old maid if I didn't find someone—and fast. But after Willie and James, I was gun shy.

What I really needed was some kind of distraction to keep those thoughts—and Mama's persistence—at bay.

Just about that time, the Nantucket Cottage Hospital started offering training for nurses. This seemed a perfect thing to do, taking into account my experience during the war. And I relished the idea of finally having a profession—being a sister instead of a nurse. I applied and was accepted into the three-year program: two years of training on Nantucket and one year in Boston at the city hospital.

We had courses in anatomy, dietetics, obstetrics, the history and theory of nursing, and cooking for invalids, among many others. Sam enrolled in the program with me, but after the second year, she dropped out for an odd reason: coconut oil.

It was the spring of 1921—early April, I believe—and Sam and I were eating lunch in the staff room at the hospital when Abigail burst in with the news.

"You've got to come, quickly."

"What is it, Abigail?"

"Coconut oil."

"Coconut oil?"

"Yes. The whole town has dropped everything and is heading out to Quidnet and Wauwinet. Bernard's waiting in the Maxwell to take us out there."

Sam and I looked at each other, thinking Abigail had lost her mind.

"Abigail, slow down. Now start from the beginning."

"There's no time for that."

"What are you talking about?"

"Come on. You'll see soon enough. We'll be rich!"

As I'm sure you've figured out by now, it didn't take much to convince me to ignore authority, so long as disobedience led to adventure. Sam, on the other hand, was apprehensive. "But we can't just leave the hospital. We're in the middle of our classes."

I wasn't about to listen to her calls of concern.

"You say the whole town has dropped everything?" I asked Abigail.

"Yes. Now come on. We're losing time. We've got to get our share of the oil. Your Mama has already gone to the store and is buying as much lye as she can. She says there could be a big market for soap, and she's ready to start making it."

I was keen on playing hooky, but I could tell Sam was not, so I tried to convince her. "They won't miss us for an afternoon. Let's do it."

"I'm worried, Amelia."

"I bet everyone in the hospital is already on their way out there."

"It's not that. It's something else."

"What is it?"

"Things will change."

"Of course they'll change. We might be a little richer. Now are you with me or not?"

She gave in reluctantly, and we ran out of the staff room, down the corridor, and out of the front door of the hospital. Bernard was waiting right outside, and we piled in the Maxwell and drove toward Wauwinet.

"This better be good, Bernard."

Abigail, excited as a whale on the line, went on to explain. "A British ship got stranded on the Great Round Shoal last week, and they tried to get her off, but they were unsuccessful."

"What's that got to do with it?"

"They didn't get the ship off until they pumped the cargo out of the hold of the ship."

"Coconut oil," I guessed.

"And now it's drifted with the currents onto the shores of Quidnet and Wauwinet, and everyone is heading out to retrieve it, because it's got to be worth something."

Bernard interjected, "Or at least good for making soap."

Bernard was driving so fast, it seemed as if we were on a Nantucket sleigh ride.

When we got to the eastern shores of Wauwinet, we could see nothing but miles and miles and piles and piles of white, congealed oil lapping up against the shores. Bernard and Abigail were correct: the entire town seemed to have shown up to gather the chunks.

We took buckets that Abigail had gathered and ran down to the shore. Bernard had placed a tarp in the trunk, and we filled it until it could hold no more.

"How much of this stuff are we going to take?" I asked.

"As many buckets full as we can," Bernard said. "Then we'll come back for some more."

Literally tons and tons of the white oil surrounded the shoreline, seemingly without end. As much as you would pull out, that much more came in. It was an unending sea of little white cakes.

The only problem was that the chunks were very greasy to handle, and in no time, we were covered head to toe in the oily stuff. We piled back in the car and sped off to make the first delivery back home to Mama.

"How much oil they say is out there?"

"About nine hundred tons."

"And everyone's going to make soap with it? We'll have soap to last a lifetime and then some."

We got back to our house, and Mama was ready for us. She and Da had emptied out an old washtub and put it in the backyard. We dumped the load and went back out to gather more oil.

Just as we were heading out of town, Mr. Boyer yelled to us that the oil was spotted at Brant Point. We decided to go out there, as it was a lot closer to home.

We made several trips back and forth to Brant Point throughout the evening. On our last trip, we were so covered in grease, as were the car door handles, that we couldn't get back into the car. We tried wiping our hands off on our clothes, but they too were covered in oil. It was like trying to catch a fish with your bare hands. Every time we thought we were about to release the door lock, our hands slipped off it. We tried wiping our hands off as best we could on the grass by the side of the road, but it too was trampled in oil. After several attempts, we finally got the door open—only to trip and slide out of the car on account of the oil on our shoes.

And we weren't the only ones with this problem. So much oil was tracked up and down the streets and sidewalks of Nantucket that automobiles went to and fro in the street, most of the time narrowly avoiding each other. Main Street nearly became a game of bumper cars.

As for people on foot, they fell to the ground on the sidewalks—and some couldn't get up again. It was as if they were slipping on the same banana peel over and over. Everywhere you looked, there was some silly slapstick skit being played out. It was as if the town had been transported into some kind of Buster Keaton picture. The comic lack of physical equilibrium brought on by the oil made for many a bellyaching laugh.

The next morning, Da said he had heard that we might get five cents a pound at a soap factory on the mainland for the stuff. News spread like wildfire, and it didn't take but a few hours before every ship out in the harbor went out to scoop it all up. We decided to stick to the shoreline.

Sam and I were walking up an embankment with our buckets when she slipped and went sliding down. As she did, she barreled bow on into a real looker of a man, who lost his footing and tumbled down with her. The lard tub he was holding went flying through the air, and the oil in it rained down on them. Sam and the young man rolled down together, coming to a stop just at the shoreline. Sam was on top of him, and they were covered in grease. His lard tub came crashing down beside them.

I ran down the embankment to see if she was hurt. "Sam, are you all right?"

Sam was wiping the grease away from her eyes and laughing when she made eye contact with the man.

"Sam?" he squeaked.

"I suppose I should get off you."

"That would be lovely."

She rolled off him and lay on her back, laughing. He wiped the oil away from his lips. He looked very familiar, although I wasn't sure where or when we had met. He reached out and wiped the oil away from her cheek. I stood above the two of them.

"Are you all right?"

He was about to speak when Sam winked at me and interrupted. "Yes, Amelia, we're fine."

He smiled at me as if he knew me and nodded in agreement. Sam grabbed his arm. "I'm sorry."

"Are you all right?"

"Yes, and you?"

"Fine, I guess."

He got up on his knees, picked up his empty lard tub, and stood up. He held out his hand to help Sam up. "What's your name?"

"Samantha Witherspoon. And you?"

"Scudder Simmons."

I was not one to play invisible. "And I'm Amelia."

"It's nice to meet you both, although I've met you before." He looked directly at me.

"I thought you looked familiar, but I can't place it."

"I asked you to dance at the party to celebrate those who served in the war."

I looked away from him in embarrassment. "Yes, of course. Well, it's nice to finally meet you."

I thought we'd leave it at that and hooked my arm into Sam's, but Sam shook my arm away and kept up the small talk. "Do you live here?"

"I moved from Chatham a couple of years ago to fish and scallop, but I didn't count on the coconut-oil harvest being bigger than the scallop harvest."

Sam, all greased up and smitten for Scudder, beamed underneath a layer of Nantucket's latest bumper harvest. "I must look a sight."

"No, you look some nice."

"What are you doing with your oil?"

"I hope to sell it. There are some men from New York coming in to settle the score. I think they think we should give it to them for nothing."

"Captain Killen wouldn't let that happen."

"I don't think any of us will let that happen. We have some rights to it."

"Are you going to the meeting?"

"I wouldn't miss it for anything."

"Amelia and I will be there too. You should look for us."

I looked at Sam as if I'd been hit by a boom. I couldn't believe how forward she was. Quite frankly, she was acting more like me.

"I'll do that," he said.

With that, Scudder Simmons bowed (he actually bowed!), winked at the two of us, and went about his business of collecting oil. We went in the opposite direction. Sam grabbed my arm and dug her claws in like a cat in heat. "That man is going to be my fiancé."

I wasn't prepared for that prediction. "Sam, this isn't a time for jokes."

"I'm serious, Amelia."

She rarely made such predictions about her own life; she usually kept them to herself. "He's the one. I know it."

I didn't want to hear it. You see, I had taken a fancy to him as well—and I was first. He had asked me to dance two years ago. She had completely dominated the conversation with him. I just couldn't get a word in edgewise to make any headway with him.

"But the sad thing is, Amelia, it's going to cause a big rift between you and me."

This consequence was already brewing inside of me.

"Don't get ahead of yourself, Sam. I don't find him the least bit attractive."

Of course, I was fibbing. She was head over heels in love. I wasn't going to tell her that I thought the cut of his jib seemed more to my tastes than to hers. How could this happen?

Sam and I attended the meeting on the old north wharf, in front of Captain Killen's office. Everyone from town was there; anyone who had harvested the oil had a stake in the arrangements that were to be made.

"Do you see him?"

Sam eyed the crowd like a red-tailed hawk looking for a rabbit.

"No. Maybe he didn't come."

"He's here, Amelia. I know it."

She was grating on my nerves.

"Well, if you know it, then you should know where he is."

"There he is."

Standing some fifty feet away was Scudder. She waved her arms in the air. He noticed her (it wasn't too difficult, as she stood out like a sore thumb) and returned the wave. He made his way through the crowd toward us.

"You're here," he greeted us.

He stood between Sam and me. I took the first initiative. "We wouldn't miss this for the world."

Sam grabbed his arm and turned him toward her. "And I'm not here for the coconut oil."

He stood back, looking at her, confused. "Why else would you be here?"

She smiled and blushed. "It's seeing you." Sam batted her eyelids, he smiled, and I was keeled out. If that didn't beat the pattern.

Despite Sam's flirtations, continuous gibbering, and sudden lack of interest in coconut oil, most of us had an interest in how much money we were going to receive for our labors. But the New York cargo surveyors had no intention of paying a fair price—or any price, for that matter—and nearly accused us of stealing.

Sam and Scudder were all smiles, laughs, and rosy cheeks. You'd think they were hooked in. I couldn't concentrate on what was happening at the meeting. My blood was boiling. I had to stop the two of them. Finally, I interrupted. "What's he saying?" I asked sharply.

Scudder took his eyes off her and looked over at me. He fidgeted like a school-boy caught writing love notes instead of practicing his algebra. Sam frowned at me in disapproval as Scudder looked over at the younger man from New York who was speaking.

"He said it doesn't belong to us, and he could legally take it away. He's got another thing coming if he thinks we're going to believe that. Salvagers have rights too, you know."

The crowd burst into a collective moan. A shout came from the crowd. "We know our rights! This isn't the first time cargo has washed ashore. How much is it worth to you?"

The New Yorker yelled back in a pissy tone, "Absolutely nothing."

The crowd responded with a mix of groans and laughter. Scudder yelled to the gentleman, "If it's worth nothing to you, then why are you here?"

Everyone in the crowd started clapping and stomping their feet. The New Yorkers had met their match.

Defensively, the other agent tried another scare tactic. "We could throw you in jail for taking that oil."

Scudder laughed and jeered at the agent. "We'd love you to try, sir. The Nan-tucket jail only holds two people. Where will you put the others?"

The crowd erupted in laughter as the agents scowled. The meeting was clearly going nowhere. Mr. Wood suggested the meeting adjourn until the evening.

The crowd dispersed. Scudder asked Sam if she wanted to get a spot of tea at the Sunset Tea Room.

"Sure. You don't mind, do you, Amelia?"

"Why would I mind?"

The two of them walked off the wharf. I stood there as the crowd dispersed. In a matter of minutes, I was alone, save for the gulls circling overhead, crying out for attention.

What was wrong with me? Sam was my friend. If she was happy with Scudder and knew that he'd be her husband, then why should I be feeling so grouty about this? Because I knew from this moment on, as long as Scudder was around, I wouldn't see much of Sam ... and because, deep down inside, I had feelings for Scudder that I wouldn't admit to at the time.

I went to the meeting Friday night. I was hoping that Sam would be there. I could accept her being with Scudder, but I would have preferred just Sam. Well, as you can guess, there was no sight of Sam or Scudder. I kept my weather eye peeled on the entrance, but they never came through that door. I could hardly pay attention to the goings-on. I felt completely abandoned. I was blue and didn't really care that an agreement was made on the price we'd get for our oil (which, after much arguing, ended up being thirteen dollars and fifty cents per ton).

I spent the next days walking around like a dog caught in the rain. I went back to the hospital to continue my studies. Sam never showed up again. Her nursing career was over.

United States Coast Guard
Special Report upon the
Incident on the Steamship *Uncatena*
October 16, 1921
Excerpt, Testimony, Ms. Catherine Moorland questioned by
Deputy Officer William B. Madden

"You know she served in the war."

"Yes, your husband told me."

"She wasn't old enough to enlist. We had no idea she did it, and wouldn't have allowed it if we did. She's got some imagination and can be very persuasive."

"How so?"

"Well, it's like I said. She convinced the Red Cross she was old enough and got herself enlisted. That takes creativity. Imagination. Persuasion."

"Do you think she's made this up?"

"Is that something you should ask a mother?"

"You know her best."

"If you're asking me if I think she is capable of making this up, I'd have to say yes. But if you're asking me if she really did so, in my heart of hearts, despite all the trouble I've had with her, I'd have to say no."

"But we've found no body."

"I think she thinks it really occurred, whether it did or not."

"I don't understand."

"I don't think she's well. Did my husband tell you she survived the Spanish flu?"

"Yes. Do you think that had something to do with it?"

"I'm not a doctor, but it only seems reasonable to think that the war and the flu overcame her. There's no family history. I'll tell you that much. We're always healthy. We're strong as bulls, at least my side of the family. I can't speak for my husband."

"So it is your belief that she had a nervous breakdown of sorts."

"I think it's possible that it all got to her."

C H A P T E R XIV

I'm getting thirsty again. I have a visitor who comes around about now. He's my old uncle Jim Beam. He's always on time, and I've yet to miss him. I need just a nip. It's a nice way to finish the afternoon and start the evening. He doesn't bite … or at least, he's never bitten me.

Oh, how I'm going to miss him. I can never get enough of him. He's caused me to do some wild things. He's stripped me naked and made me dance through the moors. He's also made me argue with people over God knows what. I've lost quite a few acquaintances because of him, but I never had the heart to let him go.

Then I started having heart troubles. The doctor begged me to give him up: "You'll live longer if you get off the drink."

I took his advice and tried to avoid him a couple of times over the years, but it never took. In the end, I couldn't give him up. He has this manly scent that makes me crave him.

It wasn't as if I never saw Sam. It's just that our friendship never was the same. She had one thing on her mind, and that was Scudder. It didn't matter if we crossed paths on Main Street, or had lunch, or went for a walk out in the moors; it was always Scudder this and Scudder that. It brought back memories of Willie and James. And Mama didn't make it any easier for me.

"You know, you're not getting any younger. This nursing thing is nice, but it won't take the place of a warm body next to you and someone to share your life with."

That was the first time Mama had spoken to me of any kind of intimacy. Little did she know, I was desperately longing for a warm body next to me every night. But her comment was lost on account of my stubbornness, frustration, and anger at Sam's newfound love.

I stormed out of her kitchen and walked briskly up Main Street and out of town. I passed the old Quaker graveyard, crossed the open fields where the Voornevelds grew the flowers that they sold at their shop on Centre Street, and walked all the way out to Hummock Pond.

I sat gazing at the glassy, smooth pond and the blue ocean in the horizon. It was all very clear to me: I was ready to find someone again.

"Hello, Amelia."

I turned around and saw Scudder. "Hi, Scudder."

He stood in front of me. "I've been meaning to come see you."

I looked at the fields surrounding us. We were the only ones there. "Did you follow me out here?"

He squatted down and looked directly in my eyes. "We never seemed to get to know each other very well."

His physical proximity made me uncomfortable. I backed away. "Well, you've been busy with Sam."

He sat down next to me. "I've often wondered why you wouldn't dance with me that evening at the Red Men's Hall."

"You took me by surprise that night. I didn't know how to react. But I did come back to look for you."

He picked a tall blade of grass and brushed it ever so delicately against my arm. "Do you ever think how things might have turned out if we had?"

I was getting aroused. "That's ancient history now, isn't it, Scudder?"

"It doesn't have to be."

"What do you mean?"

He put his arms around me and kissed me. I turned my head away from him. "Scudder, we shouldn't ..."

Before I could finish the sentence, he was kissing me again. I attempted to stop him, but my effort was feeble. In all honesty, I wanted him to kiss me. I wanted as much as he was giving. He held me tight in his arms. All I could think about was Sam and how this might hurt her. I thought about Lena and James and how I had felt at their betrayal.

I pushed him away. "I'm serious. We shouldn't do this, Scudder."

"Why not?"

"Because of Sam."

He kissed me again. I tried to push him away, but he was too strong for me. I didn't want him like this. I became agitated and angry, and I slapped him across the face. Stunned, he pushed me away and wiped the smart off his cheek. He was breathing heavily in frustration. He turned his back to me and clenched his fists.

"I'm sorry, Amelia."

I knew in my heart that I did the right thing by stopping him, but I also knew I wanted him.

I stood up and straightened my blouse. "No harm has been done."

He came toward me. "I don't know why you play so hard to get."

Startled, I began to walk away. "I'm not leading you on, Scudder."

He grabbed my arms. "I wanted you, Amelia. Not Sam."

I tried to shake free. "You don't mean that."

He took hold of my chin. "Don't tell me what I mean or how I feel."

I knocked his hand away. "Why have you spent so much time with her?"

He let go of me. "To get to you."

"You'll never have me, Scudder. Not like this."

He kissed me on my forehead, then walked away. I remember hearing the dry grass crunch as he took each step away from me and thinking he must be twenty feet from me. Now thirty. Forty. Fifty. Was I going to call out to him and beg him to come back? I was speechless. Then I couldn't hear his steps anymore. I only heard the tall grasses swaying around me.

I sat there as the sun set and the cold, early evening air enveloped the land-scape. Had I really let him get away? Shouldn't I feel repulsed at the thought of him trying to have his way with me at the same time that he was seeing Sam? I had let him go because of Sam. Why didn't that make me feel good? Why did I feel angry—and at Sam, no less? What about my feelings for him? I couldn't be true to them. They must remain a secret.

I got up as the sun's last rays saturated the western horizon. I brushed off my dress, trying to get Scudder's scent off me. I left the field in the dark and walked home—once again, alone.

United States Coast Guard
Special Report upon the
Incident on the Steamship *Uncatena*
October 16, 1921
Excerpt, Testimony, Ms. Cornelia Thompson, passenger, questioned by
Deputy Officer William B. Madden

"I'm very nervous."

"There's nothing to be nervous about. I'm just going to ask you a few questions, and all I want is for you to answer them truthfully. If you don't know the answer, just tell me you don't know."

"OK."

"Do you know Ms. Amelia Moorland?"

"Yes."

"And did you see her on the ferry?"

"Yes. We spoke."

"What did you speak of?"

"We said some niceties ... you know, like how the summer season was, what my plans were for the autumn, where I was going that evening ... the usual things one talks about on the ferry this time of year."

"Did you notice anything peculiar about Ms. Moorland?"

"She seemed distracted, so I asked her what was wrong."

"What did she tell you?"

"She started crying and was fighting back the tears, poor little lamb. She said it was nothing and then walked away. I thought it was probably nothing more than a young woman's romantic problems, and the best thing I could do was stay out of it."

"What happened next?"

"Well, you know she took a dive off the boat."

"Yes."

"That caused a great delay. You can imagine I was fit to be tied, because we were late coming in to New Bedford, thanks to Amelia's aquatic adventure. And then the crew gathered all of the passengers around and were taking down all of our contact information—I'm assuming for you and the investigation—and because of all of this nonsense, I missed a very important dinner engagement in Providence."

"Is there anything else, Ms. Thompson?"

"Well, while we were gathered around the crew, I spotted what appeared to be a woman—no, it was a woman—coming off the plank and slipping off into the dark night. I'm almost certain it was the one Amelia supposedly jumped in after."

"And you're certain?"

"Yes. It had to be her. I've known her for years."

CHAPTER XV

I've got a leftover lobster in the refrigerator. I'll probably just eat one of the claws; I'm not really that hungry. There's something about contemplating the last hours of your life that takes your appetite away. I thought I'd want to eat a big feast to ready myself for the journey. But it's probably best to go on an empty stomach; there'll be less for the undertaker to contend with.

It's already cooked. I boiled it last week. I realize that was a while ago, but I have a cast-iron stomach. I can eat anything.

I always thought that I'd serve lobster Thermador at my wedding. But I never got around to it—getting married, that is. Yes, there was that incident, but as I told you, it counted for nothing. In the end, no one asked me, and I never found anyone I'd ask myself. I was never able to say those two cherished words, "we're engaged," and really experience it.

"We're engaged. Can you imagine that? Scudder and I are getting married."

A little over a month had passed since my episode with Scudder at Hummock Pond. He sure moved quickly.

It was all I could do to muster a smile. "Congratulations. I'm so happy for the two of you."

"We thought we'd tell you on your birthday."

What a way to ring in my twentieth birthday. "Was that necessary?"

Scudder forced a smile. "We're telling you in honor of your birthday."

"Well, it's quite an honor."

How could Scudder be so mean? Not to mention that I felt as if my birthday was upstaged by this news.

"Will you be my maid of honor?"

Now they were pouring salt in my wounds. "I don't know what to say."

"Say yes."

"I …"

I looked at the smiles on their faces, taking in Sam's wide-eyed puppy joy. She was so happy. But I could have been engaged to Scudder … it should have been me. Scudder appeared happy. Had he forgotten that day? He held Sam's hand tenderly. They were Willie and me, going from moving pictures to nights walking hand in hand. They were James and me, sharing a secret wink and a smile amid the chaos of the evacuation hospital. I couldn't say no.

"Yes."

The three of us embraced. Scudder rubbed his hand up and down my spine. Was it a sign of affection, or was it merely a friendly pat on the back? If he asked her to marry him, surely he no longer held feelings for me. I had lost Scudder before ever having him. And now, I was sure to lose Sam.

About a week later, I ran into Scudder down on the docks. Mama had sent me down to see what fish had been caught that day and to pick one up for supper. Scudder had just come back from an overnight trip. I saw him as I walked past his boat. I looked the other way, hoping he wouldn't see me, but to no avail.

"Amelia."

I ignored him. If he did catch up to me, I could always say I was in my own little world and didn't see or hear him. But he grabbed my arm.

"Amelia."

"Scudder. I …"

There was something about his eyes that made me feel weak in the knees. I couldn't have these feelings. I had to stop.

"I hope Sam and I didn't offend you by telling you of our engagement on your birthday."

"Not at all."

"About the time out at …"

"It's completely forgotten."

How could I mask the outright lie of that comment? Could he believe such a statement? Sadly, he'd never know that I still dreamed about that day at Hummock Pond and wished for a different outcome.

"I wasn't myself, Amelia. I don't know what got into me. Maybe I was scared that Sam and I were moving so quickly, and I was trying to find something to slow it down. But at least you brought me to my senses."

He took hold of my hands and squeezed them.

"I'm glad I could help."

We looked into each other's eyes. The entire conversation felt like a lie. Could he tell I wanted him? Did he still have feelings for me? I couldn't bear his touch any longer, and I pulled my hands from his.

"Mama will have a fit if I come home without a fish. I'd better get moving before it's all gone."

I walked as fast as I could away from him. This had to end. I convinced myself that once Sam and Scudder were married, all of this would go away. Our feelings would be sealed away forever. The wedding couldn't come soon enough.

About one month before the wedding, Sam and I packed a lunch and our bathing costumes and took Pud Smith's dory from Madaket Harbor over to Tuckernuck Island. For those who don't know, Tuckernuck is very close to Nantucket. In fact, you could swim to it if you wanted to. But most people boat over.

Sam and I hadn't been over there since before the war. It was an excursion that we had both treasured in the past; this particular trip came at my suggestion to ensure that our friendship would endure, even in marriage.

We got started early. Looking east, the sun was just above the tip of Great Point lighthouse. We loaded the dory and shoved off.

I took one of the oars, and Sam took the other, and we rowed out across the harbor and over to the northernmost tip of Tuckernuck. We didn't say much of anything on the way over. All you could hear were the oars dipping in and out of the ocean, the lapping of waves at the bow of the boat, and our breathing.

"Does this look like a good place?"

"Yeah. Let's go ashore."

We rowed as close to the shore as we could before hitting sand, then jumped out of the boat and pulled the dory ashore. Once we got everything settled, we looked back at Nantucket.

An osprey floated above the water. It suddenly dove in and came back up with a very large fish.

"Breakfast."

"That's more than breakfast, Amelia. That's for sex," she said matter-of-factly.

I nervously laughed. Given what had happened with Scudder, I wasn't comfortable talking about love, sex, or intimacy with Sam.

"The female holds back until she gets what she wants from the male."

I smiled and looked away. "Let's change into our bathing suits."

We spread out our picnic blanket and changed right on the shore. We didn't have to worry about being seen; no one was there to bother us. Sure, there were a few homes, but you never saw anyone out and about.

We went for a quick swim; the water was freezing, but refreshing. We came back, toweled off, and lay down, letting the sun warm us up.

Sam turned to me. "I know this has been hard for you, Amelia."

"No, it hasn't."

"Call a spade a spade. You know that I know these things about you."

I began to wonder if she knew about those times with Scudder. She had powers; it certainly was plausible. I had to change the subject. "I feel like I'm losing you, Sam."

Sam took my hand. "You're not losing me."

Tears began to well up. "You've been my soul mate since I can remember."

"It's going to be different."

I wiped away a tear. "I don't want it to be different."

Sam smiled. "I'll always be there for you, Amelia."

"Am I going to find someone? A husband?"

Sam looked down, avoiding the question. "You know I can't tell you that."

I sat up. "But you know the answer, don't you?"

She turned her back to me. "I don't, Amelia."

I grabbed her shoulder, turning her toward me. "You always keep things from me. You're so secretive. Why?"

She furrowed her brow. "I don't keep secrets from you. It's you who have kept a secret from me."

I was taken aback. "I have not."

She stood up, towering over me. "I've tried to ignore it, but I can't anymore. You're harboring feelings for Scudder."

I looked away. "How can you say that?"

She pressed on. "You've had them since that night he asked you to dance."

I started edging backward. "That was a long time ago. He's marrying you, not me."

She gritted her teeth, holding back tears. "But he still has feelings for you."

I stood up and went toward her. "That's impossible. We've barely gotten to know each other."

Her face was beet red with anger. "You've been with him, haven't you?"

She had me against the wall. There was no escaping it: my feelings had shown through.

"Not like you think. Nothing happened."

She looked deep into my eyes. "I know, Amelia."

I looked away, guilty as charged. "He loves you, Sam. He chose you, not me."

Sam began to cry.

"Don't cry."

"I've been so emotional over the last two months. I cry at anything."

I embraced her. "You're under a lot of pressure, getting things ready for the wedding."

She pushed away. "It's not that."

"Sure it is, Sam. Things will settle down once the wedding is over."

"No, they won't."

"How can you be so sure?"

Shaking, she cried out, "Because I'm pregnant, Amelia."

That took me by surprise; it was the last thing I expected to hear.

"Scudder fed me a lobster dinner, and I gave him the keys to Hotel Chevrolet."

"Your daddy's car? Does Scudder know?"

"No one knows. You have to promise not to tell … my father would kill me if he knew."

"I won't tell a soul."

I held her hand. "Are you going to tell Scudder before the wedding?"

"I don't know. I don't want to scare him off."

"You have to tell him, Sam."

"Something terrible is going to come from all of this. I just know it."

"Don't say such a thing."

"You know I'm rarely wrong about these things."

That was what troubled me.

I took both of her hands and led her back down on the blanket. "You're about to get married and have a beautiful baby. There's nothing terrible in those things."

Sam was not convinced. "I'm exhausted, Amelia."

She buried her face in the blanket. I lay down beside her, curling up into her backside, and embraced her. She tightly held onto my arms. I was her protector that afternoon. I wasn't going to let anything hurt her.

She fell asleep in my arms. I couldn't sleep. I felt helpless. There was nothing I could do to stop whatever Sam knew was going to happen. I had to be strong. I had to help her through this.

For a brief moment, Sam and I were closer than we'd ever been before. I didn't want the day to end, but it was time to head back. As we rowed back to Nantucket, the sun was setting over the western shores. A light breeze blew through the tall shore grasses.

"Promise that we'll go over to Tuckernuck together every summer," I said. "Just the two of us, just like today, until the day we die."

"I promise, Amelia. I promise."

We rowed the dory into Madaket Harbor as the evening sky turned blue, orange, purple, and honey gold. I was hell bent on remembering the color of that sky. And then once again, I had this feeling: a terrible feeling that Sam and I would never go to Tuckernuck again, and that this would prove to be the last such sunset that we would share together. I felt uneasy.

We stood at the edge of the harbor arm in arm, watching the evening light turn to darkness.

"I love you, Amelia."

"I love you too."

With that, we got into her father's Chevrolet and headed back to town.

United States Coast Guard
Special Report upon the
Incident on the Steamship *Uncatena*
October 16, 1921
Excerpt, Testimony, Mr. Hollis Stevens, passenger, questioned by
Deputy Officer William B. Madden

"And you saw her get on the ferry?"

"Yes. She was distraught."

"Distraught?"

"She was weeping. You know, crying and lugging a heavy suitcase."

"Was anyone with her?"

"No one got on with her that I saw. I asked her if she was all right, and she said that she'd be fine—that she was going away. I asked if she would come inside with me, and she said no, she wanted fresh air."

"And that's the last time you saw her?"

"I thought I saw her get off the ferry in New Bedford. She was maybe three or four people ahead of me."

"Are you sure?"

"Yes. I believe it was her."

"Unfortunately, when the crew took down the details of all of the passengers, the crew didn't get her name or address."

"Is that so?"

"Yes. There's no record of her being on that vessel."

"That's funny. I could swear I saw her."

CHAPTER XVI

I've always loved fires in my fireplace. I have so many memories of being by the fire—like when Bernard and I were children, and we used to lay as close to the fireplace screen as possible. We got quite hot after a while, but we made a little game of it: who could stand the heat the longest? I always won. During the Depression, we used the fireplace to heat the house during the winter; Mama, Da, Bernard, and I slept on the living-room floor under multiple layers of blankets. It was like camping out. And still other times, I stared into the flames to warm myself with memories of those who have gone before me, like Sam, Bernard, Da, and Mama.

I don't know how they made fireplaces back then (the house is over one hundred and fifty years old), but I've never had a problem with the draw. That, coupled with a stash of really dry and seasoned wood, makes it easy for me to tend the fire myself.

I think one last fire is called for ... and also, a little Uncle Jim to make me comfortable. I always sit by the fire and sip Uncle Jim. It usually helps me sleep. But I haven't been sleeping well these past days. My heart has been doing funny things. Stopping and starting ... beating fast, and then slowly. Be that as it may. It's giving out. I'm resigned to that; it's destined to happen.

But I'm running out of time. I have to tell you about Sam's wedding.

I didn't sleep well during the weeks leading up to the wedding. I convinced myself that I had to prepare for whatever bad events Sam said was coming. I spent as much time as I could with her—partly out of a maid of honor's duty to assist with the wedding arrangements, but mostly because I had decided that if something were to happen to Sam, I was going to be there to right whatever went wrong.

The wedding date drew closer without any sort of catastrophe. Perhaps Sam had been overwhelmed by the pregnancy, her engagement, and all the wedding arrangements. Perhaps she was tired and wasn't thinking straight when she told me that something bad was going to come of this. I have to say I was relieved. I let down my guard.

Sam and her mother planned a very simple wedding. Sam didn't want bridesmaids or groomsmen. She only wanted me as maid of honor and Fitzy, Scudder's brother, as best man.

Fitzy lived in Chatham and worked in a boat yard. He was ten years older than Scudder and quite large. At one time, he must have been built like a racehorse. But too much eating and drinking and gravity had punctuated his distended stomach, which poured over the top of his belt.

Fitzy came over a week before the wedding to spend time with Scudder. They had gone out fishing for the day, which entailed catching few fish and consuming large quantities of booze. They came back after sunset drunk and, for whatever reason, decided to stop by my house.

My da had asked me to adjust the focus of the headlights on the Maxwell. You see, in those days, you had to properly adjust the headlight bulbs, or you'd have trouble seeing while driving at night. I was in the garage when Scudder and Fitzy dropped by. I had just finished removing the lamp glasses when they barged in.

"Amelia?"

Scudder slurred his words, and I could tell they were crocked, so I decided to continue the chore at hand, hoping that might prompt them to leave.

"Hi, Scudder."

I walked over to the driver's side of the automobile, got in, and turned the headlights on. I went to get out of the seat, but before I could, Scudder came up to the door and blocked my exit. He stuck his head into the automobile, reeking of bathtub gin.

"You know, there's still a part of me that wonders what would have happened if the two of us …"

I interrupted him. "You've had too much bug juice, Scudder."

He turned around and yelled to Fitzy. "You hear that, Fitzy? We've had too much to drink."

Fitzy lurked a couple of feet away. He glanced around and cleared his throat, shifting his weight from one foot to the other and back again. "Come on, Scudder. Leave her alone. Let's get out of here."

I hoped that he'd take Fitzy's advice. "That's right, Scudder. You've had a long day. Why don't you go home and sleep it off? You're getting married in a couple of days."

"I could still get out of it."

"Don't say such a thing."

"I'm just pulling your leg."

"There's nothing between us, Scudder. Leave well enough alone."

I wanted to smack him. I wanted to tell him he was going to be a daddy and shouldn't be thinking such things. I was angry and frustrated. I'd never have him; he was engaged to Sam, and she was having his baby. If he continued to behave this way, I would probably lose Sam. I pushed him out of the way. He stumbled and fell to the ground. He and Fitzy laughed. I ignored them and placed a card over one of the headlights, then worked on the bulb that wasn't covered. I moved the bulb so that a V-shaped image shined on the back wall. Scudder rolled onto his back.

"Am I finally going to get to dance with you at my wedding?" He would not, but I didn't want to ruffle his feathers. With some help from Fitzy (and some difficulty), Scudder stood up.

"One dance, Scudder," I said, just to get him moving. "That's all."

As I was adjusting the other lamp, he came up to me and put his arm around my shoulder, pressing his weight against me as if to try to find his equilibrium. I had to hold him up, as he was a bit light on his feet.

"That's all I want, Amelia. Just a dance."

Scudder couldn't hold his head up very well.

"Fitzy? Help me get him in your truck. I'll get my da to drive you two home."

Fitzy nodded in agreement. We walked Scudder out to the truck and put him in the passenger seat.

"Wait here while I get my da."

"I'm sorry about this. He was determined to come over here. I tried to stop him."

"We'll mention none of this to anybody."

"You're a peach, Amelia."

I went into the house and called for Da. As I did, I heard an automobile engine turn over. I ran out of the house and looked down the driveway. Fitzy drove off into the night.

I thought to myself, "I hope he's all right and knows where he's going."

I was so uncomfortable around Scudder. Would his flirtations end once he and Sam were married? I tried to convince myself that he was just nervous about getting married and was taking it out on me. But something inside me knew that wasn't the case. I didn't know how I was going to manage his forwardness and my close friendship with Sam.

That night, I had the most unexpected dream. Scudder and I were alone in a dory on Long Pond. The sun sat low in the western sky. There wasn't a breeze or cloud in the sky; it was eerily weatherless. I dangled my hand in the water as he rowed.

We came upon a sea of swans swimming in the water. With all of his might, Scudder pulled the oars forward into the deep water and followed through, raising the oars out of the water and holding them up in the air. Heave-ho. The dory almost lifted out of the water and lunged forward. He put the oars down as we glided through the water.

The movement upset the swans. They took off in flight in a panic. The sky was filled with the great birds retreating. It turned white, with wings flapping on top of each other, row upon row of swans. They screeched and screamed to get out of our way. I was overwhelmed by the number of birds and felt frightened, thinking they might attack.

I ducked down and crawled into Scudder's arms, placing my head under his chin for protection. He took hold of me. His warmth was inviting. He began to caress my hair. I arched my back in acceptance of his touch and curled myself closer to him like a cat to its master.

Suddenly, the swans disappeared. There was nothing around us. It was just Scudder and me, floating. But there was no dory, and we were naked. We were floating above the water. He took my face in his hands, lifted me up, and kissed me. I melted in his arms. He started kissing me all over my body. He lay on his back and lifted me on top of him. I wanted him. There was nothing to deter us— not a thought nor a person present. We embraced and entwined. Our legs knotted together.

As I lifted my body off him, he suddenly fell beneath me. I tried to catch him, but his arms and legs slipped out of my reach. We were no longer over water; there was nothing to break his fall. He crashed with a violent thud in the middle of a cobblestone road and cracked his skull open. Blood poured out of his head, inching its way around his body. A scarlet halo formed around his head. I tried to reach him, but I was being pulled upward, over houses and trees, into the black night. All I could see was a sea of blood flowing around him. Then I heard Sam calling.

"Amelia?"

"Sam?"

She was distressed. "Please come. It's Scudder."

I woke, shaking. Had Sam been aware of my dream? Why did I have these feelings for him? He was hers, not mine.

I got dressed and ran to Sam's house. All of the lights were on. As I entered the house, I heard Sam let out a loud, bone-chilling wail.

"Nooooo."

I saw Mr. Witherspoon rocking in a chair in the parlor. Tears ran down his cheeks.

"Mr. Witherspoon, what's wrong?"

He continued to rock in the chair, looking straight out at nothing, as if oblivious to my presence.

"What happened?"

He never looked at me, but finally spoke. His voice cracked. "Did you hear?"

"No. Tell me. Is Sam all right?"

"Scudder and his brother ... they ... they were in an accident." He stopped rocking and took a deep breath, then cleared his throat and continued. "The truck turned over and crushed them. They're dead."

I heard Sam let out a bloodcurdling wail. I ran upstairs and hurried into her room. Her mother sat on the bed, crying. Sam slowly paced the length of the room. Back and forth. Back and forth.

"Sam."

I embraced her. It was like holding a corpse—stiff and lifeless.

"What am I going to do?"

"I don't know, Sam. But we'll get through this."

"I knew something was going to happen."

"We'll get through this together."

"I just didn't know it would be this."

I pulled back her hair. "I'm here for you, Sam."

She finally looked at me. "He didn't love me."

"That's not true."

"He loved you."

I began to cry. "No, Sam. No, he didn't. You're upset."

"It's all right, Amelia. I don't blame you. I blame him."

She put her fingers in her mouth and began to shake uncontrollably. "What am I going to do?"

I knew she was talking about the baby, and with her mother in the room, I couldn't say anything. I went to embrace her again, but she let out a loud wail. "Noooo ..."

I stepped back. Her voice trailed off until it sounded hoarse and gravelly. When she inhaled, she collapsed on the floor.

Mrs. Witherspoon and I sat her up. Mr. Witherspoon burst into the room. "What happened?"

"Help us get her into bed."

Mr. Witherspoon picked her up. We tucked her under the sheets as she came to.

"I don't know what to do." Mrs. Witherspoon fought back tears.

Mr. Witherspoon decided to take charge. "I'm going to call the doctor."

Sam shot up quickly, protesting. "No. I don't want to see the doctor. No."

I understood her urgency. There was no telling how her parents would react (especially Mr. Witherspoon) if a doctor, while examining her, discovered she was pregnant and informed them.

Mr. Witherspoon would hear nothing of Sam's protests. "You've suffered a terrible shock, Samantha, and you're not yourself. I'm calling the doctor before you lose your mind completely. I'll hear of nothing else."

Sam fell back and buried her face in her pillow. She was weeping uncontrollably.

I didn't know if I should tell her parents about the baby. If I told them, and Dr. Whitefield didn't discover it or mention it to her parents, I would never forgive myself. It was up to Sam to tell them; it had to be on her terms. We would have to hope for the best.

Mrs. Witherspoon kissed the top of Sam's head and then looked up at me. "Amelia, you'd better go."

"Are you sure you don't want me to stay?"

"There's nothing you can do. The doctor will take it from here. We'll talk to you in the morning."

I looked at Sam and touched her shoulder. She grabbed my hand and squeezed it.

I walked out of Sam's bedroom, down the stairs, and out of her house. I don't remember walking down the street, but I got to the corner of Ray's Court and Main Street and stood there, numb.

I couldn't comprehend that Scudder was gone. He couldn't be gone. Just hours ago he had come to my house. And Fitzy too? Impossible. This was some kind of nightmare. It couldn't be real. I knew that Fitzy shouldn't have been driving. I should have driven them home instead of going in the house to ask Da to take them home. But Scudder was being too forward. I didn't want to be around him. This was all my fault. Would I ever be able to bring myself to tell Sam?

A wind whipped through the chestnut trees and scattered the dead blossoms off their branches. I looked down the street. There wasn't a soul around.

The next morning, I went over to the Witherspoons to check on Sam. As I knocked on the door, I heard shouting. No one answered my knock. I looked in the window and saw Mr. and Mrs. Witherspoon arguing. Mr. Witherspoon was pointing his finger at Mrs. Witherspoon. They must have found out. I had to see if Sam was all right. I pounded on the door. The shouting stopped. Mr. Witherspoon opened the door.

"I came to see how Sam is doing."

"She's resting."

"What did the doctor say?"

Agitated, Mr. Witherspoon ignored the question. "It's not a good time, Amelia."

With that, he slammed the door shut. They knew.

There was some confusion over what to do with the bodies. Scudder and Fitzy's parents were deceased, but they had distant relatives on the Cape. Should there be a funeral service on Nantucket? Who would arrange it? It wasn't as if Scudder and Fitzy had family here, and Scudder hadn't tied the knot with Sam, so the Witherspoons weren't obligated. He wasn't religious either, or a Nantucketer, so no one in particular felt any urge to send their souls off to heaven (if that be God's will). In the end, Scudder and Fitzy's bodies were shipped back to their cousins in Chatham for burial.

The day the brothers were to be transported, I went down to the wharf to pay my last respects. The two coffins sat on the wharf among other boxes and items to be shipped over to America. Sam was there with her mother. I walked toward them and caught the eye of Mrs. Witherspoon. She waved her hand at me, shooing me away. I acquiesced and kept my distance. I didn't want to upset Sam.

When the men came to load the coffins, Sam jumped on one of the coffins and lay down on it. She was on the edge of breaking down. "No! You can't take him yet."

It was distressing to witness. I wanted to run up to her and hold her. I wanted to comfort her, to be there for her as she had been for me after the war. She was beside herself.

I couldn't help but wonder how I could have had the thoughts I had about Scudder. Why did he continually taunt me? Sam was the most important person in my life. How could I let him tear us a part? I was glad he was dead. That sounds terrible, but I'm telling you the truth. It served him right, getting drunk and coming on to me.

Mrs. Witherspoon had to pry her daughter off the pine coffin. As the men loaded it on the steamship, Sam collapsed on the ground in a fit of tears. The steamship pulled out into the harbor. Once it rounded Brant Point, her mother lifted her up and helped her home.

I stood on the empty docks and wondered if Sam and I would ever be the same again.

I went to Sam's house every day, and I was turned away each time by her mother.

"She doesn't want to see anyone."

"Not even me?"

"I'm sorry, Amelia."

This couldn't be Sam's wishes … or could it? Maybe she knew what had happened with Scudder.

But maybe it wasn't Sam. Maybe Mr. and Mrs. Witherspoon were holding something against me. I started feeling guilty. But guilty of what, I couldn't say.

I had to see Sam, but I didn't know how I was going to get past her parents. And I didn't want make her parents any more upset than they already appeared to be.

Then one night, as I was dozing off, Sam finally came to me. "Amelia?"

"Sam?"

"They know."

"I thought so."

"My father doesn't want anyone on the island to know. That's why he won't let me see anyone."

"What are you going to do?"

"They're sending me away."

"Where?"

"My father wants me out of the house. He won't even look at me. He's so ashamed."

"Come live with me."

"I can't do that."

"Sure you can. I've got to move to Boston for the last part of my training. You can come with me."

Sam spoke as if in a fog. "It's not possible."

"It is possible. I'll take care of you."

She was lethargic. "It's not finished."

"What are you talking about?"

"I won't be with you much longer."

"Sam? What are you saying?"

I woke up and saw Mama standing over me. "What are you saying?"

I was disoriented.

"You were talking in your sleep. You're flushed. You must have had a nightmare."

"I don't remember."

What was Sam saying?

I finished the term of my nursing school at the Nantucket Cottage Hospital and was a few weeks away from moving to Boston for the last ten months of instruction. I had to convince Sam to move to Boston with me.

I went to Sam's house and was turned away every day. I would look up at her window and see nothing but closed curtains. It was as if she wasn't there anymore.

The week before I was to leave, I went over to her house at the usual time, but something was different. Mrs. Witherspoon, instead of turning me away, ushered me into the parlor and sat me down. She was as jittery as a June bug.

"I don't know how to ask you this, Amelia."

"Ask me what?"

"I just don't know how to react."

"React to what?"

"My husband would be so angry at me for asking."

She gripped her hands together tightly. She looked at the floor, to the left, to the right, and up at the ceiling as she fought off tears and avoided looking me in the eye. I tried to gain her confidence.

"You can ask me anything, Mrs. Witherspoon. It's all right."

She pursed her upper lip, took a deep breath, and exhaled her question. "Did Samantha tell you she was, you know?"

I took hold of her hands. "Pregnant?"

She jerked her hands away from me and stood up. "So she did." She raised quivering hands to her face to cover the tears.

"It's all right, Mrs. Witherspoon. We'll all help her."

"She's lost the baby, Amelia." She turned away.

"What?"

"Samantha had a miscarriage."

I felt as if I'd been punched in the stomach.

"It was awful. She didn't know what was happening to her. She was screaming and running around naked. Her father came in and blew up. He called her a sinner and a whore and told her he wanted her out of the house and out of our lives forever. He stormed out, and she started shaking and screaming. It was all I could do to calm her down. She frightened me."

"Is she all right? Can I see her?"

"It's terrifying being in this house. Samantha is out of sorts. She rambles on about nothing, as if possessed. She's not my little girl anymore. And Mr. Witherspoon can't find it in his heart to forgive her. He's disowned her; he can't bear to be in the same room with her. He's doing everything he can to ignore her and spends all of his time out except the early hours of the morning, when he sleeps. He's insisted that she move to the mainland. He wants her out of the house and out of our lives. I'm going to have to let her go."

"You don't have to let her go."

"He'll have no other way."

"And if you stand up to him?"

"I don't have the strength, Amelia. You can't imagine what he's capable of doing to me, let alone what he's done to Sam."

"You can't let this happen."

"It's a matter of survival. I've no choice."

I embraced her. She was trembling and began to weep uncontrollably.

"Can I see her?"

Mrs. Witherspoon kissed me on the cheek and took me by the hand. She led me up the stairs to Sam's room. The door was shut and locked. She took a key out of her apron pocket. "I keep it locked because I'm afraid she'll run away."

Sam was lying in bed, asleep on her stomach. "Samantha? Dear? You've got a visitor."

Sam turned over and stared at me.

"Your mother told me about … well, you know. I'm sorry, Sam. Really I am."

Sam's face was blank. It was as if she couldn't hear a word I said. Mrs. Witherspoon placed her hand on my back and nudged me toward the bed.

Sam turned over and placed the blankets over her head, as if she wasn't interested in my presence. This person wasn't the Sam I knew. This person was in a deep, dark place that made it impossible for her to make any kind of contact with the living world.

Who had taken my Sam? I was completely beside myself. I understood why her mother was so distraught. How could we bring her back? Would she ever come back?

Mrs. Witherspoon took my hand. "I can't let her leave in this condition, but now that she's not pregnant, I fear her father will put her on the next ferry."

"You can't let him do that."

"And how am I supposed to stop it?"

"I'll take her to Boston with me."

"You'd do that?"

"She'd do it for me."

Sam turned over and sat up in bed. She spoke in a weak and faint voice. "I've told you I can't go with you, Amelia."

"You don't have a choice, Sam. You've got to come with me."

"I'm going away ... but not to Boston."

"Maybe in time, your father will come to his senses," I said, "especially when this blows over."

She ignored me. I pleaded, "Sam, we'll always be together." She didn't respond. I put my foot down. "I won't hear of anything else. You're coming with me."

I went over to the bed and hugged her, not letting go. She was as limp as a rag doll. All I could think about was saving Sam as she had saved me.

But how was I going to get her on the ferry in her condition?

I plotted night and day to get Sam off the island with me. I decided that we'd try to leave within the week. I couldn't tell my parents or Bernard for fear that they would think I was crazy for taking on such a responsibility. My plan was simple: I would get the ferry tickets. Mrs. Witherspoon would bring Sam down to the ferry while Mr. Witherspoon was out of the house, and we would cross to the mainland. I just hoped that Sam wouldn't ramble on the ferry. And if all went well, the only other hitch was finding a flat to rent in Boston and hoping Sam wouldn't appear cuckoo in front of prospective landlords.

I didn't know what the future held, but I was prepared to do whatever I could to help her. Everything seemed to be in order—but it's the circumstances you can't plan for that have a way of throwing you off balance.

A few days before my mission was set to launch, I went over to Sam's house for a visit. It was a gray and dreary day, and the house was dark and cold, except for a glow from Sam's bedroom. I knocked on the door and cautiously walked in.

"Hello? Mrs. Witherspoon? Mr. Witherspoon?"

No one answered. I walked up the stairs and heard dresser drawers being opened and shut. The door to Sam's room was no longer locked. As I entered, she was busy packing a suitcase.

"You got sprung?"

Sam continued packing. "Daddy decided to let the cat out."

"Are you packing for Boston?"

"Daddy wants me out of here and on the next ferry." Sam slammed the suitcase shut and walked past me, out of her room, and down the stairs. I followed her into the parlor.

"Where are you going?"

"I'm leaving."

Sam walked over to the Victor, cranked it, and placed the needle on a record. "After You've Gone" began to play.

I had to think quickly. "But I can't leave today. It's too soon."

"I'm not going to Boston."

I went over to Sam and tried to take her hands in mine.

She pulled away. "Amelia, don't make this harder than it already is."

"It's doesn't have to be hard. You know that."

"The only thing I know is that it's time for me to go."

"But where? Where are you going?"

"You'll never see me again, Amelia."

"Please don't do this, Sam. Let me try to make it better."

"I lost everything that mattered to me. Why don't you understand?"

"I know it's hard. Losing Scudder. The way your father has treated you. And then to lose the baby … I don't know how anyone can deal with such loss. But let me try to help. You've got me, Sam."

"Do I?"

"You know that you do. We've had our disagreements in the past, but I've always loved you, Sam."

"Then you'll understand why I must go."

"But I don't understand."

I was frustrated; I had no idea what she was talking about. She walked over to me and took my hand.

The music ended, but the record kept spinning. All I heard was static as the needle scratched and skipped. Sam placed her hand on my face. Her eyes were so sad—bloodshot from too many tears. She moved closer to me, and we embraced. She felt limp and lifeless in my arms.

Suddenly, she pushed me away and ran her fingers through her hair nervously, righting her appearance. She went over to the Victor and took the needle off. The static stopped. The house was silent.

She avoided eye contact. "I've got to get going."

"You haven't told me where you're going."

"I'm leaving on the ferry." She gave me a hurried hug. "Good-bye, Amelia."

I didn't let go of her. "I'm not budging from this house until you tell me where you're going."

Her jaw tightened, and she forced herself out of my grip. "You can't stop me, Amelia." She started toward me.

"Stop playing this game with me, Sam, and tell me."

"Please leave." She backed me toward the door and forced me out of the house, shutting the door in my face.

I knocked. Then pounded. "How can I leave you like this?"

She refused to answer. I decided to walk down to the end of the street, hide behind a tree, and wait for her to come out.

An hour or so later, she walked out of the house, carrying the suitcase. It seemed to weigh her down.

I kept my distance and followed her as she walked across Fair Street, onto Main Street, and down to the wharf. She immediately boarded the ferry. As soon as I was sure she couldn't see me, I went into the ticket office and purchased a ticket. I had no idea where she was going, but I had to follow her as far as I could.

"Better get a move on it … we're shoving off."

I ran up the plank and jumped on board. As I walked down the deck, the plank was being hoisted up. I was the last person to get on the ferry.

I searched from the top of the ferry down to the bottom. A smattering of passengers were aboard, and all were in the inside passenger-seating area. I ran into Cornelia Thompson and asked if she had seen Sam. She hadn't.

I went outdoors. It was freezing, but I scoured all of the decks. I ducked inside when I couldn't stand the cold. I couldn't find any sign of her. Where was she hiding?

About two hours into the voyage, I finally found her, standing at the bow of the boat on the lower deck. She dropped the suitcase. It sounded as if a bomb went off when it hit the deck, but the sound didn't faze her. Her face was distant, emotionless. She propped herself up on the safety rail. She was drooping over, exhausted, looking like a wet, heavy piece of clothing on a worn clothesline. She took a rope out of her pocket and tied herself to the suitcase. Then, she struggled to pick up the suitcase and jumped into the water.

I couldn't believe my eyes. I ran to where she had been standing and looked for her in the water. I had to save her. I couldn't just let her go like that. I jumped in after her.

"Man overboard!"

Those were the last words I heard as I hit the surface of the water.

United States Coast Guard
Special Report upon the
Incident on the Steamship *Uncatena*
October 16, 1921
Excerpt, Testimony, Mr. Phillip Witherspoon questioned by
Deputy Officer William B. Madden

"Mr. Witherspoon, can you tell me where your daughter is?"

"I suppose she's somewhere in America."

"How do you know that, sir?"

"Well, me and the missus paid for her ticket and saw her off."

"You took her down to the ferry?"

"Well, not exactly."

"Then how did you see her off?"

"We said our good-byes at the house."

"When will she return?"

"I beg your pardon?"

"When do you expect her to return to Nantucket?"

"This is a little embarrassing."

"Why is that?"

"It's that Moorland girl, isn't it?"

"I beg your pardon?"

"She's the one who has dragged us into this mess. She couldn't keep her nose out of our business."

"What business is that?"

"What happens in the privacy of my house is my business and no one else's."

"I see."

"That girl has been nothing but trouble her entire life."

"I'm more concerned with your daughter."

"Well, you needn't be."

"Why is that?"

"It's a family matter. You understand, don't you?"

"Mr. Witherspoon, I'm conducting an investigation. While your daughter has not been directly implicated in this, I have to know everything to ensure that she isn't part of this."

"We had a parting of ways."

"A parting of ways?"

"Yes. My wife and I … and Samantha … we decided it was best that she go off on her own."

"And where was she headed?"

"I told you. America."

"You don't know where in America she was going?"

"I didn't want to know. And I still don't."

CHAPTER XVII

I always say good night to Uncle Jim before I turn in. Tonight really shouldn't be an exception; he might take it as a slight, and I can't have that.

I haven't had too much to drink today. And if I did, who cares? I'm celebrating my birthday, aren't I? The drink got Mama through a lot, and it got me to one hundred. It's damn near impossible to beat that.

What should I drink to? My story? It's not finished. How about to believing my story?

Nobody believed me when I told them Sam had jumped in first, and I went in after her. The Coast Guard inspector kept asking me to recount the story over and over again. Each time, I told him the same thing, and each time he told me the crew had only seen one person jump in, and that was me.

I asked if they had contacted Mr. and Mrs. Witherspoon. He said he had spoken to Mr. Witherspoon, who stated that he and his wife had had a parting of ways with Sam and knew she was somewhere in America.

When I heard this, I stormed over to their house to confront them. How could they believe such a thing?

I knocked on their door several times before Mrs. Witherspoon opened it. When she saw it was me, she looked back into the house and came out on the porch, as if she didn't want Mr. Witherspoon to know I was there.

"How are you, my dear?"

"I'll be all right."

"You shouldn't have used Samantha as your alibi. It's your own mental breakdown, Amelia."

"But it's not a mental breakdown. I saw her jump."

"That's impossible, Amelia. She wouldn't do such a thing."

"But she did."

"We can't take anymore, Amelia. Her pregnancy and miscarriage and the shame she brought on our house … taking her own life is impossible."

"How can you be so sure?"

"She wouldn't do that to us."

She looked back at the door to make sure Mr. Witherspoon was not in earshot. "I have to believe she's alive somewhere in America. It's the only thing that will keep me going. She'll come back sometime. You'll see."

"But that's not how it happened."

"You need to go, Amelia. He's fit to be tied that you even mentioned her."

"But I saw her jump."

Mrs. Witherspoon slapped me across the face. "Don't say that! You can't say that anymore. I won't believe it. She's alive somewhere. Somewhere in America."

Mr. Witherspoon opened the front door and pushed his way outside. "What's going on, Mother?"

He saw me and his face turned crimson. "You have some nerve, trying to pin the craziness going on in your head on my family. You should be ashamed of yourself. Well, you're not welcome here, you understand? So go on, get out of here."

He tried to shoo me away like some starved, unwanted pest.

"Mr. Witherspoon, I saw her. Why would I make that up?"

"You're insane, that's why. You should be locked up in some institution, where you can't hurt anyone."

"Are you denying it because you feel guilty that you sent her away?"

He began to quiver. His voice cracked as he shook his fist at me. "Quit talking like that. I gave her money to help her out. She's gone to America to start a new life. She wanted to go. Come on, Mother."

He grabbed Mrs. Witherspoon and went back in the house.

It was the last time I spoke to them.

My parents were of little assistance to me. They had told the inspector that I had suffered during the war and that perhaps this was all related to that. This was noted in the official record.

I kept hoping that Sam would wash ashore. That perhaps her coat, dress, shoes, or suitcase would be found. There was nothing: No body. No suitcase. No piece of clothing. We found absolutely no sign of Sam. It's how she would have liked it.

In the end, not a single soul believed me. They chalked it up to the war (some kind of shell shock) and the aftereffects of the Spanish flu (delirium). No one could look me in the eye. They avoided talking to me. No conversation probed deeper than "How's the weather?"

I was told that I had been through a lot (I couldn't argue with that). And that I wasn't thinking clearly. How can anyone think clearly when they've been branded the madwoman of Nantucket?

My nursing education was put on hold for four years. The state assigned me a psychiatrist who came over to Nantucket once a week and dissected my brain. He dislodged many memories and problems I had no idea were under the surface of my skin, but he could not explain Sam's demise and my part in it. I insisted that I was not crazy.

I went to bed each night hoping that Sam would make contact. When she didn't, I tried to communicate with her. "Sam. Sam, it's me. Are you there?" But I never got an answer.

It's the only time of my life that I couldn't remember my dreams. I closed my eyes and saw black, then woke the next morning to the sun's rising, but I had no recollection of dreams in between. Is it possible there weren't any?

For months, I walked the beaches around Nantucket, searching for any piece of evidence that would clear my name. I took a dory over to Tuckernuck and then just beyond, to Muskeget. I found great mussel and clam beds and brought bountiful harvests home for dinner—not to mention scallops, when they were in season. But I never found a trace of Sam.

And then I began to doubt myself. Was everyone correct? Had I hallucinated? Had I gone mad? Did I have a nervous breakdown? If that were the case, then Sam was alive somewhere in America.

I thought of the day much later in life, when I would bump into her on a street in New York or Boston. Or perhaps she would rent a summer cottage on Nantucket, and I would see her strolling down Main Street. We would recognize each other and pick up our friendship as if no time had passed. But in my heart of hearts, I knew this wasn't true.

I've never tried to explain why she did it. She was in a place so incomprehensible that I never felt it fair to pass judgment. Some may think that I let her down because I let her go. But they don't realize that I was struggling to save her. I was running out of breath. If I had continued, I would have died with her. When I let go of her, I knew that I was incapable of pulling her out of it. Had I been able to do so, there would be no discrepancies in the official record.

Mama and Da were as supportive as they could be, but I knew that my being tagged crazy (despite any hard evidence) had chipped away at Mama's self-esteem with regard to her position in the community. It was bad enough that I had refused to be born on the rock; it was completely reprehensible that I would go mad and tarnish the Moorland name.

I remember hearing Mama and Da arguing late at night, when they thought I was asleep.

"It isn't from my side of the family."

"And you think that it's on mine?"

"It's only natural to think that a family brought up secluded on this island would drive some in their clan to madness."

"You don't know what you're talking about, Catherine."

"I know that no one from my family ever suffered a breakdown."

"Why don't you quit while you're ahead?"

"Are you afraid of the truth, Obed?"

"I'm afraid you're drunk, Catherine, and that is never a pleasant situation."

"Take the easy way out, and blame it on my drink. That's just like you and just like her. Neither of you have ever come to terms with truth."

I thought that I should go into exile. Perhaps a clean slate was what the doctor ordered. I could start anew somewhere fresh, and I wouldn't feel depressed.

But when I told my doctor my plans, he informed me that the state required me to remain under my parents' custody until he found me well again. If I tried to run, I would be sent to an institution, and that was not my idea of a good place to start over.

I was very frustrated. I couldn't move. I couldn't start a new life. I couldn't finish my nursing studies. I was chained in time, unable to get on with my life.

I resigned myself to working hard to convince the doctor that I was well enough to move on. It took four years and a false confession that I had made up the story—that Sam hadn't jumped. I knew it was an outright lie, but it was my only way out.

The Witherspoons sold the house on Ray's Court as quickly as possible and left Nantucket for good. People forgot about them in no time.

Over time, people also forgot about Sam and my insistence that I went in after her to save her. But it took much longer for them to forget that I was the lady who jumped off the ferry. They just forgot the reason why. As I outlived every one of my contemporaries, the memory of my jump completely faded.

The official record declared that I had a mental breakdown. The body of Samantha Witherspoon was never found, and her whereabouts are still unknown. But I know where she is.

Over the years, corpses, body parts, and bones have washed ashore. Some have been identified; others remain a mystery, unidentifiable. I have a picture in my mind of random bones piled high in a box in some dark laboratory. I often wonder if she's somewhere in that pile.

In recent years, I've thought about telling the authorities about her, especially now, considering what they can do with DNA. But I've decided that they, like everyone else back then, would not believe me; it might prompt them to commit me. I would lose everything. They would probably think my madness had come back.

It took some time, but Sam eventually visited me again. She is here with me now. But she never speaks.

How do I know she is here? The hairs on the back of my neck stand straight up. See, just as they are doing now.

I'm the only one who has kept Sam alive through my memories. For almost eighty years, I have kept her close to my heart when no one else seemed to care. After tonight, if you would be so kind, will you keep both of us alive?

You must be wondering how you can verify whether my story is true. It wouldn't please me more than if I could give you a list of people and places you could go to confirm what I've told you. But they do not exist. You cannot verify it.

I've already told you what the official record states, and it conflicts with my own account. My parents and the Witherspoons kept all of this out of the newspapers, so past issues of the *Inquirer and Mirror* will be of no use to you. I'm the last one alive from that time. Even if there were someone alive, they would probably tell you that I was something of a character, a pisser, and that I had a spell.

You must rely on what I've told you. You must trust me. You have to believe that I would not make this up. I'll be dead soon. It is the truth.

You do believe me, don't you?

United States Coast Guard
Special Report upon the
Incident on the Steamship *Uncatena*
October 16, 1921
Excerpt, Conclusions

Having interviewed the crew on the vessel, employees of the ferry company, passengers on board, and the family and acquaintances of the subject, and having found no body, clothing, or any such article related to Ms. Samantha Witherspoon, and having exhausted all methods at the investigation's disposal to contact Ms. Witherspoon with no success, it is the conclusion of this investigation that Ms. Amelia Moorland jumped off the *Uncatena* alone, apparently suffering from a nervous breakdown due to the distresses of her participation in the Great War and contraction and survival of the Spanish influenza. Further, the investigation notes that Ms. Witherspoon's whereabouts remain unknown, but recommends that this case be closed.

The Inquirer and Mirror
Wednesday, June 20, 2001

Amelia Moorland Dead at 100

One of the oldest living residents of Nantucket and a feisty old timer, Amelia Moorland died early Sunday morning in her sleep. She had celebrated her hundredth birthday the day before. Ever the recluse in her last years, she declined an invitation from the Nantucket Chamber of Commerce, the Nantucket Yacht Club, Our Island Home, and the Unitarian Church to celebrate her milestone birthday. "We really wanted to do something special for her, but she just wouldn't hear of it. It breaks my heart to know she's gone," said Millie Levy of the Chamber of Commerce.

The daughter of Obed Moorland of Nantucket and Catherine Cannon of Brooklyn, New York, Ms. Moorland was born on the steamship *Island Home* on the morning of June 16, 1901, as it headed into Nantucket Harbor. She grew up on the island, went to the Academy Hill School, and served in the Red Cross in World War I. During the war, she contracted the Spanish flu but survived and returned to Nantucket after the war.

Because of her experience in the Red Cross, she decided to study nursing and graduated from the Nantucket Cottage Hospital Nursing School in 1926. She worked at the hospital off and on for more than fifty years.

With the outbreak of World War II, Miss Moreland enlisted once again in the Red Cross. This time stationed in England, she served from 1942 until 1945.

With the news of the death of her mother, Catherine Cannon Moorland, Ms. Moorland returned to Nantucket in December 1946 and took up residence with her father at her parents' house on Pleasant Street. Her father died in the summer of 1947.

In 1950, she moved for a brief period to Aspen, Colorado, where she took a nursing position at the local hospital. The altitude, however, did not agree with her, and Nantucket beckoned her back. In the spring of 1951, she took the position of head nurse at the Cottage Hospital.

In the early 1960s, she traveled to Asia, visiting such places as Hong Kong, Bangkok, Singapore, and Tokyo, briefly working with the Red Cross in Bangkok during the early part of the Vietnam War. It was on this trip that she began collecting Asian art and Chinese export, amassing over 350 paintings and ceramics. She graciously left her collection to the Nantucket Historical Society, which plans to auction the items off later this year in an effort to raise funds.

The autumn of 1967 brought tragedy to Ms. Moorland as her brother, Bernard, was killed in an airplane accident. Mr. Moorland was coming in for a landing at Nantucket Airport when his engine failed. He was badly burned and taken to the Cottage Hospital, where he died with his sister, wife, and son by his side.

In the early 1970s, Ms. Moorland was an active member of the National Organization of Women, raising funds and awareness on Nantucket and the Cape. In one of her more colorful moments, she staged a protest against the inequalities she found between men and women by burning her bra in front of the United States Post Office on Federal Street.

In December 1979, she retired from nursing after more than fifty years of service. Her retirement hardly slowed her down. "I can remember the day after her retirement party, she showed up on the steps of the Nantucket branch of the Massachusetts Society for the Prevention of Cruelty to Animals and offered her services. She supposedly said to the veterinarian on duty, "'They may think I'm too old to touch humans, but I can't be too old to touch a dog or cat, now, can I?'" recalled Lila Mayhew, a volunteer.

President Ronald Reagan paid tribute to her lifetime service in the Red Cross in a ceremony in the Rose Garden at the White House in June 1983. Her sister-in-law, Abigail Smith Moorland, and nephew, Bernard Jr., accompanied her to the ceremony.

Ms. Moorland spent the latter years of her life recounting tales of old, but never allowed anyone to record her on video or audio tape. "We really tried to get her on tape, to talk about her Asian art collection and her life, but she proved too difficult," said Historic Society archivist Biff Marlborough. "It's really a shame."

On Main Street, the news of her death brought tears, reminiscences, and regrets from those who knew her well and those who knew of her. "She was one of a kind. She will be missed," offered summer resident Marcia Buckner.

Ms. Moorland was predeceased by her father, Obed; mother, Catherine; brother, Bernard; sister, Nora; and sister-in-law, Abigail. She is survived by her nephew, Bernard Jr., of Nantucket.

A memorial service will be held this Saturday, June 23, at 10:00 AM at the Unitarian Church, 11 Orange Street. Reverend Ted Anderson will preside. In lieu of flowers, donations to the MSPCA are encouraged.

At her request, Ms. Moorland's ashes will be scattered in Nantucket Sound by her nephew in a private ceremony.

CHAPTER XVIII

We are in the dory together. We are lying next to each other, side by side. She takes hold of my hand and kisses my forehead.

"It's OK. Despite it all, I still love you."

I hear the gentle lapping of water against the wood frame of the boat and the shrieking cry of an osprey overhead. The bells faintly toll in the far-off distance. We are drifting out to sea. Asleep, we are together.

978-0-595-42033-9
0-595-42033-8

Printed in the United States
84848LV00004B/1-75/A